Grampa Jack

Grampa Jack

a novel

Rocky L. Doubenmier

Cover and author photography by
dean brittingham
lavender lens photography
707.823.7351
www.lavenderlens.com
lavlens@yahoo.com

To order additional copies of this book, contact:
Xlibris Corporation
1-888-795-4274
www.Xlibris.com
Orders@Xlibris.com
30727

To Gary for sharing twenty-three years of
his love and life with me.

Chapter One

It was in January of 2002, Monday the 14th to be exact. That was the day when my six-year-old grandson, Jamey Fitzpatrick, came to live with me.

Overnight, a light rain had fallen on the southern coastal town of Laguna Beach, California, a haven for tourists, artists and someone like me who took pleasure in the smells of the ocean's breath in his own backyard. That morning, I cooled down after a two-mile run on the beach with a brisk walk along Laguna's deserted sidewalks. Rows of sagging, sun-bleached awnings not only distinguished each store front from the next, but also sheltered me from the rain as I hurried back to my beach house.

I ran past several trendy beachfront restaurants; banners in their windows announced, "We'll Be Back In The Spring". Christmas and New Years in Laguna had come and gone, as had visiting sons and daughters and grandchildren. Having eaten and unwrapped their way through one more Christmas holiday, they bid sentimental farewells to Moms and Dads and Grammas and Grampas and then headed home to Wisconsin or Nebraska or North Carolina or wherever their roots had been transplanted. As for me, I welcomed the holiday exodus. Even the seagulls shared my sentiment; they hovered above the lonely streets along Pacific Coast Highway, feasting on seasonal leftovers. Together we reclaimed our coastline, at least until Spring Break. The gulls had the right idea, get life back to normal. But I had no idea how my life was about to change.

Late as usual, I arrived at my daughter's house that morning, still in my running gear. Annie and Jamey lived in the private, beachfront community of Monarch Bay, a challenging four-mile weekend run from my place in Laguna. On school days, however, I chose to drive my old convertible instead. Jamey attended first-grade at Emerald Cove Elementary, a California Distinguished School and I was his daily ride. Today Annie and Jamey were waiting on their wet lawn, watching for my car.

As I rounded the corner, my car's bald tires screeched against the wet pavement. Jamey spied my convertible and sprinted toward the sidewalk. Little boys seldom walk when they can run instead. He waved his spindly arms above his head to flag me down. Wearing a bomber jacket that hung below his knees, he looked like a kid who had borrowed it from an older brother; Jamey was my only grandchild. I pulled into the driveway. He slammed the heavy car door shut and wriggled into the car's bench seat, cranked the window down and shouted, "Bye Mom, I love you!"

"I love you too, honey. Have a good day at school and no junk food, either of you. Go on you guys, it's almost eight o'clock," she said, then with a flip of the hand motioned for us to hurry along.

"Hi Grampa," Jamey said and then yawned. He struggled with the seat belt. I locked him into the seat and asked him, "How's my best buddy this morning?"

Before he answered, he tested the stiffness of his self-styled spiked hair. Satisfied with the results of his handiwork, he finally replied, "Good. Are we gonna have you know what?"

"Shh, your mom will hear," I warned him. Jamey quietly gathered a crumpled pile of breakfast food wrappers that we had tossed on the floorboard of the car and then ditched them under the front seat.

Annie had eyes in the back of her head like most moms. Standing fifteen feet from my car, she said, "Don't you think it's time you cleaned out the inside of that car?"

I swallowed and then nodded; Jamey fidgeted with his seat belt and tightened the loose strap.

Shivering from the misty winter beach air, Annie stood barefoot on her front lawn. She was still in her pajamas and robe; she wrapped her arms around herself to keep warm. I watched her standing there through my foggy windshield; her youth weathered like a garden statue exposed to too many salty winter rainstorms. I gestured with my hand for her to come to the car. "How are you doing, baby?" I asked.

"Just fine, Dad," she said, but her tone wasn't very convincing.

"How about a lift to Dr. Shapiro's office today?"

Annie folded her arms again. She tucked her left hand beneath her right elbow indicating mind your own business, and scorned me with a look she might give Jamey if he'd done something wrong. "No thanks. I'm canceling my session today," she said and stared at the vacant house across the street.

"Why?" I asked bluntly.

Jamey's thumbs gyrated like a whirling dervish playing his Super Mario Game Boy but he was taking in every word of the exchange between his mother and me.

"Dad, I am not up to talking about Derek today."

"Honey, I know that you miss him. Dr. Shapiro explained to me . . ."

"I'm not going, Dad."

"Not even for your old man?"

"Just make sure you pick Jamey up after school on time."

"Yes M'am," I said, saluting her. "You need anything?"

"Not one thing. Go on now, you're gonna be late. And Jamey has already eaten a bowl of cold cereal and some toast. No snack stops along the way; got it?"

Hiding our secret behind a grin, I winked at Jamey. He leaned forward to make certain that his mom was not watching and then winked back.

Annie inherited her playful green eyes, wavy auburn hair, and sharp tongue from Margo Evans, her mother. Inherited from me, Annie's willowy figure and stubborn independence seemed more like a curse. Her hollow cheeks and unsteady hands indicated to me that she hadn't eaten for a couple of days. Dark circles framed her haunted eyes; prescription medication had clouded her sense of humor. I missed her playful teasing. Whenever I looked at Annie, I saw the resemblance to her mother, a mirrored image I have tried to forget. We haven't seen nor heard from Margo for twenty-five years. She deserted us when Annie was only five months old.

"You be careful driving that old clunker down the coast," Annie hollered as we backed out of the driveway.

"The way you talk about my classic," I said, blindly honoring the bucket of bolts that I called mine. Annie ran up to the car, leaned through the window and kissed me on my forehead. I reassured her, "I'll pick Jamey up after school today, on time."

I drove Jamey to school every weekday morning; it was one less hassle for Annie. Jamey and I shared a Breakfast Jack and an OJ on the way, a morning ritual and a sworn secret between grandson and Grampa.

We cruised down Pacific Coast Highway through the morning drizzle. Jamey agreed that I owned the coolest wheels of any of his friends' Grampas, maybe a bit too cool. The convertible top on my '56 Chevy leaked like a sieve. Disguised by layers of duct tape the soft-top's color remained a mystery. Annie had pleaded with me countless times to sell and I always flatly refused. Her husband, Derek Fitzpatrick, on the other hand, had volunteered to help me restore it. Computer software programming was his work but vintage car restoration was his passion. Five years later my Chevy remained a bucket of bolts, a piece of shit, an eye sore.

I had taken great pride in having him for a son-in-law. But Derek was taken from us in March of 1995. He had driven to San Francisco to attend a soft-ware convention. Early morning road conditions through the Central Valley on California's Interstate 5 can be unpredictable during springtime. The Tulie fog had reduced visibility to zero between Coalinga and Tulare. Instead of pulling off to the side of the road, he continued driving through the soupy fog. Traveling north bound at 40 mph, one-half mile behind Derek, the driver of an 18-wheeler fell asleep at the wheel. He plowed over Derek's new convertible. A sixty-car collision left forty people dead. My son-in-law didn't make it home to celebrate his son's first birthday.

One week later, Annie and I shared a somber celebration for Jamey. That evening Annie's depression began. I blamed her in-laws for Annie's illness. To keep their son at the top of his game they hounded Derek daily about climbing the corporate ladder regardless of whose job it might cost. They tossed my small town girl into the world of the pretentious wives of the Balboa Bay Club driving their pricey BMW's and Mercedes, shaming my kids into debt up to their ass. After Derek's death, the insurance paid off their mortgage and left Annie and Jamey on easy street. Somehow, that wasn't enough to erase my daughter's addiction to medication and psychiatrists or ease her depression.

Her in-laws, Peg and Rob Fitzpatrick, apologized the following morning for not coming by to wish Jamey a happy birthday. The mayor of Newport Beach had hosted a dinner honoring their philanthropic work for the homeless in Orange County. The event had been planned months before Derek's fatal accident. Construction for the Fitzpatrick Center, a new forty-bed homeless shelter, broke ground in Anaheim, the day following the Fitzpatrick's award ceremony.

Rob boasted about the center's state-of-the-art kitchen, private shower facilities for men and women, and a 52" widescreen projection television with satellite, a right-wing conservative philanthropist's tax write off. They were front-page news in the *Santa Ana Register*, a conservative newspaper which carried my syndicated weekly.

Two words described Rob Fitzpatrick—pompous ass. His desirable Newport Beach address suited his status as a corporate attorney for Micro Com, one of NASDAQ's premiere Southern California based wireless communications companies. I envied his lifestyle. However, his staunch support for the Moral Majority, the Republican Party and the Christian Coalition's dogmatic definition of the American family kept us at odds. I didn't fault Peg's clouded judgment for marrying Rob, but I did disagree with her willingness to support his beliefs. The Fitzpatricks tolerated my family because it produced a grandson for them. But my gay lifestyle challenged their tolerance toward me.

I drove straight home after dropping Jamey off at school that January morning. When I stepped onto the back porch, I nearly tripped over his sneakers that were stuck to the cement steps. My tennis shoes were missing. A neighborhood dog had probably buried them in another neighbor's yard. Our soiled socks and wet beach towels were still draped over the washing machine. We had shared the previous day together digging for sand crabs and chasing seagulls down the beach.

I searched the house for Maria. Her '72 Beetle remained parked in the driveway, but the grocery list we had collaborated on earlier was missing from the kitchen table. She preferred to walk to the market located across from the beach, three blocks from my house.

Peace and quiet around my house was a luxury short-lived. Stumbling over the dirty laundry basket, Maria made enough racket to wake the dead. "Mr. Jack, you must ask Jamey not to leave his tennis shoes on the back steps. I nearly tripped over them just now!" Maria scolded me. Her Genoa Italia temper had softened over the years along with her 4' 11" figure. Even her English grammar had expanded since the day she came to work for me twenty-six years ago. Her heavy Italian accent had all but disappeared, probably a result of living with me and listening to my American slang all these years. However, whenever Maria got a little hot under the collar her accent resurfaced and echoed throughout the house.

I lightened the burdensome grocery bags Maria toted and snatched the Chee-tos and Oreos teetering on the top. "Okay, I'll tell Jamey to park his sneakers elsewhere. So Maria, what's for dinner?"

"We're having Pasta con Pesto Genovegnese with asparagus. Save some room for dinner in between your cookies."

"Even between cookies, Maria, I save room for your pasta bellisima!" Maria nabbed one of my cookies, sandwiched it between her lips, flashed a self-indulgent grin and then disappeared through the kitchen pantry door.

Despite Maria's cucina bella, I maintained my college weight of 178 lbs. I ran three miles a day and worked out at a local gym, lifting weights three times a week. Most of the gym's clientele consisted of young, buff, gay men, but I held my own against them. At 52, my 6' 1" lean build still looked pretty good in a tank top and running shorts even though I had dined on Maria's best since the mid-seventies.

I remember my naiveté, desperation, and sleep-deprivation when I hired Maria on the spot. Somehow, she had found her way to me in 1975, when I was a young, still wet behind the ear newspaper reporter and a single father with a new baby. After more than two decades, Maria's cockiness had evolved into an unspoken mutual affection that endeared her to me.

Harboring that affection, I hid my face behind the morning newspaper minding my own business. "Maria," I said, "did you read my column today?"

Maria wedged herself into the over-stocked pantry to unpack her shopping bags. "Of course I read your column; it's part of my job description," she reminded me.

"Cute," I said, snapping the paper, but she didn't hear the noise, the pantry door was half closed. "What did you think?"

"*Middle Age Baby-Boomer Investments Retrogress*? Really, Mr. Jack, isn't that a bit of a stretch?"

"Did you read the entire article?" I asked, not surprised by her reaction.

"Your article would deny your peers from living a dream, buying a new car that reminds them of when they were teen-agers. Owning a dream is "misguided spending"? Instead, they should be investing in their futures: retirement, and the stock market? Maybe, but having some fun before it's time to check out is worth every penny spent. Try it. You could benefit from acquiring a little fun yourself."

"My point, Maria, is that conspicuous consumption is fueled by skillful and enticing marketing. I guess you don't agree with my point of view. And by the way, I do have fun."

"If you say so. Then again, you might be right," she said.

"I knew you'd see it my way."

"Some retro cars might be better off in a wreckage yard, instead of parked in a driveway," she said, pointing to our driveway. "As a matter of spending, a new car would be fun."

"The old beast is just fine for me to drive."

"Suit yourself," she said, "but what does matter is that Mr. Fitzpatrick called this morning. I told him that you were taking Jamey to school."

I chuckled under my breath as I listened to an avalanche crashing in the pantry. Maria spilled coffee beans and crushed my hidden bag of corn chips beneath her feet. Holding back my laughter, I peered over the paper's edge and asked, "Did he say why he called?"

"No, you know Mr. Fitzpatrick, always to the point. Just call him back," Maria replied testily. She was not amused by my amusement and fired back in her dialect, "Movete e alsa il tu culo and help me clean up this mess."

I moved my lazy ass and forced myself to return Fitzpatrick's call instead. "Rob, this is Jack."

"Jack, old man, how are you? How's my grandson doing?"

His phony cheerfulness annoyed me to no end. "We're both fine. It won't be long before that bomber jacket you bought him will fit. What's up?" I asked, inferring, get to the point.

"I need to meet with you this morning."

"I'm busy," I said, "maybe some other time during the week."

"Sorry old man, that won't do," he persisted.

Motivated by purely selfish reasons, I easily gave in to his persistence. "Okay then," I said, "meet me at the Little Shrimp at noon."

"Where's it located?" he asked.

"Right on Pacific Coast Highway just down from my house. It's a quiet, laid back café. You'll like it; they have a full bar."

"12:00 straight up," he said and hung up without a goodbye.

The Little Shrimp was in fact a gay bar and restaurant where I had cruised away many Saturday nights in vain. I would be forcing Rob to endure a setting that was emblematic of all that he abhorred. His urgency to meet with me allowed me to score off his blatant homophobia. I'm certain his idea of the Little Shrimp was like eating at a Denny's that featured a sea food grand slam.

But I was not looking forward to the encounter as I walked toward town. I seldom missed an opportunity to needle Rob, and a part of me knew that was not such a great idea.

Even in winter, the pink bougainvillea that scaled the west side of my beach bungalow maintained abundant blossoms. The flowerless ice plant bordering my neighbor's property reminded me of a sprawling, sea green carpet of giant sea anemones. I walked toward Pacific Coast Highway just a couple blocks from my house and breathed in the fragrance of damp eucalyptus leaves that mingled with the crisp, salty ocean air. Inhaling the concoction woke me up like a morning cocktail. The rain had moved south, leaving scattered cumulus clouds that filtered the morning sunlight on the town that I called home.

I ran across Pacific Coast Highway against a red light and hollered good morning to Captain Walt, an old friend of mine. I caught him leaning against his '57 T-Bird, a punishable crime for anyone else who dared to do so. I slowed down once I hit the sidewalk and waved hello to two moms that I recognized from Jamey's school. They entered Walt's espresso café, whispering between them.

"Captain!" I hollered. He shook my hand and embraced me like a seaman greeting an old chum.

"Hey, Jack," he said then stepped back from his car and caressed the turquoise fender being careful not to streak the morning condensation. "This is Derek's finest restoration," he beamed with sentiment and respect for my son-in-law. "By the way, how's your Chevy coming along?"

"Annie wants me to sell it," I said.

"Maybe she'll change her mind. Then again, I'm not so sure. Your Chevy needs more than a little TLC," he said, sniggering under his breath and his mammoth mustache, yellowed from smoking too many cigarettes, one after another.

"Bite your tongue," I said.

He clapped me on the shoulder and guided me toward the front door of his café. He said, "I saw that grandson of yours last week. That little weasel conned me into sponsoring his soccer team's banner; not bad for his first soccer season."

"That's my boy!" I said; my chest puffed out with pride.

"It was good to see Annie. She's not around town much these days."

"Jamey keeps her pretty busy." Changing the subject, I said, "Now that you're the Sharks' sponsor, maybe I can con a free cinnamon-walnut croissant."

"Get out'a town," he grinned. I loved Walt's laugh. It bellowed from the depths of his well-fed waist; his scruffy beard and mustache widened his toothless grin. He repositioned his tam covered in baking flour, to hide his receding hairline. "You and Jamey drop by Sunday; I'll see what I can do."

"We'll pop in Sunday." I checked my watch, 12:10. "Gotta go, Captain. I'm late for a meeting."

Rob waited inside his Mercedes 500 SL parked across the street from the restaurant. I tapped on the windshield. He raised a finger letting me know he'd be a minute while he finished his phone call. He slammed his car door shut, pressed his remote, the headlamps blinked and the horn beeped twice. He wedged his hefty build between his car and the small pick-up parked in front of him. He yanked the door handle twice assuring him that his car was locked. He said, "Thanks for meeting me. Shall we?"

"After you," I said, gesturing toward the entrance.

The smell of stale booze and tired cologne filled my nostrils the moment he and I passed through the bar. The tropical print upholstery on the banquettes along the back wall hadn't escaped the smells of thirty-five years of anniversary, birthday, and New Year's Eve celebrations. Rob followed behind me with his hands hidden in his trouser pockets, fingering his keys. "A gay bar, huh?" he asked and kept his hands tightly tucked into his pockets to avoid any male contact.

I shrugged my shoulders in response then recognized a friend, Tim Higgins, who was sitting with a gentleman as the host guided us toward our table. Before being seated, I had to say hello to Tim, which invited the added pleasure of shaking the hand of his handsome companion. An intimacy hangover glazed their eyes. They were in love. I raised my left eyebrow and pursed my lips into a half-grin, expressing my approval and envy. I introduced Rob to the new couple, but his guarded handshake fell just short of cordial; I apologized with a visual gesture and whispered to Tim, "See ya at the gym."

The Little Shrimp appeared to be hosting an alumni reunion of sorts. Seated at nearly every table, middle-aged and older gay men carried on like a bunch of old hens. Endless Tequila Sunrises and Mai Tai's supporting cocktail umbrellas added a hint of color to an already colorful crowd. A scotch and water helped calm Rob's uneasiness; the house decaf-mocha eased my rising anxiety.

The owner of the Little Shrimp discriminately hired good-looking, well-built men only, much to my delight. It delighted me even more observing Rob's reaction to the gay, middle-aged, graying couple sitting at the table next to ours. They held hands while they reminisced in detail about their recent Caribbean vacation. Rob's composure began to crumble as he listened to the younger of the two, probably forty-five, describe the passion and love they had shared with one another on a private beach, on a small island, south of St. Thomas. They shared together what I longed for, a relationship with a man.

Rob's second scotch and water faired better than his first. He spilled less of it onto his yellow, cotton chambray shirt.

"So Rob, why the urgency to meet?"

His scotch and water had loosened his tongue, but his manliness remained uptight. I sipped at my mocha and skimmed over the familiar menu. Rob pushed his menu aside, snapped his watchband against his wrist and replied, "We're here to talk about Annie. How is she managing her depression?"

I closed the menu and then motioned for the waiter. "Annie's hanging in there," I said.

"Are you gentlemen ready to order?" the waiter asked.

"Give us a few more minutes," I said.

"Certainly," he said. Before he tucked his order pad into his apron, he asked us, "Can I freshen your drinks?"

"I'm fine," I said and continued to mindlessly stir the foam in my mocha.

Rob ignored the waiter's courtesy. Once our server was out of ear shot, Rob cleared his throat and sipped the last of his drink. "Annie," he continued, "she still in therapy with that psychiatrist, Dr . . . ?"

"Shapiro," I filled in the blank. "Last week Dr. Shapiro informed me that Annie's recovery is progressing, but still advises that she continue the medication."

"I see. Peg and I stopped by her place last night around 5:30. Jamey answered the door, said his mother was sleeping."

"I'm sure she was sleeping, between running that big house by herself and taking care of Jamey. You know, since Derek's death . . ."

He leaned forward and tipped the bistro table with his over indulged gut. I rescued my espresso before it spilled; Rob's drink never left his hand. The volume of his voice raised when he said to me, "We're not here to reminisce about my son."

I pushed the bridge of my specs closer to my eyes and responded, "What a shame."

The couple sitting next to us turned their heads; I wanted to leave but refused to back down.

Rob leaned back into his seat; the table settled except for the toppled salt and pepper shakers. He lowered his voice a notch and continued, "Peg and I question Jamey's lack of supervision. We're concerned for his safety. We're filing an action in court to remove Jamey from Annie's care."

"Like hell you are," I erupted.

"Listen to me, old man. Most of the time Annie is so wired from the drugs she takes that Jamey has to fare for himself."

"That's bullshit! Jamey is going to stay right where he belongs—with his mother, in his own home. I check on Annie twice a day, sometimes three. I see to it that Jamey gets to and from school everyday. If Annie needs a break, Jamey spends the night with me."

"That's another issue Peg and I are concerned about."

I clenched my fists and shouted, "Stop right there!" The conversations in the dining room silenced; heads turned; stares traveled from Rob then to me and then back to their personal affairs.

Rob slouched into the worn banquette, crossed his legs, and rocked his scotch and water with his left hand. Had he been sitting closer to me I would have shoved his opinions and his cheap bar drink down his throat. I stood up from the rattan chair, pushed it away with the back of my knees, gripped the sides of the empty bistro table and leaned forward until I felt his breath against my glasses. I lowered the pitch of my angry voice. "Annie and Jamey are my family," I threatened and leaned closer to his face. "I love my grandson and I will continue to help care for him. If you have issues with me then just say what's on your mind. If you and Peg feel the need to help with Jamey, then I suggest you take it up with Annie."

Rob downed the last half of his scotch and water and flipped a twenty dollar bill onto the table. He nodded his head once. "Jack, I'm certain that this comes as a surprise to you, but this isn't about you or Annie; it's about Jamey. Peg and I will be in touch. My best to Maria," he said. Dangling his keys in his pocket, he lumbered out of the restaurant.

I cupped my mug with both hands and sipped at the foam resting on the bottom. Standing tableside, the waiter politely asked, "Sir, another mocha?"

"No thank you. I've had enough for one morning. Just the check." I tossed a ten dollar bill on top of Rob's donation and weighted it down with the peppershaker. The two lovebirds sitting next to me buried their expressions behind the morning newspaper as I walked past them toward the exit.

The host held the door open for me and said, "Have a good day, sir."

"Yeah, you too," I responded and stepped outside into the late morning drizzle.

I walked back to the house oblivious to the Captain, the weather, and my clenched fists.

I sat at my desk and tried to calm down. With an hour and a half to kill before Jamey's school let out, I shuffled through a stack of unpaid bills, Jamey's handmade Christmas card to GRAMPA, a Breakfast Jack wrapper, and a recent copy of the *University Times* from California State University at Los Angeles, my alma mater, to find William Broderick's telephone number.

Eight years ago, William moved from Newport Beach, California to Kennebunkport, Maine; Annie was only seventeen then. The state's motto, "Maine, the way life should be", appealed to his laid-back, seacoast, lawyer lifestyle. William and I should have been together, especially now.

I finally found William's annual holiday letter with his phone number handwritten below his signature and called him. "William?" I asked, not recognizing the voice on the other end.

"No, I'm Joey. Who's calling?"

"Jack, Jack Turner."

"Oh, Jack from California. Billy talks about you all the time. Hang on; I'll get him for you."

More minutes passed than I thought necessary before William came to the phone. "Jack, sorry to keep you waiting. How are you?"

"I'm alright. Billy? Since when do you go by Billy?" I had to ask. No one called William, Billy, not even his mother.

"It's Joey's idea. I think it's sweet."

"Hmm," I moaned silently, "and Kevin? Did you and he . . ."

"Breakup? I'm afraid so. He hated the New England winters."

"Mm, hmmm," I said.

"Oh, who am I kidding? I can't bullshit a bullshitter can I? It was time for Kevin and me to move on. He moved back to California a couple of months ago. He told me that he was looking forward to a warm Christmas. Actually he's living in your neck-of-the-woods, Newport Beach."

"I don't know what to say, William. I figured that you guys would grow old together, collect your social security, clean your teeth in a glass, and drive an SUV."

"I did too, but you know me, I plan to keep my own teeth," he joked. But I could sense the loss in his voice when he mentioned Kevin's name.

"I need your help, William. It concerns Annie and Jamey."

"Do you need money?"

"God, no! Fitzpatrick called me this morning insisting that I meet with him for lunch. He wasted no time getting to the point once we sat down at the restaurant. He insinuated that Annie isn't well enough to take care of Jamey. He's filing a court action to take Jamey away from her. Then the prick all but accused me of impropriety with my grandson because Jamey spends nights at my house."

"He's out of line," William added with conviction.

The fear of losing my grandson caused me to fire back, "That may well be, but he's rich, influential, and the son-of-a-bitch is an attorney."

"Calm down, Jack. Nothing is going to happen overnight. Put your apprehension and fears aside about Fitzpatrick. There's very little he can do during the next two weeks. By then Joey and I will be in California."

"What's the occasion?"

"Disneyland," William moaned. I could feel William's eyes rolling back in his head.

"In January?" I asked.

"Joey wants to go. Anyway, why don't you and Jamey join us? Jamey can ride the rides with Joey which will save my old back. Besides, it'll give us a chance to catch up with one another. I'll talk to you more about how I think you should proceed with Fitzpatrick when I see you. Sound like a plan?"

"It sounds like a great plan, William."

"Give my love to Annie, Jamey and Maria. I'll see you soon."

William had a knack for calming me down.

Chapter Two

I cleared my desk. Week old food wrappers landed in the leather trash basket already heaped with crumpled paper. I pinned Jamey's card with thumbtacks onto the cork bulletin board hanging cockeyed against the wall near the glass slider. The January sun beating through the single paned glass warmed my bare legs. Maria called for me to come to lunch, but I told her to start without me. I read the headlines on the front page of the university newspaper; it took me back a few years, years that I longed for even for just a moment.

Maria snuck up on me, tapped my shoulder and whispered in my ear, "Mr. Jack, your lunch is getting cold."

My thoughts had wandered to a place other than the present before Maria touched me. Startled by her unexpected intrusion I said, "Maria, you damn near scared me to death." The newspaper slid from my lap onto the parquet floor. I haphazardly gathered up the sections and began to organize them in their rightful order. Dazed, I said to her, "Lunch? I already had lunch, well, sort of. You look nice. Where are you going?"

"I volunteer at the battered women's shelter on Mondays and Wednesdays," she reminded me then glanced at the quartz digital clock setting on my desk. "Oh dear, it's nearly one-o'clock, I'm going to be late."

"Then I'll see you around six?" I asked, hopefully.

"Yes, and if Jamey wants a snack after school there's fruit and cheese in the refrigerator." Maria slung her purse over her shoulder. After the back porch screen door slammed behind her she ordered, "Find another resting place for Jamey's tennis shoes." She cranked over the cylinders of her Beetle; I tossed Jamey's sneakers aimed at the foot of his bed and then followed my nose to the microwave oven.

Cold macaroni and cheese seemed better suited for the garbage disposal rather than my unsettled stomach even though I hadn't eaten; so I swallowed a few Oreos and then cleaned up the back yard. My missing tennis shoes had been scattered along the rain soaked lawn that bordered my side of the neighbor's fence. I raked the shredded rubber soles and shoestrings into wet piles then shouted loud enough for my neighbor to hear, "Keep your damn dog locked up!"

The neighbor's whiskey-tenor voice echoed over my fence, "Jack, she is locked up."

I grabbed a rake from the shed and cleaned up the remains of my shoes. No sense arguing with Mrs. Jarret; by noon she was always half cranked. Her husband discreetly stacked their empty whiskey bottles into the plastic-recycling bin near the front of their driveway. Two weeks before, while warming up before a morning run, I had counted twelve empty booze bottles hidden beneath a stack of newspapers. Mr. Jarret must have heard me snooping through his stash. I caught him peering through his dining room window and imagined him grumbling under his breath, "Nosey old fart, mind your own business." I recall waving good morning to him, no response, and then I jogged toward Pacific Coast Highway.

Mr. Jarret's addiction to booze was the least of my concerns at least while I raked up what was left of my tennis shoes. Forty mile an hour gusts blew my clean-up job back behind the garage. Earlier that morning the weatherman had predicted a winter storm would hit Laguna by midday. Unfortunately, they were right. I ran around the backyard in shorts and a sweatshirt; goose bumps raised the hair on my legs warning me to zip-up my sweatshirt and pull the hood over my head.

Mrs. Jarret called for her dog to come into the house while I stuffed the pooch's evidence into my trashcan. My soggy shoes left muddy prints as I walked down the driveway. Tuesday was trash pick-up and I hated getting up before five am to take the cans out. I had an hour before Jamey's school let out, enough time to sweep the sidewalk before picking him up. The cold damp air locked my grip around the push broom's handle. With each sweep my muddy shoes slid against the slick eucalyptus leaves.

It started to sprinkle, dotting the leaf stained concrete and my glasses. I propped the broom against a eucalyptus tree and pried my cold hands loose from the handle. As I dried the raindrops from my specs with my shirttail, the broom fell forward just missing the fender of an Orange County Sheriff's patrol car.

Lieutenant Hank Beyers, an old high school buddy of mine from Los Angeles handed me the broom. "Afternoon, Jack. What are you doin' out here in the rain?"

I returned the broom to the old eucalyptus tree and wedged its handle between the weathered peeling bark. Shrugging my shoulders, I replied, "A piss poor job of sweeping. What brings you to my place on this dreary afternoon, Hank?"

A tall, lanky gentleman stepped out of the patrol car; his cheap gray suit hung three sizes too big on his thin build. Hank introduced him to me, "Jack, this is Reverend Tom Whitman, he volunteers his time for the precinct as a chaplain."

I wiped my cold, grimy palms on my shorts and shook his hand. "What's this about, Hank?"

Whitman's handshake warmed my cold palm. His gaunt face and rather somber expression was softened by his low and warm voice. "Mr. Turner, why don't we go inside out of the rain?" he suggested.

I scraped my upper lip with my teeth. "What the hell is going on here?" I asked while searching Hank's troubled eyes for an answer.

Hank had been like a brother to me back in high school. Just as he had once led me away from a school ruckus, he touched my arm to lead me to the house. "Jack, what d'ya say we get out of the rain?"

I jerked my arm from his hand. "I'm fine right here," I said coldly.

Hank ran his hand across his crew cut; raindrops trickled down his tanned forehead and nose. "I've known you for a long time, Jack," he said then paced the lawn that edged the sidewalk and the street. He nervously turned his wedding band, hesitated, and then continued, "This is tough for me, Jack. I was dispatched late this morning after responding to a 911 call from Annie's neighbor. She reported hearing a gunshot."

"Not from Annie's house?"

Hank nodded confirming my fear. I sunk to the curb, sat on the cold cement and wrapped my arms around my shins. My eyes focused on a rainbow circling a small oil spill in front of the patrol car. Hank knelt beside me and said, "I recognized the address from the Christmas party."

"What address?" I asked.

"Jack, it's raining pretty hard. Come on, let's go inside."

"What address, Hank?" I persisted.

The weight of Hank's troubled eyes rested on mine. He folded his hands and drew them to his lips. His words cautioned, he slowly said, "I found Annie lying on her bedroom floor. She's gone, Jack."

I stepped away from the curb; my disbelief churned into rage. "Gone my ass. I just saw her this morning, she was fine!"

Hank rested his hand on my shoulder. "The coroner told me he thinks it was suicide."

Rain, death and denial echoed against the silence in my head. My eyes remained fixed on the rainbow circling at my feet. "Jamey," I whispered to myself. I dug for the car keys buried in my pocket. I backed away from Hank and Mr. Whitman. "Gentlemen, please excuse me, I need to pick up my grandson."

My piece-of-shit car refused to start. I kept pumping the throttle while I held the ignition on until it finally blew a cloud of exhaust onto the driveway. Hank's reflection in my rear view mirror blocked my view. He stepped aside as I started to back the car out of the driveway.

"Stop the car, Jack," Hank ordered.

I slammed the gearshift into park and gunned the throttle. "Move out of the way!" I demanded.

Hank ran his hand along the driver's side of my Chevy until our eyes met through the driver's door window. "You're not thinking straight, Jack. Please, get out of the car; I'll drive you to the school."

I rolled my window down and unloaded on Hank. "You come to my house and tell me that Annie is dead and stand there and tell me I'm not thinking straight. Move away from the car, Hank. I am not pulling up in front of Jamey's school in some goddamn police car!"

Hank stepped aside. Running for my life, I spun the rear tires against the oil-slicked pavement then raced toward Pacific Coast Highway.

Fifteen minutes passed like hours as I followed the coast to Emerald Cove Elementary. Memories of 8mm black and white home movies fucked with my head. I saw Annie's naked two-year-old cracker butt splashing water from a plastic wading pool and drowning Mrs. Zucker's roses. At two she talked a mile-a-minute, "Daddy, Daddy, watch." She squinted and blinked her eyes every time the water splashed her face and scolded me, "Daddy, you didn't watch," so she splashed some more. The movie running in my head moved to fast forward. On Annie's wedding day she and I waited inside the back porch of my beach house. I cradled her train in my arms and kissed her forehead. The smell of lavender stayed on my mustache all day. The wedding march sounded flat but a local band was all we could afford.

Reeling from the images of Annie's childhood I drove through a red light. An oncoming car swerved to the right missing my front fender. I deserved the gesture I caught in my rearview mirror, but I didn't give a shit. I didn't give a shit about the other driver or me or anyone until I reached Jamey's school and heard him shout, "Grampa!" as he ran toward my car.

Jamey buckled up and sunk into the pad-free, snagged seat covers; he could barely see over the dash. The engine finally turned over. Frustrated and scared I asked Jamey, "How was school today?"

He bounced off the bench seat to see out the windshield. "It was good. I'm hungry."

"I'm hungry too," I said. The Oreo sugar high had passed a while ago. "How 'bout burgers?"

"Okay. And fries too," he added.

"You're on dude," I said. We high-fived and drove to the drive-through window of a fast food joint across from Aliso Beach and then parked near the pier. The clouds began to break up. Some afternoon sun peeked through the tears in the clouds like an old torn sheet hanging on a clothesline. Sitting on one of the pier benches, we looked like Mutt and Jeff. We crossed our legs in unison and raised our burgers to the sky and saluted a toast to the begging gulls.

Above the pier, safe from the rising tide, ice plant and pickle weed crawled along the cliff's edge, cascading like a suspended waterfall showering the moss between the crevices. An offshore breeze carried a salty mist with it, fogging my glasses, distorting my view of the cliff. The mist frizzed my thinning curly hair which amused my grandson; Jamey laughed at the sight. His laughter made it all the more difficult to find the words to tell him. I wanted to shelter him from my nightmare and drive us far away from that day, away from my image of Annie's lifeless body and sorrow that I failed to mend.

The words by which I made my living flowed easily for me, but the words I sought to tell Jamey that his mother was dead burned in my throat. Instead, I hedged the issue and told him, "You just wait. Someday you're gonna look just like your old Grampa, frizzy hair and everything."

"Na, uh!"

"Na, huh!" We bantered back and forth like two kids on a school playground.

Our childish exchange challenged us as to who would get the last word in. I gave in first. My mind wandered beyond the ocean, drowning until the burning words in my throat surfaced. I asked Jamey, "Do you remember the story I told you about your dad?"

Ketchup drizzled down his chin. "I don't know," he said.

"Remember when I told you he died in the bad car accident?"

He wrinkled his forehead, remembering, "Yeah, you said my dad could see me 'cause he was an angel in heaven."

"Do you remember what else I said to you?"

"My mom loved my dad and when he died it made her sad," he said, concentrating on the remaining fries that were buried in the bottom of the greasy bag.

"That's right, Jamey. Come here and sit by Grampa; I'm gonna tell you another story."

He scooted across the bench. We sat hip to hip. "Can I eat my French fries first?" he asked.

Jamey munched down the rest of his fries and then pointed to my chin. "You got ketchup on your beard," he said, giggling at me.

I ruffled his hair and hugged him close to my side. "Okay, no more silly, this is real important."

He sat up straight like a little soldier and uncrossed his legs. Seeking my approval, he asked, "How's this?"

"You're too much, Jamey."

Facing my grandson, I clenched my hands together and tried to gather my wits. "Jamey, your mom isn't sad anymore." My racing heartbeat pulsed at my temples. "She's gone to heaven to be with your dad."

Jamey's stillness leaned into my lap. He whispered, "Mom won't have to take medicine anymore, huh Grampa?"

"No, honey, not anymore."

*　　*　　*

Before walking onto the back porch at home I could hear the annoying intermittent beep from the answering machine. I played back the two messages, one from Maria and the other from William. "Mr. Jack, I'm spending the night with friends, see you tomorrow. Please tell Annie I'll be by in the afternoon with lunch and dinner."

On some selfish level I was relieved that Maria didn't know. But when I heard William's tearful voice say, "Jack, Hank Beyers called me. He told me about Annie. Hang in there, Jack. I'll be there just as soon as I can." I wished he had been there with me at that moment.

I busied myself in the kitchen and made myself a cup of tea, something William would do to calm him down. Jamey wandered out to the front porch and found Mrs. Jarret's dog sleeping on the welcome mat. Jamey plopped down on the wooden steps next to the Golden Retriever. The dog laid his head on Jamey's lap. I heard Jamey say to him, "I won't make you go away." I stood quietly in front of the living room window and watched Jamey coddle the dog; he rocked the retriever's head in his lap like a baby. I folded my arms around the vision of my family and rocked in unison to Jamey's innocent affection.

After I put Jamey to bed, the late evening quiet and soft light from the fireplace brought on a flood of memories as I blew cigarette smoke past my lips. The wispy gray haze hung motionless above the living room until I exhaled. Eerie silhouettes traveled across the ceiling then vanished into the corners. I heard Jamey's slippers scuffling against the hardwood floor down the hallway. He stood in the doorway; pillow creases indented his cheeks. "Grampa, I can't sleep," he said.

I stretched my neck over the back of the couch to look at my grandson. "I can't sleep either, Tiger." I patted the cushion and motioned for Jamey to sit next to me. He crawled onto my lap and yawned and laid his head against my chest. He looked up at me and wiped the tears from my cheek. "It's okay to cry, Grampa," he said and then laid his sleepy head on my chest again.

Within minutes Jamey fell asleep. I carried him to bed and then dragged myself to my room. The dim fluorescent numbers on the clock radio illuminated the darkness of my room and a photograph of Annie setting on my nightstand; a photograph that said good night to me every night, a Kodak face that started my good mornings, every morning.

At 7:00 am the following morning Jamey bolted into my room. He shook my bed and rocked my shoulders and yelled at me, "Grampa, get up Grampa. It's time to go to school."

Trying to escape the glare from the 100 watt ceiling light that Jamey switched on, I buried my face in my down pillow. Yawning, I asked, "I thought you'd want to stay home today?"

"It's Johnny's birthday," he reminded me. "He's my best friend and there's a party at school today."

Mr. Ready and Anxious had already dressed himself. He had tucked his Spiderman shirt into his jeans that were on ass backwards and had smeared a glob of toothpaste across the action hero's masked eyes. Jamey had also applied enough hair gel on his spikes to lubricate the chassis of my car. He looked a fright, but I allowed him to make certain choices. I did suggest, however, that he turn his britches around.

"Okay, okay, okay," I repeated, dragging my groggy ass to the edge of the bed.

Stretching on his tiptoes, Jamey unhooked my bathrobe from the closet door and draped it over my head. He succeeded in coaxing me out of bed with his relentless insistence, "Come on, come on, get up!"

I curled my toes into the plush carpet. Rummaging for my glasses, I knocked an ashtray and Annie's picture off the nightstand. Impatient with me, Jamey put his hands on his hips and interrupted my search. "Grampa, they're on your nose!" he said. I had slept with them on all night.

On the way to school Jamey's denial about his mom troubled me, but I didn't question him about it. We parked curbside behind a school bus and waited for the kids to exit. Jamey yelled out to Johnny and two other classmates, "Guys, wait up."

"Hold on a minute, slugger. Your friends can wait," I said. Jamey blew through his lips rumbling like a motorboat, pouted, then slumped down in the seat. "Jamey, look at me. Are you gonna be okay today?"

He turned his head toward me, his eyes focused downward. "Yes, Grampa." He unbuckled his seat belt, gathered his schoolbooks and opened the car door.

I rested my hand on his shoulder. "I'll pick you up after school. Tell your teacher to call me if you need anything, okay Tiger?"

Jamey slammed the car door and ran to meet his friends. He didn't hug me goodbye that morning.

My old Chevy idled, choking, anticipating its death while I waited for the school bell to ring. Jamey mingled with his friends. I waited until they entered their classroom then drove toward Annie's house. He needed school clothes and I needed, I wasn't sure what I needed.

*   *   *

I pulled up to the entrance of Monarch Bay. The security guard left his station and knelt beside my car door. "Good morning Mr. Turner, I'm so sorry to hear about Annie."

Appreciating his genuineness, I simply nodded my head. He opened the gate to let me through. "Thank you," I said.

The slower I drove the louder the muffler under my car rumbled. Only the sounds of seagulls circling the houses showed any signs of life around the quiet manicured neighborhoods. The overcast sky shadowing the beach intensified the volume of the pounding surf against the rocky cliffs of Monarch Bay. I pulled into the driveway and felt my heartbeat against the bows of my glasses. I waited in my car and remembered Annie scolding me to hurry along earlier that morning. And from a distance, I read the yellow tape that blocked the front door, "Police Line—Do Not Cross."

After closing the front door, the smell of ripe cantaloupe reminded me that I hadn't eaten. The police must have disarmed the security system when they broke into the house; the warning signal from the alarm panel lay silent and void of light. One of Jamey's jackets hung on the banister of the staircase where he had tossed it coming home from school and then tore ass upstairs to say hi to his mom. My tennis shoes squeaked across the foyer's marble floor as I inched my way to the kitchen. My trembling hands picked up the thinly sliced cantaloupe cradled in its rind still neatly arranged on a salad dish. Rimming the inside of the stainless steel carafe, airless froth from souring milk waited next to the espresso machine. I made certain that the French doors leading outside to the pool were locked and then unplugged the espresso machine before I climbed the stairs to Jamey's bedroom.

Avoiding the doorknob, I pushed his bedroom door open with my shoe. Rushing cold air flushed my face taking my breath away. The window above his bed was wide open and puddles of rainfall had dripped onto his pillow drenching a packed duffel bag setting on the comforter. I pictured Annie folding Jamey's size 5x running shorts and matching tank tops, a pair of flip-flops, a tooth brush and his Pooh Bear while I unzipped the duffel bag. Jolting my sweet remembrance of Annie, thunder rattled the open window and rocked the house. I heard my teeth grinding and fought the tears beginning to well in my gut and struggled to swallow so they wouldn't reach my eyes. Lying on top of Jamey's clothes was an envelope. In Annie's handwriting, the word "DAD" pierced through my denial and tears flooded my eyes as I pressed the envelope to my lips. Clutching Annie's letter to my chest, I emptied Jamey's dresser and stuffed the duffel bag with his underwear, socks, sweatshirts and jeans and then closed the window.

I followed the grooves imbedded in the carpet left behind from the Coroner's gurney that led to Annie's bedroom. The double doors had been removed so that Jamey could come in without knocking. I stood at the entrance to Annie's bedroom; my fear paralyzed my legs. I remembered challenging Derek's decision to buy a .38 caliber

Smith and Wesson handgun. He was adamant about protecting his family and locked the gun in a closet drawer safe from Jamey's reach. My eyes scanned her room in horror as I witnessed Annie's young life splattered against the ceiling and walls. Her blood lay pooled in the carpet next to her bed. I felt my soul ripping my heart from my chest. I begged her to stop, and then fell to my knees and cried out to Annie, "NO!" I wept from a place deep inside my soul I had not known until that moment. My tears burned my cheeks from the fire roaring in my gut. I gripped Annie's letter in my angered fist. Unfolding the crumpled parchment, I leaned against the doorless entry and mimicked her words out loud.

> *Dear Dad,*
>   *I know exactly what you'll think when you read this. "Baby, this is really chicken-shit!" You always did use such eloquent words to describe your feelings. My words are far less eloquent than the sorrow that I leave you with, but Dad, I just can't do this anymore. I failed my husband and have abandoned my son. I'm weary. I have one regret, not knowing who my mother was. If you ever see her again, tell her she has a grandson.*
>   *Take care of my son; he loves you so.*
>   *I love you. Bye Dad,*
>   *Annie*

Each time I read her letter, Jamey's voice screamed in my head, "I want my mom, I want my mom!"

I screamed out, "I want her too, Jamey!"

I tucked Annie's letter into my pocket, grabbed Jamey's duffel bag and headed down the stairs one step at a time. Before I reached the foyer I heard a crash of shattering glass from the adjoining library. Picking up the pieces from a shattered crystal vase, Peg cut her finger. "Jack, I'm so sorry about the mess," she stammered.

"What are you doing here, Peg?"

Fumbling with a tissue, Peg wrapped her bleeding finger. "I was visiting a friend on the next block and when I drove by I saw your car."

"How long have you been here?" I asked.

"I just walked in." Peg stepped aside from Derek's desk. She steadied herself near a bookshelf. Tears welled in her eyes. "Jack, we're so sorry."

"Sorry my ass! Not according to your husband."

Peg stepped away from the bookshelf and walked toward me. "I don't know what you're talking about," she said.

"Is that right?" I backed away from Peg and lowered my voice. "It doesn't matter, Annie's gone now."

"It does matter." Peg stared through me, pleading, "We have to think about Jamey."

"We? According to Rob there is no we."

Peg shrugged her shoulders inward and stared toward the ceiling. Compressing the tissue around her bleeding finger, she said, "I don't know where you're coming from, Jack."

"I suggest you talk to your husband about it. He knows. He has it all figured out."

"I will talk to him." She held onto a photograph, caressed its polished frame and told me, "I'll talk to him tonight."

"You do that."

Peg sat down on the armchair facing the cathedral window; I watched the reflection of her tears mingling with the raindrops settling upon the windowsill. "Jack, none of us saw this coming. Annie's mother left her when she was just a baby, and then she lost . . . she lost her husband . . . even her baby wasn't enough . . . enough to fill her loss."

She stared out the window that had a view of the ocean, but the sheeting rain covered the glass like a shroud. She pressed the framed photograph of Derek holding his five-month-old son, against her bosom. Her eyes followed the rows of framed awards lining the library walls that Derek had earned and then focused on his master's degree from Cal Poly that hung above his desk. Mirroring my sorrow, she laid the picture of her son on her lap. "I lost my son too!" she cried out.

"I know," I said, concealing Annie's letter in my fist.

"What can I do to help, Jack?"

I reached behind me for the door. "Stay out of my life and leave my grandson alone."

"That's not fair. Jamey is my grandson too," she fired back at me.

"Lock the front door when you leave." I left her sitting alone in the library. I ripped the yellow tape from the front door and threw it into winter's dead garden and drove home.

*   *   *

Somehow I was being protected from having to tell Maria about Annie. Maria left another message on the machine. "Mr. Jack, I've gone to Santa Barbara with my girlfriends. Sorry you have to cook again. I'll be back by noon on Wednesday." In bold red print Maria's cell phone number hung next to the kitchen telephone; I hadn't even called William.

But to be home alone with Jamey was a blessing especially during rainy weather. Normally, at his suggestion we would build a fire and play *Harry Potter and the Sorcerer's Stone* board game. He remembered the minutest details from the story that I read to him and relished winning every time we played. But that evening, he made no mention of it; maybe it was the weather that clouded his usual playfulness.

The storm must have been centered above my house. I closed the screen door at the back porch to muffle the noise. Running off the roof, the winter deluge drowned the hum of the electric can opener as I prepared our gourmet peaches.

"Jamey," I shouted from the kitchen, "dinner's almost ready. How do hamburger steaks, cottage cheese and canned peaches sound?"

"It sounds good," he echoed back.

"Run along and wash your hands. I'll set the table."

He wrapped up his spelling homework and piled his papers and books in a stack and carried them to his room. I busied myself in the kitchen while I listened to the storm bombard my house. Jamey dawdled in his room for twenty minutes before coming back to the kitchen. When he returned, he stood next to his place at the table and rearranged the knives and forks. "Where's Maria?" he asked.

"She's on a little trip with her friends. She'll be back tomorrow. You were in your room a long time. What were you doin' in there?"

"Stuff," he said. He sat down at the table, placed his napkin on his lap and waited for me to join him.

I served up his meal restaurant style. Pretending to be a waiter, I asked him, "What can I bring you to drink, sir?"

"Nothing, Grampa."

"Not even Gatorade?"

"No."

Ruffling his hair, I sensed his pain through my hands. "You're sure down in the dumps. Wanna talk about it?"

"No." He pushed his plate away. "Grampa, I'm not very hungry. May I please be excused?"

"Jamey, I'd really like you to eat something."

He folded his arms and then hunched his back against the chair. He grit his teeth and hid his face with his hands. Tears began to moisten his pouting eyes when he shouted at me, "My mom doesn't make me eat if I don't want to."

"Jamey . . ."

"And you can't make me either!" He jolted from his chair knocking it on its side and ran to the living room.

"Jamey, come back to the table," I called out angrily.

"No! I'm going home. I want my mom!"

Jamey slammed the front door before I could reach him. He ran like a thoroughbred into the sleeting rain. Wearing his Spiderman T-shirt, his small frame was easy to see even through the downpour. I fought my emotions and the images of my daughter to keep up with his pace. I shouted through the rain and howling wind for Jamey to stop and caught my shoe on the uneven pavement. As I watched Jamey turn the corner I fell onto the concrete and scraped the skin from my elbow. I got back on my feet unaware that I was bleeding and ran like hell to catch up to him. He was only five feet from my reach when I lunged forward and grabbed his shirt collar. Like a racehorse fighting to flee, he continued running from me. He kicked at me and flailed his arms trying to escape my hold. I tightened my stronghold on his shoulders and turned him around until we were face-to-face.

Powered by his anger, he hit me again and again with both of his clenched fists. "Let me go! Let me go! I want to go home. I want my mom, I want my mom!"

"It's okay, Jamey. Hit me. Hit me hard, hard as you want. Let it out. Let it all out!"

His beating fists gave in to exhaustion. He clutched my shirt, buried his face on my drenched clothes, and touched my soul. I lifted his shivering body from the sidewalk and wrapped my sweatshirt around us both. He nestled his head against my neck and said to me, "I'm sorry, Grampa."

I whispered in his ear, "Let's go home, Tiger."

Chapter Three

Middle age had dimmed my eyesight; when I woke up, the view from my pillow was a hazy blur. Wednesday morning's sunrise glared through the paned windows above my bed, casting abstract shadows onto the walls. Even without my specs I clearly saw silhouettes move across the ceiling. No, I wasn't crazy, just not a morning person. So I covered my head with the comforter and waited for the passing sunrise to banish the shadows from my room. Above the hum of the alarm clock I listened to the creaking eaves overhanging the windows. Hibernating spiders sought shelter between the weathered cracks while dew laden silk webs bridged flowerless bougainvillea to the window frames. The storm had passed overnight and the storm in my head began to calm.

Across the hallway, Jamey slept, clucking his tongue against the roof of his mouth, a habit he had acquired as an infant. After last night, I didn't have the heart to wake him up to go to school. I snuggled into my down comforter and listened to the noises of my house, my life and my grandson and recognized a woman's voice leaving a message on the answering machine. "Hello Jack, this is Margo. William called me and told me about Annie. I flew out yesterday. I'm so sorry, Jack. If there is anything I can do, please call me. I'm staying at the Newport Hilton."

I deleted her message from the answering machine. After hearing Margo's voice, I was reminded of the day she walked out on her infant daughter,

Annie, and me. Twenty-six years of bent-up anger and bitterness flooded my head as I fell back into my pillow and cursed her, "How fucking dare you call here. Damn you, Margo, you have no right to console your soul over your daughter's death. And I'll be go to hell, you will not do it my house!"

"Grampa, who are you talking to?" Jamey asked.

I glanced over my shoulder and saw my grandson standing at my bedroom door. He rubbed the sleep from his eyes while he curled his toes into the carpet. The hall light stretched his shadow across the floor. "No one, Jamey," I said, "I was having a bad dream."

He dangled his Pooh Bear by its stuffed claw, worn and shabby from the love of a child. Dragging Pooh behind him, Jamey, still half asleep, slowly walked to the edge of my bed. Wearing his pajama bottoms ass backwards, he said, "Grampa, I'm hungry."

"Me, too," I said, and then he jumped onto my bed, clung to my back and shoulders, and together we made a bee-line to the kitchen.

With an appetite like an NFL linebacker, Jamey scarped down a full stack of pancakes. He soaked up the last bit of maple syrup, sponging the soggy cakes, and then guzzled down his glass of milk. "I'm full. Can I go outside and find Willow?" he asked.

I drizzled a tad more syrup onto my last pancake. "Who's Willow?"

"Mrs. Jarret's dog, silly!"

After twelve years of living next door to the Jarrets, I finally learned that the shoe thief had a name. Jamey lured Willow into the back yard. When I heard Maria call out to Jamey, "Don't forget to shut the gate behind you!" I hurried to load the dishwasher before she came into the house. Maria slammed her car door in the driveway while I made a mad dash to clean the remnants of the sticky syrup off the granite counter before she came into the kitchen. There were two household bugaboos that sent Maria into orbit, Jamey's dirty tennis shoes left on the back porch steps and a messy kitchen that I often left for her to clean up.

Grinning with approval, Maria passed the clean counter, then me, and laid her overnight bag on the dining room floor. "Looks like I'm a little late for breakfast," she said.

"Are you hungry?" I asked. "I'll whip you up some flap-jacks."

"I had a drive-thru breakfast earlier this morning. Traffic on the 405 makes me jittery. Maybe a decaf latte if you're brewing?"

Having mastered frothing the milk into a thick and creamy consistency without air bubbles, I prided myself as the latte king. After one sip of her espresso, Maria sported a mustache as white as the hair that shaded my upper lip. "Oh, Maria!" I said, pointing to her upper lip and then gestured with my thumb and forefinger across my mustache.

"Oh, this," she said then pretended to groom a mustache of her own. "I think I'll keep it, thank you."

I reached for my pack of smokes and repeatedly flicked the disposable lighter. "This damn thing never works," I said.

"Mr. Jack, it's childproof. Maybe it's Mr. Jack proof too. Push the button in on the side first."

"Aren't you clever," I snarled, finally lighting my cigarette. "Maria, there's something I need to tell you while Jamey's outside." I continued wiping maple syrup where there was none. I held back tears that had been damned up for three days, and then reached for Maria's hands. "Maria, Annie's gone."

"Gone where?" she asked, setting her cup on the table, noiseless but deafening.

"Gone." My thoughts wandered; tears flooded my eyes. Barely audible, I murmured to her, "She died . . . on Monday."

Peacefully, Maria spoke Annie's name as she motioned the sign of the cross. She knelt beside the chair, praying, "Nome di Padre, Figlio espiritu, Santo, Amen. Poverina!" She wiped her tears on a lace handkerchief and then pleaded, "Why didn't you call me?"

"I don't know, Maria. When Hank came by the house on Monday, I thought only of Jamey and Annie, and well . . ."

"You should have called me. Henry would have understood. I would have come home right away."

"Henry? I thought you were in Santa Barbara with your girlfriends."

"Mr. Jack, now is not the time. I'll tell you about Henry later. How is Jamey, is he okay?"

I watched Jamey from the kitchen window as he played with Willow in the back yard. I reassured both Maria and myself when I told her, "Jamey is handling this better than any of us."

Witnessing Maria's tears, as she wept for our loss, made me realize, she was my family.

No one read my feelings better than Maria; she volunteered to call our friends, including William. Holding both of my hands, she comforted me, "You take care of you and Jamey and Annie's needs; I'll manage the rest."

Maria's selfless consideration lightened my burden for the days ahead. Even with her passing, Annie gave to me the same consideration. She had prearranged her own funeral, something people seldom consider until they reach my age. She wanted to be buried next to her husband. Even during her long illness, she had organized her affairs, making my transition to care for Jamey a no brainer. Annie had hired an attorney to file the documents designating me as legal guardian of Jamey and executor of his trust. The sale of the house funded the majority of his inheritance. After the house sold, the money remained safe in the trust waiting Jamey's twenty-first birthday. Little did Annie know that the Fitzpatricks and I had started a college fund for Jamey, one of the few things that we, the in-laws agreed upon.

*   *   *

Friday morning, five days after Annie's death, American Airlines flight 1294 from JFK International to John Wayne International Airport had been delayed an hour and a half. Wandering idly around the terminal, Joey read his Disneyland brochure while mapping his Magic Kingdom adventure. Joey was young, immature, unemployed, and gorgeous, and William was smitten with him. William called me on his cell phone, "Jack, we're gonna be late getting in to Orange County. The added security here since 9/11 slows everything down to a snail's pace," William told me. "There's been some kind of problem and all flights out are being delayed."

My mind moved twenty paces too fast that day. Listening to William, reviewing the funeral arrangements in my head, and anticipating the gang arriving, I asked him, "Do you remember Richard and Tommy, my old neighbors from West Hollywood?"

"That far back, huh? Let's see, I recall a health nut and his good looking boyfriend?"

"Yes, that would describe them. Richard still dines on food with names I associate with wilderness foraging. I have to hand it to him though, he looks ten years younger than I do and we're the same age. Tommy probably sneaks a burger every now and then, but his workout ethic keeps him fit. I think that if he didn't, Richard would force feed him tofu salads as his punishment. They're arriving tonight around six to set up a buffet at the house for tomorrow. I haven't a clue what they will bring."

"Tell you what, if you find nothing on the menu you like, I'll take you out to dinner."

"I'll hold you to it."

"What about Mr. and Mrs. Zucker?" he asked.

"The old Jewish couple who lived behind Tommy and Richard. I thought I told you, Mr. Zucker passed away a year ago, lung cancer. He never smoked a cigarette in his life. They were such dear friends to Annie and me when she was just a little girl. Anyway, Mrs. Zucker is coming with the guys this evening to help out before the funeral tomorrow."

"There was someone else who lived by you, some crotchety old man."

"Mr. Thomas. Oh, yes, the old curmudgeon will be here too. We'll have to listen to his boring war stories, but Annie wouldn't have it any other way. At four years old, Annie was the only child who could weasel the old bastard into doing anything she wanted."

"He sounds like the life of the party. Anyway, has Kevin called yet?"

"Actually he stopped by last night. It was good to see him again. God, it's been nine or ten years since I last saw him; I'd forgotten how handsome he was. Wanted to know if there was anything he could do. He's gonna drive us to the cemetery tomorrow."

"Jack, they just announced that our flight is beginning to board. I'll call when Joey and I arrive at the hotel."

"I'm anxious to meet him," I said.

"He's anxious to meet you too."

"By the way," I said, "Margo's in town."

"I know. I called her and told her about Annie. Gotta go, Jack. Love you."

"Love you too," I said, then listened to the monotonous hum after he hung up.

While I was talking to William, the faucet had overflowed the kitchen sink and countertop, saturating my trousers and underwear. As I peered out the window to check on Jamey, I felt two strong hands grab my waist and a pair of chafed lips kiss me on the neck. I wrung out the front of my trousers and shouted with delight, "Tommy! You big lummox. You're not supposed to be here until six."

"We're a little early," he said with his eyes glued to my dripping trousers. "Did we have a little accident?" he asked, teasing me.

"Get out'a here. I brushed my britches against the wet sink while I was talking to William," I said, wringing out the excess dish soap from my pockets.

"You and William, when are you two ever gonna tie the knot?"

"He has a new boyfriend," I said with objection.

"Oh, do I hear a little jealousy?"

"I'm not the jealous type. And speaking of boyfriends, where is Richard?"

"Mr. Nuts and Twigs is unloading the car."

"I should go help him," I said. As I took two steps forward, a yelp at my bare feet scared the bajeezes out of me. "Holy God, what have we got here?"

Tommy scooped his eight-month-old Papillon puppy from the floor. "This is Nikki."

"She's no bigger than a fart in a mitten," I said. "What does she weigh, four pounds?"

Tommy kissed Nikki's dwarfed black nose and loved on the puppy as if she were his baby. "Her's a big girl now, almost five pounds," he said and kissed her butterfly ears. "Here, take her, I'll help Richard unload the van."

Smudging my glasses with her wet nose, Nikki clawed at my beard with her miniature paws. I held her at an arm's distance from my face and then spoke directly to her, "I don't have fleas little bit, so knock it off." Dogs and I got along better from a distance, but this furry gerbil settled right into my arms. "Tommy, where are the other two dogs?" I asked as I coddled Nikki in the crick of my arm.

"Lady and Sandy are in the van. Can they come into the house?" he pleaded.

"Let's try the back yard first," I suggested. "Jamey's out there with the neighbor's dog."

I was grateful for all the commotion in and out of my house that afternoon. It helped to keep my thoughts of Annie at bay, at least for the moment.

Toting an overflowing laundry basket under one arm, Maria pushed open the kitchen door with her hip. Her face lit up when she saw Tommy. It did my heart well to see her smile again. Two days of crying had left her eyes swollen, but seeing Tommy melted away the puffiness. He had that affect on her even when we lived next door to him in West Hollywood. She stretched on her tiptoes and with a motherly squeeze, hugged her six-foot-five buddy around his middle. She caught a glance of Nikki from the corner of her eye. "Oh, look at this," she said, and then began nudging noses with the puppy like an Eskimo. "Tommy, un' bella canina. What is she?"

Tommy lifted the puppy's ears to imitate its namesake and then replied, "She's a Papillon, Maria."

"Papillon, little butterfly," cooed Maria.

Maria handed me the laundry basket and I handed her Little Miss Darling, a fair trade. Hearing these two carrying on was a bit much for me to stomach. "Honestly," I said, "there's enough syrupy sugar in this kitchen to sweeten one of Mrs. Zucker's bitter rhubarb pies. If you need me, I'll be out front helping Richard unload the van."

Heaped to the headliner in the back of their van, stacks of foil wrapped serving trays filled the air with a variety of tofu aromas; none of which had been disturbed; the dogs must not have been vegetarians. Richard chased Lady and Sandy into the backyard and then hollered at me, "I'll be right there."

Buried beneath food, table cloths, and overnight bags, Mrs. Zucker pleaded, "Jack, please help an old woman out of this van."

"You are such a dear to help out," I told her, as she struggled to free herself from the barricade of food containers that cramped her space.

Patting my hairy chin with her arthritic hands, she said, "I don't know about you, but tomorrow I want more than nuts and twigs for dinner. I'm roasting you a turkey and baking a home made rhubarb pie, Mr. Zucker's favorite, God rest his soul," she said, lifting her eyes to the heavens. "The roses on the seat are for you, Jack. And this is for Jamey," she said as she tucked a blue envelope into my shirt pocket."

"What's this?" I asked.

"A little something for Jamey's education. You put this away and when Jamey goes to college, you tell him this is from Mrs. Zucker."

"I hope that he will be able to thank you in person when he starts college," I said.

"Are you insinuating that I am an old woman," she said, and then laughed until we both had tears in our eyes.

Balanced upright in a cardboard box, three dozen long-stemmed yellow roses rested in a crystal vase. "Are these from your garden?" I asked, knowing better. And then buttering her up, I kissed Mrs. Zucker on her rouged cheeks.

"All those years that you and Annie lived next door to me, you didn't learn one thing about gardening. My roses don't bloom in January, you ninny. These are the best hot house roses money can buy. I spent a little of Mr. Zucker's money he left me."

"They're beautiful, thank you so much," I said and then looked upward toward the heavens to thank Mr. Zucker as well. She steadied her walk with her cane and then clasped my hand as we climbed the front porch steps together. Without a free hand to wipe her tears, she welcomed my home with her roses and smeared, rouged cheeks. Mrs. Zucker was an inspiration; at 82 she still cleaned her own apartment, baked pies, and during Hanukkah gave Jamey a twenty-dollar US Savings Bond in a sealed, blue envelope, a tradition she began with Annie when Annie was six-years old.

*   *   *

On the day of Annie's funeral, Saturday morning's sun, hidden above a thick coastal cloudbank, rose to the sounds of winter. Before Willow beat them to the trough, backyard blue jays battled with squirrels over unshucked peanuts that I had donated to the birdfeeder. Resting seagulls scratched on the roof tiles with their beaks, contemplating breakfast at the shoreline while early risers in the neighborhood planed their singing tires along the wet pavement. The heat from the old floor furnace expanded the iron grate cover, creaking, waking me from a half-sleep. 12:00 flashed red from the alarm clock; a power failure must have visited during the night. I lay there in bed under the comforter, fighting the upright position until I smelled fresh espresso wafting through the house. Maria's attempt to make a latte dragged my slumber into the kitchen; the corduroy tie dangled from my robe, dusting a narrow path along the hardwood floors. Maria and I sipped in silence until Jamey clicked on the TV and began channel surfing for cartoons.

Competing with the deafening, warring "Transformer" laser battle, blaring from the television, William banged on the screen door, hollering, "Is anybody home?"

Jamey muted the mutilating sounds with the remote control and then shouted, "Uncle William!" Jamey nearly succeeded in tackling William to the floor. "Grampa, Uncle William's here!"

William's strong arms reached from rib to rib around my lean chest. He hadn't grown any taller, my chin still rested comfortably on his thick bushy hair; his nose poked my Adam's apple. "I'm so glad you're here," I said.

"How do you stay so trim, Jack?"

"Metabolism and a six-year-old grandson," I confessed.

Joey cradled his chin on William's shoulder and introduced himself, "Hi, I'm Joey."

I reached out to shake his scrawny hand. "Nice to meet you," I said. At 5'9" he and William stood nose to nose. Kevin was 6'3". Evidently, youth had replaced William's attraction for aging jocks.

"So you're the legendary Jack," Joey said. "Billy sings your praises everyday."

"Billy shouldn't sing! Legendary? More like ancient," I said.

"I don't know. The gray is pretty sexy," he said, eyeballing me from head to toe.

His innuendo was inappropriate in front of Jamey. I swallowed a comment meant for him. "Hmm," I grunted, indicating my disapproval and then said to him, "This is my grandson, Jamey."

Joey grit his teeth to hide his embarrassment. His apology shone through his immature but expressive brown eyes. Plopped in front of the blaring TV, Jamey zoned us all out; the Transformers reigned supreme. I pulled the area rug from under his butt and said, "Jamey, say hi to Joey."

With his eyes glued to the battle on the screen, he said, "Hi."

"Hey, Jamey. What are you watchin'?" Joey asked.

"Transformers," he said; his concentration was impenetrable.

Joey plopped his butt right next to Jamey's on the rug and talked a language only Jamey could translate. I wrapped my arm around William's shoulders and said to him, "As one kid to another. Come on, Maria is anxious to see you."

Together, we headed toward the kitchen. William asked me, "Did you call Margo back?"

"I haven't spoken to Margo for more than twenty years. I don't intend to begin now."

"She was Annie's mother, you know," he reminded me.

"Yeah, right." My gut began to burn. The images of the day that lay ahead flashed across my mind like a tired video, the tracking out of sync and on fast forward. I sank into one of the dining room chairs and fussed with the morning newspaper, organizing the sections. Newsprint blackened my cheeks as I smudged the tears beneath my glasses. "William, I cannot do this day. I miss Annie so much."

"I know," William said. He handed me a box of tissue and told me, "Kevin just pulled in. Why don't you and Jamey get ready before everybody comes into the house. Besides, I need to say hello to Maria."

While Jamey and I dressed in our gray suits with matching blue silk ties, William and Maria helped Mrs. Zucker carry her roasted turkey and baked pies that she had prepared at Kevin's condo the night before. Maria then excused herself to her room to freshen up. Richard and Tommy locked the dogs in the back yard. Mr. Thomas sat on the sofa and razzed Joey about his earring. Somebody put on a CD, Karen Carpenter's voice graced the house with calm only I seemed to appreciate.

With his lawyer preciseness, Kevin made the seating arrangements; he drove, Mrs. Zucker and Jamey rode up front while William sat between Joey and me on the back seat. Richard, Tommy and Mr. Thomas followed behind us at a car's length. We passed few cars as we crawled along Pacific Coast Highway. A veil of dark coastal clouds wept onto the highway as if to mourn our loss. William held onto my hand and caressed my knuckles with his thumb. My stare followed the gray shoreline until we turned away from the ocean toward the cemetery.

Beside her husband's name, Derek Fitzpatrick, was engraved upon the same headstone, Elizabeth Anne Fitzpatrick, February 20, 1975-January 14, 2002.

Jamey hand carried a single yellow rose from Mrs. Zucker's centerpiece that she had arranged for the dining room table earlier that morning. Following the eulogy, given by William, Jamey walked near the edge of the open gravesite and stood next to the headstone that towered above him. His fingers traced the smooth engraved edges of his mother's name and laid the rose onto the wet grass. He looked past Rob and Peg to find my eyes and said to me, "I wanna go home, Grampa."

"Soon," I said.

Mesmerized by the mahogany casket that hid his mother from view, Jamey watched as Annie's memory was lowered beneath the sculpted lawn. Peg saw Jamey silently watching and motioned with open arms for him to come to her. "Give your Grandma a hug," she said.

Staining her St. John knit dress, nylons and Ferragamo shoes, Peg knelt against the rain soaked lawn. Watching her embrace Jamey, I realized how much she loved her grandson. Rob remained stoic and unmoved, but never left Peg's side. I read Jamey's stiff posture as: his tie was too tight and his black leather shoes were cramping the beach lifestyle that he imitated from me. When he kissed his grandmother on her cheek, Peg said to him, "Jamey, honey, you can call me anytime; you know the phone number. You can come and spend the night or weekends, whenever you want."

"Okay," he said. "I'll ask Grampa."

She lowered her eyes to hide the hurt she felt from Jamey's response. She then raised her eyes to find mine. At that moment I remembered her sitting in Derek's library asking me what she could do to help. She kissed Jamey on his forehead then followed a short distance behind Rob toward their car. Rob turned, grabbed Peg's hand and said to me, "Jack, sorry about Annie."

My swollen eyes watched Rob and Peg walk across the cemetery lawn. A woman who was parked in front of them drove away in a white limousine. When she rolled the rear window down, I recognized her face. Jamey stayed with Maria and William as I walked alone toward the curb. Margo's perfume lingered as I watched her limo turn onto a quiet residential street.

By mid afternoon we were all pretty full of turkey, pie and tofu chicken style sesame salad with tahini dressing. The afternoon had warmed to a pleasant sixty-five degrees, inviting an outdoor smoke on the front porch and a sit-down in an old wicker rocking chair that I had cherished since West Hollywood. From inside the house I heard Tommy telling some obscene tale, Mrs. Zucker laughing so hard she had to blow her nose from laughter induced tears, and Mr. Thomas butting in about some floozy he courted in Thailand during shore leave. Jamey had his fill of our friends, the funeral, and the unfamiliar feast, even with me, so he played with Lady, Sandy and Willow in the backyard; Nikki never left Tommy's lap.

Little boys possess an innate joy, a capacity that most adult men seem to outgrow. When Jamey gets tickled inside his laughter begins at his toes and ends up tickling my insides just from listening to him. All of that joy from being licked from head to toe by three dogs. I nestled my head against the back of the porch chair. Jamey's laughter reminded me of my little girl, Annie, giggling and splashing in a blow up pool. I realized that innate joy doesn't have an exclusive on gender.

Minutes later, I heard a car door shut waking me from that sweet memory. My head didn't budge from the comfort of the porch chair as a part of my past arrived, uninvited. The limo I'd seen earlier pulled up in front of the house. Margo asked the chauffeur to wait. She took only a few steps onto the walkway and stopped. "Hello, Jack. It's been a long time."

I walked to the edge of the porch, widened my stance and gripped the wooden handrails that were in need of a coat of paint. "Hello, Margo," I said. My rigid posture and unforgiving stare warned her not to come any closer.

Life in New York City had been more forgiving to Margo's beauty than my beach bum lifestyle had been to me. Rumor has it that gray hair on men is considered distinguished; the rumor is full of crap, gray hair just makes me look old. Neither crow's feet nor gray hair betrayed Margo's age; she was still as stunning as I remembered. Her auburn hair, shorter now, styled like so many anchor women on the news, trendy and ruffled, worked with her hip hugger jeans. At 52 she pulled it off.

"I'm so sorry about Annie, so sorry that I never got to know her," she said.

"I'm sorry for you too," I said. The silence of our voices increased the visual volume of our locked stare. Allowing her to enter my life again was not an option for me. "My friends are waiting inside," I said. Widening my stance, I blocked the porch entrance; Margo stayed her distance, frozen on the walkway. I reached for the screen door and with my back to Margo; I said to her, "You're not welcome here."

"Jack, please don't." Nearing the bottom of the porch steps, Margo began to lose her composure. Indignant, she refused my goodbye. She lowered her eyes and then muttered loud enough for me to hear, "I was Annie's mother."

"You gave birth to Annie. That's all you did. She was my baby. Do you understand that? My baby! Have a nice ride, Margo," I said then moved my stare to the limo. Despite my cold words, I longed to embrace her, but too many years had passed preventing me from reaching out to her. I butted out my cigarette, missed the rim of the ashtray, and then turned away from Margo to go back into the house.

Margo edged her way closer toward the steps; her eyes followed my stare. Her quivering voice insisted, "I'm not leaving yet, Jack."

Near enough for me to see her green eyes, emerald and unguarded, I blasted her, "What the fuck do you want from me?"

"To hear me out."

"So you can cleanse yourself of guilt? I never expected you to help me raise Annie. Margo, you fucking left. You didn't even say goodbye or why you left."

"Jack, please, let me explain," she pleaded.

Jamey came bolting through the screen door letting it slam and plowed right into my behind.

Margo's eyes lit up when she saw Jamey. A maternal voice spoke from her lips. "Who is this handsome devil?" she asked. I watched the anxiety in her face melt away.

Jamey nuzzled into my side like a chick finding shelter beneath its mother's wings. Clutching my shirttail, he introduced himself, "I'm Jamey. Grampa, who's that?"

Jamey's blond hair lay like silk beneath my lanky hand. I held him close to my side and answered, "Someone who knew your mom a long time ago."

Margo pursed her lips, perhaps to smile, maybe to repress a tear. Before turning away to leave she focused her attention on my grandson. "It was nice to meet you, Jamey. Maybe we can meet again sometime?"

Margo disappeared through the rear door of the stretch limo. She rolled down the tinted window and leaned through the opening. She uttered words that I had once read in a note left behind in Annie's crib, "I'll call you."

In slow motion, the limo glided away. The darkened window remained closed as I stared at the taillights reflecting their red glow against the wet pavement, trailing toward the ocean.

With Jamey still at my side, the image of Margo had imprinted a new memory onto my old worn out brain like a negative from an old photograph, there but not there. I mumbled, "She looks so much like Annie. Grandma, huh?"

"What Grampa?" Jamey asked.

"Nothing," I said. "I need a piece of Mrs. Zucker's rhubarb pie. How 'bout you?"

"I already had some, Grampa."

I picked him up by his waist and swung him around the front porch, his feet just missed the chairs and wicker table that Willow had chewed to bits. "I bet you could eat another piece."

1974-1976

Chapter Four

L ife before Annie seems so long ago now. I'd sell my soul to go back to 1974 before all of this happened, back to when I first met William Broderick.

It was sometime in April during my junior year at California State Los Angeles when William caught my eye for the second time. I recall him squatting on the lawn sandwiched amongst a crowd of gay men and lesbian women. His bushy mane, dark as ebony, stood out amongst the sea of blondes with tanned shoulders, his eyes hidden behind a pair of dark sunglasses. I stared at him for the longest time until the gentleman sitting next to him caught my glance and smiled back at me; William hadn't noticed my stares. His focus was on the speaker who had just walked onto the stage. The applause from the crowd diverted my unintentional attention from the gentleman who had smiled back at me, while William remained sprawled along the grassy quad in front of the new student union building, unaware of me.

The Gay and Lesbian Organization on campus held a rally that afternoon. The guest speaker, a candidate for California State Representative and a proponent of gay rights, detailed the recent Supreme Court's debate on the Sodomy Law referendum. Near the rear of the liberal crowd, Margo and I paced back and forth, heckling the protesters. They waved picket signs, screaming their conservative and unoriginal right-wing rhetoric, "Fear Queers!", "Lock the closet!", and "God hates faggots!"

Margo Evans, my best friend and roommate, flipped them off and yelled out, "Fuck you too!"

"Margo, what the hell are you doing? That's exactly the kind of reaction they're hoping for," I said.

"They piss me off with their self-righteous, right-wing bullshit," she replied testily.

"Yeah, me too, but you need to exercise a little restraint here, okay?"

"You invited me along to support you, not to be apathetic," she reminded me. Determined to get the last word in, she flipped off the protesters one last time.

In spite of her sharp tongue, Margo was stunning to look at, a Rita Hayworth with a sassy walk and a petite figure all wrapped up in a lovely but arrogant package. Not your average profile of a female certified public accountant with an MBA whose goal was to profit from American corporate greed. I jumped at any opportunity to be seen with her in public. But her behavior that afternoon was over the top; all I wanted was to remain anonymous as I covered the story for the paper. With Margo at my side, anonymity became impossible; so I gave in, gave up, and flipped off the protesters as well.

My interest soon turned to a group of young men who were visiting from USC with their shirts wrapped around their trim waistlines as they soaked up the warm April sunshine. My eyes followed their tight, lean naked torsos as they moved across the lawn.

Without inhibition, their bodies seemed to dance to private melodies that played in their heads. Margo was too busy chatting with her lesbian friends to notice my interest in the men who were parading near us. The guys who were "out" had wrapped their arms around each other and were kissing on the mouth in order to get a rise out of the protesters. They succeeded and continued their display of sensual consent. Margo's flirtation with her lesbian friends fed additional fodder to those picketing the rally. I overheard her invite two gay women to our place for Sunday dinner, not to annoy the picketers, but to annoy me instead. I had tolerated these two women before as guests in our apartment, a small sacrifice on my part to keep Margo happy; however, she invited them to our place at least once a month. Whenever they were guests, I cooked, they drank cheap wine, and I always ended the evening getting loaded on some killer weed from Margo's stash because it helped me to get through an evening of female dominated male bashing.

Once the rally dispersed, Margo joined her friends in conversation while I sought shade beneath a blooming jacaranda tree to cool off and to jot some notes for a story that I was writing for the *University Times*. My bias against organized political rhetoric influenced my commentary regarding the rally. Some radical gay men and lesbian women labeled me a hypocrite because I resisted aggressive participation in the cause for furthering gay rights. Mainstream homosexuals applauded my passive resistance because I chose to live my life without flaunting my homosexuality to the world.

Too many of the spectators had chosen to gather around the same jacaranda tree that I had quietly nestled under. So I weaved my way through the thick crowd of testosterone and sought another quiet place to sit where I could organize my notes without interruption; not an easy task when surrounded by so many good-looking men. Away from the crowd, I settled onto the grass near a hedge of flowering honeysuckle and star jasmine and began writing; a mistake because I was allergic to star jasmine. My vision began to blur through my wire-rimmed glasses. I sat in the lotus position and blew my nose on a handkerchief that had seen better days. Before I stood up to move away from the hedges, I noticed a pair of knobby knees staring me in the face. Above the knees, a baritone voice broke my concentration, "Aren't you Jack Turner?"

"That would be me." My watery eyes were glued to his shorts. As I blew my nose again, I thought to myself, "who wears seersucker these days?"

I uncrossed my yoga position in order to stand. He insisted, "Please, don't get up. I didn't mean to interrupt what you were doing."

"You're not interrupting anything. Just scribbling some notes about this rally for an article I'm writing. I can finish this later."

He reached out to shake my hand. "By the way, I'm William, William Broderick. You don't remember me do you?"

"Not off hand," I lied, having delighted in his good looks earlier.

"A couple months ago I agreed to an interview with you for your article on the Nixon Watergate scandal."

"Of course you did. How could I forget you? I heard you speak at a luncheon on campus a while back. Your opinions about impeaching the President helped to shape my story. I remember quoting you, "I'm not fully convinced of President Nixon's connection with Watergate; however, his recent firing of Special Prosecutor Archibald Cox coupled with the Justice Department shake-up indicates an unstated admission of guilt.""

"Hmm, word for word," he said, impressed that I quoted him verbatim.

What he didn't know was that his opinions were only secondary to my motivation; I had found him attractive and wanted to ask him out. But by the end of the interview, William had excused himself and left me standing with a pen in my hand, a pad tucked under my arm, and a missed opportunity.

"Of course, I'm a newspaper reporter," I said.

"That explains it then," he said with a half-grin. "But I guess time and our justice system will eventually uncover the truth, unless Nixon resigns," William assured me.

I continued to egg him on, "Even so, his resignation will not exonerate him if he's found guilty."

"I predict that he will resign and walk away from the White House scott-free," William said in a tone of absolute certainty.

His prediction was unnerving, especially since I believed that Nixon was abusing his constitutional powers and was guilty as sin.

"I hope that you're wrong, but I fear that you are right," I said. Despite William's doom and gloom and his sun starved legs, his well-read conversation and confident masculinity made him easy to be with. I liked him.

Margo kissed and hugged her girl friends goodbye. Like a school girl with a crush on a new boyfriend she moved toward William and me. Margo preferred men when it came to the bedroom, but adored the attention she received from her lesbian friends. As Margo inched her way closer to us, Karen Carpenter's angelic voice blessed the airwaves with, "Rainy Days and Mondays". Rock and roll music irritated me to the point of distraction; but whenever I heard Miss Carpenter's voice, I became putty in anybody's hands.

"They must be playing this one for you, Jack," Margo said, razzing me. She worshipped rock and roll and coerced me into accompanying her to loud, smoke-filled, electrified concerts. I returned the headache whenever the opportunity permitted; I shamed her into accompanying me to easy-listening, intimate music concerts around campus.

Eyeing me first and then William, she introduced herself, "Hi, I'm Margo." She then snuggled up to me and slid her hand into the rear pocket of my shorts.

William, the gentleman, stood to shake her hand, "Nice to meet you," he said.

"The pleasure is all mine," she said and then passed me an approving smile.

"Are you and Jack . . . ?"

Before Margo could answer him, I interrupted and said, "No, we're friends, roommates."

Before Margo removed her hand from my rear pocket she pinched the cheeks of my bony derriere and then stepped aside. "If you're not busy, why don't you join Jack and me at our place for lunch?" she asked William.

"I'd like that," he said while I held Margo's hand away from my pockets.

Margo and I lived off campus. We shared the rent for a furnished, two-bedroom hovel. Her fascination for incense, lava lamps and macramé lent a distinct taste to a San Francisco's Haight-Ashbury address. The living room doubled as a hot house for growing potted plants that regularly thirsted for attention. She smoked like a fiend, filling three hollowed abalone shells with butts and spent roaches; the incense she burned failed to disguise the patchouli-like odor that lingered in the rental furniture. Our combined incomes paid the rent on time and we stashed enough cash each week to go clubbing on Friday nights, Margo's excuse for me to have a social life.

William and I strolled across campus back to my apartment while Margo walked ahead of us. She turned her head and hollered, "I'll meet you guys back at the apartment." She left in a dead run, her way of saying, "I'll leave you two alone for awhile."

William and I shared stories about ourselves for nearly thirty minutes before we reached the apartment. I remember his face lighting up when he told me that he had recently passed the State Bar Exam. "Congratulations," I said. "An attorney. What area of law do you want to pursue?"

"Family law, so that my mother can brag about her lawyer son at her garden parties."

"Have you interviewed with any of the law firms in town?" I asked.

"Actually, I start my new job on Monday. The law firm where I interned for a year hired me as a junior associate."

"Impressive," I said.

"This Sunday, Mother is hosting an evening soiree in my honor. But she embarrasses me every time she introduces me to her friends' unmarried daughters. One day she'll understand that I am not interested in her debutante friends."

"Maybe you should bring me along," I said, inviting myself.

"That's not a bad idea. Mother would love you. She has a thing for tall, handsome hairy men."

William's cheeks flushed pink as I buttoned my shirt. I watched his reaction from the corner of my eyes. I wanted to reach out to him and draw his face near my chest; but instead, I asked, "What about your Dad?"

"He divorced Mother ten years ago; it was Mother's decision. He remarried and moved to Arizona; we don't communicate."

"Why not?" I asked.

"Because I failed his expectation of me. My father has given the anachronism W.A.S.P. a whole new twist. To him it represents *Will Not Accept Sexual Perversion.* His narrow view on life does not accept homosexuality as a respectable alternative lifestyle. He refuses to speak to me, his little queer mistake. He even returned my graduation invitation from law school without a postmark. So after I passed the bar exam, I didn't bother to let him know."

"What a shame for you not to be able to share your accomplishment with him," I said and then sat down on a bench near the grassy path we had been mindlessly following. I breathed in the faded scent of the Pacific Ocean that lingered on the afternoon breeze while two wayward seagulls soared above the canopy of maple trees that lined the pathway.

"Yes, I suppose so. But if you can see beyond his prejudice and narrow mindedness, he's really not such a bad guy," William said.

"Maybe he'll come around and see this differently," I said as I looked up at William.

"I won't hold my breath. He's a stubborn old fool, has more money than good sense. But in spite of his beliefs and his well-funded bank account, I'd like that. But enough about my dysfunctional family. What about you? I'll bet you and your father have a great relationship."

"We did."

"Past tense?"

"My dad was killed when I was twelve. And you're right; we shared a relationship that most kids envied when I was growing up."

"Jack, what happened to your father? Unless of course you're uncomfortable talking about it," he said, apologetically.

I hedged for just a moment before I answered him, "No, I suppose I don't mind talking about him."

Until that afternoon, my private life had belonged to me, only. I wasn't one to divulge or share personal details of my life to anyone especially with regards to my childhood or parents. And now that I think about it, it's no wonder that I have lived most of my adult life without a significant other. But William had a profound affect on me even though we had just met. He sat beside me on the bench, his bare knees inches from mine. A flood gate of emotions opened inside of me that hadn't been dredged up since I was teenager. "I only know what my Aunt Janet, his sister, told me several months after his funeral," I began. "My dad was an alcoholic. He only drank on the weekends though. He enjoyed spending his Sunday afternoons in a neighborhood bar where I grew up. To this day I wish he hadn't gone there on that particular Sunday afternoon. I recall my aunt telling me that some of the local regulars, a bunch of beer drinking, foul mouth drunks, fucked with my dad's head when they tormented him about me. Witnesses later recounted hearing one of the men saying to my dad, 'Understand your son is queer, one of those sissy boys, little fruitcake, takes it up the ass.' And with that, all hell broke lose in that bar."

"Jack, if you don't want to talk about this . . ."

"Really, I don't mind. It's been a long time since I've spoken my dad's name or shared my memory of him with someone who cared enough to listen. My dad was a simple man," I continued. "He felt comfortable wearing a pair or 501 jeans, hoisted up by a leather belt with a turquoise and silver buckle, a white undershirt, and a pair of cowboy boots. He visited his barber twice a month to keep his crew cut clean and short, just like his conversations, to the point and without a lot of fluff." I continued to reminisce. "His name was Robert, Robert Turner; his friends called him Cowboy Bob. Unfortunately, not one of his friends was at the bar that afternoon. My dad shoved the guy who had insulted my character through a flimsy glass window. The shove escalated into a brawl and a physical battle between my dad and this miserable soul who provoked him. My dad was stabbed to death with a dagger of shattered glass."

"Jack, I'm so sorry, I can't imagine how you and your mother must have coped."

"Don't feel sorry for my mother. I don't, even now. The day following my dad's death my mother delivered me to my aunt's house with one suitcase filled some underwear, a tooth brush, a pair of sneakers, and one pair of jeans. She left town without leaving a note, a letter, or a phone call. My Aunt Janet raised me. Thirteen years later, I still don't know where my mother lives and frankly, I could care less."

William remained still but attentive; his eyes focused on mine.

"William, forgive me for dumping all of this on you," I said.

"Jack, don't apologize. I'm glad to be here with you. And you're not dumping on me."

"Forgive me," I said again, "all of this has been stored away in my head for more years than I care to think about. I'm sure you've heard enough."

"Actually, your life sounds much more exciting than my predictable privileged upbringing could compare with. Your mother, what happened between you two?"

"My mother was a miserable bitch. She hated her life. She hated her husband and resented me. She spent her life trying to reconcile her bitterness through religion. She changed denominations annually. One year she was a screaming Holy Roller, another year a Bible Baptist, the list is too numerous to mention them all. She finally found solace in Jehovah. Jehovah's Witnesses visited our house each Sunday for bible study, preaching their doctrine of rejecting the supremacy of government and religious institutions over personal conscience. What a bunch of crap. They do not celebrate birthdays. Whenever my birthday came around, Dad hid a gift under my bed and swore me to secrecy. In order to keep my mother from confiscating the contraband, I left all of my gifts at my Aunt Janet's house. Jesus, I'm surprised Dad stayed married to my mother. They slept in separate bedrooms. She must have been between religions when I was conceived. I'm convinced that she knew that her newborn son was homosexual. I must have been eight or nine at the time when I first heard her express her disappointment in me. Her bedroom was next to mine. I overheard her praying for the salvation of my dad and me. She prayed to Jehovah to save her son from the sins of sodomy."

"Oh my god, Jack," William said with disbelief.

"I hadn't a clue what sodomy meant until I looked it up in the dictionary. I was mortified. Couldn't talk to my mother about it and was afraid to say anything to Dad, so I confided in my aunt. I remember her gentle hands lightly cupping my ears and her sweet voice whispering to me, 'Jackie, put those thoughts out of your head. No one is going to hurt you; I won't let them. I want you to always be proud of who you are and of the young man I know you will grow up to be.'"

"I want to meet your Aunt Janet," William said.

"She lives in Florida now, but comes out to California every couple of years for a visit. Next time she's here, I'll make sure that you get to meet her. I don't think that I can forgive my mother for leaving me, and yet, if she were standing here before me, I'd probably thank her because my aunt loved me as her own son . . . Wow . . ." I said with a long-drawn-out sigh. "William, I'll bet Margo thinks that we've been abducted by some anti-gay activist, lurking on campus. How 'bout some lunch?"

Having talked myself out, we headed back to my apartment in silence until William asked me, "Jack, are you seeing anyone?"

"No. School takes up most of my time. If I'm not writing, I'm submitting articles to periodicals, and then wallpapering my room with their rejection letters. That's enough rejection for me to deal with. How about you, are you seeing anyone?"

"Not currently. But if the right guy came along, I'd take on the risk of rejection."

I buried my feelings of attraction toward William and felt them churning in my gut. After my dad was killed, I struggled with two demons, the fear of loss and commitment's inevitable death. "Hang in there," I said to William. "I'm sure the right guy will come along."

Once we reached the apartment complex we said hello to two pre-school young ladies, each of them wearing neon colored bikinis adorning their little figures of childhood's shapeless innocence. They giggled as we passed them and then resumed their playful little girl antics. After climbing thirty-seven steps to reach the second floor, I fumbled with my keys to unlock the front door while William waited patiently on the landing in his seersucker shorts.

Balancing a tray of margaritas, Margo emerged from the kitchen. She took precaution not to snag the avocado green shag carpet with her shoes even though the carpet hadn't been raked for over a month. William emptied the heaped ashtrays, wiped the black soot from his fingers onto his shorts and then said to Margo, "I should have told you earlier that I don't drink. Sorry."

"Not a problem. I'll drink this one and make you one without booze," she said and poured his drink into her glass and then disappeared into the kitchen. I sat on the floor and filed through my vinyl collection, searching for the "The Roche's" album. After I blew the dust off the record, I carefully lowered the needle onto my favorite cut and then sang aloud to "The Death of Suzzie Roche". Once Margo returned with William's drink, she threatened to pour her Margarita over my head. Her threats were typically nothing more than threats; so I continued to bastardize the song.

"Here we go, two double shot margaritas for us, one virgin slush for the new junior associate. Cheers!" Margo said then licked the salt from her glass before taking a sip.

"A toast to William," I said and raised my glass. "May you become wealthy and save the children of the world from their parents," I added.

Margo chimed in, "And may we all be saved from Jack's taste in music. Has Suzzie died yet?"

"Cute, Margo," I said and then turned toward William. "She's a pain in the ass, but she's my pain in the ass and I love her in spite of it. And she's a terrific dancer, something I am not. Actually, we're going dancing tonight. Why don't you join us? Margo and I go most Friday nights to this club in Pomona, the Alibi West. Come along with us; you'll have a great time."

"I don't know, Jack. Pomona?" he said with a tone of objection.

I gripped William's knee to halt his complaining; my real motive was to have an opportunity to touch him. I agreed with him, "Pomona leaves a bit to be desired, but the bartenders are hot and the DJ keeps the vinyl spinning without a break from one song to the next. Come on, what d'ya say?"

He made no effort to move my hand from his knee. "Well, I can't dance either and of course, I don't drink."

Margo interrupted, "Jack has two left feet, but he shakes his skinny butt well enough to get asked to dance. Besides, you can drive."

*   *   *

We left LA around 9:00 p.m. Disco etiquette commanded a 10:00 p.m. or later arrival. We drove east on Interstate 10 for over an hour, following an orange haze of taillights that illuminated the dark highway. William kept a cool head while maneuvering through the heavy traffic, but begged us to roll the windows down. The heavy scent of Margo's perfume and the cheap musk oil that I had generously splashed on, hung in the air inside the car. We gave in to William's request, even though the breeze made a mess of Margo's hair.

Honoring disco's etiquette, we arrived fashionably late. The sidewalk outside the club quaked from the sound system. Decked out in flared bell-bottom pants and snug cotton shirts leaving nothing to the imagination, four guys waited in line, dancing to the vibrating bass. William and I enjoyed the side show while Margo flirted with the bouncer, the only straight guy at the club. Her flirtatious bribe paid off. The bouncer recognized us, stamped our hands and then opened the door to let us in. Margo saved us a booth next to the dance floor; William excused himself and headed toward the men's room. I ordered drinks at the bar because tipping the bartender was cheaper than tipping the cocktail boys who waited the booths and tables.

In a disco bar certain unavoidable gay behaviors spread like a virus. Mixing gay men with alcohol and disco music concocts a cocktail that demands to be consumed one visual sip at a time. Even if you didn't dance, voyeurism was worth the price of admission. Unbuttoned polyester shirts exposed a bevy of sweet, sweaty bodies, freeing their arms to swing in rhythm to their grinding hips. Synchronized strobe lights cast shadows over the glistening faces and sensual movements of these dancing athletes.

Floor to ceiling mirrors reflected reminiscent choreography of film director Buzby Berkeley. Dancing solo, two bare-chested men gyrated to their multiple reflections until Margo butted in and asked one of them to dance. They stole center stage. The crowd acquiesced to the couple, clearing the dance floor like sprinkling pepper onto water in a glass; Margo and he paired whenever we came to the Alibi. The DJ announced over the microphone, "Margo and Jim, this one's for you," as he turned up the volume of the disco hit, "Last Dance."

While Fred and Ginger tore up the dance floor, William and I cruised the bar. We looked for a glance of approval or interest from some hopeful admirer from across the room when all we needed was to look no further than to each other. We leaned against the dance rail; Jim twirled Margo directly in front of us, her skirt brushed my arm as she blew a kiss to William. She winked at me and flung her weightless figure into Jim's arms. I chugged down a cold bottle of beer while William sipped a virgin sunrise from a tall frosted glass through a straw. I bent forward and pressed my lips to his ear, "You wanna dance?"

The soft touch from his mustache and sweet breath shot a sensual chill down my spine when he whispered near my ear, "Okay, but no laughing."

The crowd applauded as Margo and Jim brought their solo performance to an end. When the DJ announced, "Everybody, let's Hustle!" the dance floor filled to capacity in short order. Poppers were passed from couple to couple spreading a free and contagious head rush.

I planted my hands on William's narrow hips and guided him onto the dance floor. The amyl nitrate traveled from hand to hand until it reached us. We passed the liquid head rush to the guy standing next to us who immediately inhaled the fumes from the small glass vial. "William, just follow Margo's feet; she's the best hustler on the floor," I instructed him.

Shoulder to shoulder and ten lines deep the dance floor came to life as a chorus line. William and I aligned our feet directly behind Margo's. He held onto my hand and escorted me to the front line between Margo and Jim. The man, who said he couldn't dance, tore up the floor. Keeping in-step with William, I commented, "And you said you couldn't dance."

He grinned at me. "Did I?"

"Yes you did."

Without missing a step he said, "I'm not gonna tell you every thing on our first date."

Until that moment, William's subtle innuendoes had played with my head, but I resisted giving in to my feelings for him that I harbored. Dating meant commitment, a place I'd shied away from; and yet, I desired to be with William. I feared the consequence of a probable sexual fling without a future. His gentle manner, bright intellect, and budding career packaged him as a catch and I missed the ball that evening.

During the next hour, Margo and I danced with anyone who was willing. By midnight, willing was a snap, all one had to do was ask. William sat at the booth, alone, nursed a glass of water with a floating lemon wedge and watched me dance with strangers. I clammed up after he had reached out to me; I could have kicked myself right in the ass because earlier that day I had shared with William scripts about my life that I hadn't even shared with Margo.

I sat next to William as he drove us back to Los Angeles. I had not expected the feelings that were welling inside of me; I was beginning to fall in love with him. Some obscure LA radio station played classical music, William's preference. Margo fell asleep in the back seat; I nodded off while listening to the soothing orchestral sounds of violins and piano.

William dropped us off curbside in front of the apartment. After I closed the door he rolled the passenger window down. His eyes had filled with doubt before he asked me, "Jack, why don't you come back to my place with me. My house has the most beautiful night light view of the San Fernando Valley. It would be a shame to waste that view on just my eyes alone."

I rested one hand on the door and leaned inside the car. "It's late, William, and unfortunately, I have a deadline to meet tomorrow, but I'll take a rain check. I'll call you in the morning."

He focused his eyes on the empty passenger seat. I sensed the disappointment in his voice when he said to me, "Good night, Jack."

Margo waved goodbye to William and then ran up the stairs to the apartment. I waited at the curb as he sped away. Several minutes passed before I yelled to Margo, "I'll be up in a little while; I'm gonna walk around the block."

A cool evening breeze sobered my buzz before I returned to the apartment. Unaware of my passing, a young couple strolled down the sidewalk, holding hands while stealing a kiss. I thought to myself, "I wonder how long they've been together." Before I called it a night, I circled the block one last time, and imagined the sensual touch of William's mustache brushing my ear, again.

Wearing only my boxers, I stretched out on the couch and propped my bare-feet onto the worn bolstered arm. My heels dangled beyond the edge of the couch; I rubbed my ankles against the scratchy fabric. Margo lit a cigarette, brushed the ashes from her nightgown and knelt behind my head. She massaged my temples and with her lips gently blew my curly hair away from my brow. She asked me, "Do you think William had a good time?"

"I'm not sure."

"Did you have a good time?"

"I'm not sure."

Goose bumps raised the soft hair on my chest from Margo's gentle touch. As her fingers followed the outline of my right ear she said, "Jack?"

Yawning under the spell of her sweet touch, I surmised, "Oh, he's probably an out-to-dinner-and-to-a-movie kind of guy."

She butted her cigarette out and softly outlined both my ears with her fingertips. "Jack?" she asked again.

On the edge of twilight from too much booze and pot, I closed my eyes. "What is it?"

"Have you ever been with a woman?"

Lazily, I opened one eye and then asked her, "Where did that come from?"

Margo rolled her eyes toward the ceiling, but continued her sensual finger dance along my ears.

I closed my eyes and answered, "Not that I remember."

"Aren't you a wee bit curious to feel what it's like to explore a woman's naked body?"

"Margo, I don't get to explore a man's naked body anymore, but I guess that's my own fault," and then thought to myself, "I should have gone home with William tonight."

"Hmm," she said and nothing more.

She lit a joint she found hidden in her compact and then passed it to me. After inhaling two hits, my heart rate shot up several beats per minute. Smoking pot always increased my sensitivity to being touched; it made me horny as hell. I watched Margo undress; she leaned forward to kiss me. I felt her warm breasts press against my chest as she straddled my hips. My body lay still while my head spun from the pot and alcohol. Margo brushed my hair from my forehead as her long hair whispered its gentle touch along my neck. The back of my hand rubbed against the inside of her smooth legs as I rolled my boxer shorts off my hips. She made love to me on the couch that evening, but my thoughts were only of William.

*   *   *

The following morning I woke bare ass naked on the couch and scrambled to find my boxers. I smelled fresh coffee brewing in the kitchen and turned on the TV. Wyle E. Coyote had assembled his latest A.C.M.E. acquisition. He catapulted through the desert sky, crashed onto a rocky ledge, careened to the bottom of a gorge and was finally flattened to smithereens. Waiting along a dry riverbed, the Road Runner bleep bleeped and I bleeped off the TV. I read a note that Margo left on the coffee table:

> *Dear Jack,*
> *You passed out on me last night. Gone for a run. Be back soon. By the way, nice buns!*
>
> *Love, Margo.*

*   *   *

Over the next three months Margo avoided me until I cornered her in the kitchen one afternoon and asked her, "Margo, is there something wrong? We hardly talk anymore."

"I'm fucking pregnant, Jack, that's what's wrong!"

"Oh!" I said, the only word that passed my lips.

"I need to get out of here for a few days," she said as she gathered her purse, her car keys and a pack of smokes.

Feeling at a loss for words, I turned my palms up and shrugged my shoulders. I finally said to her, "Margo, you wanna talk about this?"

"No," she said and then walked out of the apartment and didn't return for two days.

After Margo left I wandered around the apartment thinking about my life without her. Consumed by my own self pity, I even felt sorry for myself that William wasn't there to help me through this. I had waited too long to tell William how much I loved him. Two weeks before Margo had slammed me with her pregnancy confession, William had introduced me to Kevin Stevens, his new boyfriend, at a garden party hosted by William's mother. Not one debutante graced the back yard of his mother's Pasadena estate that afternoon. Instead, an exclusive gathering of gay men, impeccably dressed in tailored suits, surrounded William, congratulating him on his new position as a new associate with a prestigious Orange County law firm. They raised their champagne glasses in a toast to William and Kevin, wishing them a long, happy, and prosperous life together. Kevin's *Gentlemen Quarterly* presence had been polished to a blinding sheen.

His cocky and self-confident manner disparaged his exceptional good looks. But William was crazy about him. So I raised my glass to them without uttering a word. I kissed William on the cheek, congratulated Kevin with a gentleman's handshake, and then went home. William and Kevin moved to Newport Beach, an hour's drive from Los Angeles. I spent that summer preparing for my senior year as Editor of the *University Times*, scored a job as a copy editor and staff go-fer for the *Los Angeles Times*, not bad as an entry level position with a big paper; and continued to live with Margo in our dumpy apartment.

*　　*　　*

Blowing the smog out over the Pacific Ocean, the dry Santa Ana winds greeted the fall semester. By Friday's end, the wind had ceased, the smog had returned as I looked forward to the weekend; Margo planned to stay home for a change.

My Sunday morning routine mandated a cup of black coffee, the *San Francisco Chronicle* and the couch. That morning Margo chose to sleep in rather than jog. I began to doze off when I heard the tap water running in the hall bathroom, the only bathroom in the apartment. To muffle the disturbing sound of her coughing and retching, she closed the door.

I waited in the hallway and listened for her at the bathroom door. When Margo calmed down, I tapped lightly, "Margo, you okay in there?"

"Yeah, I'm okay. Something I ate upset my stomach. I'll be out in a bit."

"Can I bring you anything?" I asked.

"I'm fine. Go read your paper," she said, gargling.

Margo emerged from the bathroom, her cheeks were flushed, her eyes were moist, her eyelids, puffy. Ignoring me, she made a bee-line to the kitchen. Margo poured herself a glass of orange juice, toasted an English muffin and joined me on the couch. She licked the jam from her fingertips and somewhere out of left field she said, "Jack, I'm going to abort this pregnancy."

I pressed my hands together and cradled my chin against my fingers as if to pray. "Why would you do that?"

"Because I don't want this child!" she screamed at me and spilled her glass of orange juice onto the carpet.

Margo walked across the living room toward the window and separated the mini-blinds to peer outdoors. She placed a cigarette to her lips but changed her mind and tapped it back into the pack. The distant expression in her eyes let me know how troubled she was. Still trim in her jeans, she laid her hand on her belly and asked, "Jack, what am I gonna do with a baby?"

I searched my emotions for comforting words of advice that Margo sought from me, but answered her with a question instead. "Have you told the father?"

"He denied any responsibility. I've confirmed an appointment with an abortion clinic for Monday morning."

"That's tomorrow! Have you thought this through? Are you absolutely certain that abortion is the right decision?"

"I'm stopping this pregnancy now while I'm in the first trimester."

Twenty-minutes of dead silence passed; only the second hand of the mantle clock could be heard. I interrupted the quiet, "Margo, I know this sounds crazy, but I'll adopt the baby."

"Are you out of your mind? You've one more year to finish your degree, you haven't any health insurance, you don't even own a car, and you're gonna raise this kid by yourself?"

"Who said anything about by myself. You and me, we'll raise the baby together!"

"Jack, listen to me. A baby does not fit into my life right now and probably won't ten years from now."

Margo's hands began to shake spilling the orange juice onto the coffee table. She picked up and laid back down her pack of cigarettes three times, then finally gave in and lit one up. I joined her even though I didn't smoke. I begged her, "Just consider it before you commit to Monday; do this for me, okay?"

Tears pooled in the creases of her mouth and rolled down her chin. Wrapping both of my arms around her sadness, I hugged her close to me. She leaned forward and dried the tears from her eyes with the corner of her blouse. "I lied to you about the father," she confessed.

I sank into the couch. I felt queasy and shaky from the cigarette. Margo sat next to me and coddled my head next to her neck. She whispered, "You don't need to adopt your own child, Jack."

Still dizzy from the tobacco, I leaned forward on the couch. "Margo, the only way I could be the father is if you and I . . ."

"You and I did. It happened three months ago after William went out with us to the Alibi."

"You told me that I passed out."

"A little pot, a little massage, a little Carpenters, you did finally pass out."

"And you let me believe that nothing happened, why?"

"It's pretty obvious. You wouldn't have believed me. Besides watching you and William together that night, you didn't need this on your head. You need to be with William, and if not William, some other guy, not me."

I gently placed my hand on Margo's knee. "Please just think it over."

"You're impossible; I'll cancel my appointment for Monday."

*　　*　　*

On February 20, 1975, Margo delivered Elizabeth Anne Turner into our lives. After fourteen hours in labor Margo slept while William, Kevin and I visited the hospital nursery. Like three love-sick homing pigeons, we cooed at my beautiful daughter through the glass window.

I wrapped one arm around William's shoulder and drew him close to my side. "Thanks for being here today," I said.

"Miss all this? Not on your life," he said, beaming. One would have thought that William was the father the way he fidgeted and jabbered without pause.

Kevin tapped my other shoulder and said to me, "Look, she pouts just like her dad."

I nudged William's ribs with my knuckles. "Yeah, but she has William's knobby knees," I said. Kevin glared at me; the expression in his eyes let me know that William's knobby knees belonged exclusively to him. I reassured Kevin with a wink; he rolled his eyes and grinned.

Over the next five months motherhood had strained Margo's mental health and our relationship. Even though the words never passed her lips, I knew that she did not want her child. Reluctantly, she breast-fed Annie while I managed to change diapers, bathe Annie in the kitchen sink and keep her appointments with the pediatrician. With graduation a week away, I was grateful for the free campus daycare. William and Kevin invited us to their peninsula retreat to celebrate; Margo bowed out, said she had flight reservations to San Francisco to visit friends. Following the commencement, I packed a diaper bag, the stroller and Annie into my new '56 Chevy convertible and drove to Newport Beach. We spent the night and returned home early the next morning; Annie had a slight temperature and I was beat.

By the time we got home, Annie and I were feeling better until I opened the front door. I cradled Annie close to my chest as my eyes panned the vacant living room. Empty toggle bolts peppered the ceiling's corners and circular water stains matted the carpet below the living room window. We walked through the sparsely furnished apartment only to end up in Margo's bedroom. A few bent wire hangers lay on her closet floor. I sat on the edge of the naked mattress and rocked Annie's stroller to quiet her down. The smell of Margo's perfume lingered in the bathroom; the cold tile floor echoed beneath my shoes. I carried Annie to my room, laid her down in her crib for a nap and found an envelope resting on the pillow. I kissed my daughter's forehead; she clutched my finger with her small hand, and at that moment, Annie's innocent presence eased my fear of commitment.

I poured myself a cup of bitter coffee reheated from Margo's leftovers, lit a cigarette and read Margo's note:

> *My Dearest Jack,*
> *I can't do this. I'll call you.*
>
> *Love,*
> *Margo*

Two weeks later Annie and I moved to West Hollywood. Margo never called.

Between diapers and dinner, I squeezed in time to read the stacks of resumes in response to my ad in the *Los Angeles Times*:

Hiring experienced nanny. Live-in, full-time position. Light housekeeping and meal preparation required. Please submit resume and references to: Jack Turner, PO Box 479, Los Angeles, CA 90069.

Maria accepted the job. I cancelled the ad that afternoon.

LAGUNA BEACH
2002

Chapter Five

B etween Mickey Mouse, Toon-Town, and Joey, a twenty-eight year-old, wiry, overgrown kid, Jamey was all in by 10:00 p.m. when we pulled into the driveway after a day at Disneyland. I carried my exhausted boy to bed, feeling grateful that the following day was Sunday. Joey sprawled out on the couch and warmed his stocking feet from the burning embers in the fireplace, another one of Maria's thoughtful touches. I tossed my jacket onto the leather Barcalounger. An envelope, addressed to me from Margo, fell from the jacket's pocket onto the floor; I had forgotten about it until then. I snatched the envelope from the floor and sat down at the dining room table while William quietly searched the kitchen cupboards for two wineglasses.

"This feels so great," I moaned a long sigh of relief. I kicked off my old sneakers under the table and curled my bare toes to relieve the stress in my calves. William saw me toss Margo's letter onto the heaped mail pile on top of the buffet.

He poured each of us a generous glass of wine then asked me, "Who's the letter from?"

I relished the first sip of the Cabernet then groaned her name, "Margo."

"Aren't you going to open it?" William asked.

"Later," I said, tilting my heavy head back against the dining room chair, beat from a day filled with Dumbo, haunted house ghosts, and a rabbit whose vocal chords needed sedation.

"You were pretty rough on her," William said.

"Maybe. I'm not sure what she expected from me. Making her grand entrance in a limo? Not a word from her for twenty-five years?"

"Let it go, Jack."

"After yesterday letting go of anything is not an option." I handed William an envelope near the pile. "Read this."

Mouthing the words of the legal jargon, William scanned the document addressed to me from the Superior Court of California. "This is a petition to terminate guardianship," he said and then choked on his first sip of wine.

"No shit! It's Fitzpatrick's attempt to take Jamey away from me."

"The allegation, what is this?" William asked and continued to read with contempt and disbelief.

"Right there," I pointed to item three on the petition. "'Jack F. Turner, as guardian of Jamey R. Fitzpatrick and the Fitzpatrick estate of the minor, should be removed as guardian and conservator for the following reasons: On the grounds of gross immorality.' What a son-of-a-bitch!"

"He has no basis for his argument unless there's something you haven't told me," he said.

"Of course he doesn't have a legitimate argument. Unless homosexuality equals immorality; I have nothing to hide, William."

"Rob is a slick attorney," William admitted. "He knows the difference between being gay and what defines immorality." Disgusted, William tossed the document onto the table and continued, "It's nothing more than his distaste for your gay lifestyle. I'm not certain what he has up his sleeve or what he thinks he can show to a judge that would prove this allegation."

After I topped off our wine glasses, I removed my specs and rubbed my eyes before asking him, "What about having sex with a male prostitute?"

"Jesus Christ, Jack. You didn't!"

"Lower your voice a little; you'll wake Jamey and Maria. I don't want them to know about this."

"Know what, Jack?" he asked abruptly. "If Rob knows about what I think you're keeping from me, it will hurt your chances to keep Jamey. Jack, did you pay this man for sex?"

"Of course not; Tim Higgins is an old friend of mine. He's a CPA now, runs his own business. When we met eight years ago he was no longer in the "business". I'll introduce you to him."

"I don't know if that's a good idea, Jack."

"You'd like Tim. After we met, we dated for about six months. Many long evenings we spent together in this house. I was ready to ask him to move in with me and that was when he told me about his past."

"Jack, you never told me about him," William said.

"No, I didn't. There was no point in telling you; Tim and I split up before we ever really got started. Anyway, enough about Tim," I said. "More importantly, the initial hearing is scheduled for February 27th; that gives me only four weeks." I offered another envelope to William that I had filed away in my desk, now yellowed from years of cigarette smoke. "I suppose this document means nothing?"

Glancing over the paperwork, William read aloud, "If at my death any of my children are minors and my husband, Derek M. Fitzpatrick does not survive me, I nominate as guardian of the person or persons of my surviving child or children, my father, Jack Franklin Turner who resides at 729 Bluebird Canyon Road, City of Laguna Beach, County of Orange, State of California . . ."

He read the rest of the document in silence. "You never told me that Annie had filed a nomination of guardianship. How long have the Fitzpatricks known?"

"About four years. Annie told them. Really pissed Rob off. Of course, she'd already filed the petition with Superior Court and the judge had signed it off."

"I'll bet that was a pleasant evening at Annie's," William grinned.

"Annie told me that Rob stormed out of the house without finishing his dinner, grumbling something about if Derek had survived. In his fit he failed to read the second half of the petition where he and Peg were nominated as guardian if for some reason I was unable to care for Jamey. Peg stayed the night. She told me later that Annie had taken two or three sleeping pills about twenty minutes before Rob left."

"How does Jamey get along with them?"

"He loves his grandparents. Jamey spends at least one weekend a month with them. Rob and Peg spoil him, but that's what grandparents do."

"And you don't!"

"Well . . . Yeah, I spoil him too, but I think they go a little overboard. His bedroom at their house is filled with electronic gadgets: Game Boy, X-Box, you name it. His room here, a soccer ball, a small color TV, and his bike. Anyway, raising Jamey is not Fitzpatrick's motive. Persecuting me? Maybe. I'm convinced he's after Jamey's estate."

"You're the executor. He can't touch it."

"If he wins, he'll try."

"Jack, Fitzpatrick is a wealthy man, he doesn't need the money."

"He's a control freak. Look how he manipulates Peg."

"You're over the edge, Jack."

"And ready to plummet. Once Annie's house is sold the trust will control over two million dollars and be out of Fitzpatrick's reach."

"First thing Monday morning I want you to make an appointment with Kevin and in the meantime, I'll help you as much as I can," William assured me.

"Kevin as my lawyer? Not a good idea. I need you to help me, not Kevin."

"Jack, I'm 3500 miles away, besides, there's a conflict of interest here. I'm too emotionally involved with you and the circumstances."

"You're right. The circumstances. God, how I wish . . ."

"Wish what, Jack?"

"Nothing," I said still hiding my feelings that I carried for him.

From the dining room table I watched Joey, Mr. Sleeping Beauty, lounging in the living room. His legs were crossed at the ankles and propped comfortably against the back of the couch. He'd cupped his hands to cradle his head. There weren't any throw pillows to cushion his head, sleeping beauty indeed. Whenever I chose to watch television in the living room, I borrowed the down pillows from my bed to cushion my head from the stiff sofa's arms, but I wasn't about to offer them to Joey.

I laid my hand affectionately on William's knee and wondered when I'd see him again. "Kevin, huh?" I asked, my eyes remained fixed on the couch.

"He's aggressive, competent, and understands California Family Law and Probate."

Not thoroughly convinced, I nodded my head in agreement and walked away from the table. I stood at the kitchen sink and stared into the moonlit backyard. William turned the kitchen lights off and joined me. "There, now you can see into the dark abyss much better," William said and then wrapped his arm around my waist.

I lit a cigarette, blew the smoke through the screen and watched it hover on the damp evening air. "Not as much to see anymore," I said with a little self-pity. I warmed William's cold hands sandwiched between mine. "William, stay here with me. Help me through this."

"If Joey wasn't here, I would, Jack."

Rubbing his deep set brown eyes and yawning, Joey shuffled his stocking feet into the kitchen. He kissed William on the cheek and then asked him, "Am I interrupting anything?"

"No, just a little chit-chat between old friends. Did we wake you?" William asked.

"I wasn't really asleep. When do you want to go back to the hotel?"

"In a bit. I need to clear up some things for Jack."

Joey kissed Billy again. "I'll watch the news. Let me know when you're ready to go."

I tolerated the kiss but cringed at the nickname.

Joey's scowl let me know that he wasn't happy with William standing alone with me in the dark. I let go of William's hand and eased away from the sink. "William, before you head back to the hotel I need to know something."

"Sure. Fire away."

"After twenty some years what happened with you and Kevin?"

William swigged the last of his wine. Shaking his head, he poured himself a second glass. "Two years ago David Hollington, one of Kevin's nightclub acquaintances, hired Kevin as legal counsel to litigate his divorce. He'd been married for twelve years, thirty years old, had three children. After I met David I understood why Kevin was smitten with him. He was young, handsome, an engineer. Tall! Kevin and I had our problems, but nothing that I thought would lead to us splitting up. After a year had passed, I'd drive by his flat on the waterfront in Portland. I missed him. I really thought that he would call me asking to come home. The drive-bys became less frequent and then I met Joey."

"Did David move in with Kevin?"

"Oh yeah. Kevin bought a condominium in Portland along the waterfront with a view of the Atlantic Ocean. As soon as title to the property was recorded, sole ownership in Kevin's name, thank God, David moved in."

"I had no idea."

William refreshed my empty wineglass. "Not long after moving in with Kevin, David began seeing his wife on the weekends. They remarried last September. Kevin accepted an associate position with Steinman, Steinman and Becker in Newport Beach and moved back to California. The firm guaranteed that he would make partner in two years if he keeps his figures high and recruits high-powered clients."

"He'll fall four or five rungs on that ladder if he represents me."

"He's a workaholic and determined. He'll make partner."

Joey waited in the car, he was either asleep or bored or both. William and I stretched out our good-byes as we meandered down the walkway. Leaning against the car, William suggested, "Come to Kennebunkport for Christmas this year. You, Jamey, Maria, and a New England Christmas."

"I can't speak for Maria; I think she has a new boyfriend."

"No kidding? A boyfriend for Maria. How old is she now, sixty-five?"

"Sixty-five this coming September. His name is Henry. A week or so ago they spent several days in Santa Barbara together. That's all she's told me."

"You'd better learn how to cook and clean," he advised with a smirk and two raised eyebrows.

"Get out'a here. Maria won't leave Jamey and me."

"Don't be so sure. Christmas? Promise?"

"I'll make flight reservations next week."

I gave William a thumbs-up as he sped away, again.

Once he was out of sight, I walked back to the porch and zipped up my sweatshirt to keep warm. Even the chilly ocean breeze failed to cool off the warmth from William's love I just waved good bye to. So I settled into the wicker rocking chair, still wearing my Levi's from the day at Disneyland and pulled out Margo's letter from my pocket. A soft amber haze glowed from the porch light which made reading a challenge. Frantic shadows of fluttering moths danced across Margo's handwritten letter as I rocked back and forth in the wicker chair and read her note.

> *Jack,*
>
> *I apologize for not phoning first before showing up at the house. That was inconsiderate and presumptuous of me. My heart goes out to you and Jamey. He's darling. There's so much I need to explain to you. I have to return to New York on Monday. I remember your love for Mexican food. Have made dinner reservations at Las Brisas for tomorrow evening, Sunday at 7:30. Please join me.*
>
> *Margo*

*   *   *

Sunday morning Maria helped Jamey finish his spelling homework. I cleaned up Willow's business from the backyard and stepped in a couple of piles I didn't see in time. William called to say goodbye before their flight departed. Peg called and left a message on the machine. I didn't play it back; I deleted it.

I locked myself in my office and stared at the screen saver on my computer, an animated explosion of construction pipes randomly connecting helter skelter. I hadn't resumed my work since the day Hank Beyers came to the house; the day Annie committed suicide. I pushed my work aside and turned off the computer. Instead, I thought of Jamey and how his innocent, selfless wisdom had comforted me that afternoon. What a kid. With Jamey's sweet image in my head, I went to my bedroom to lay out my couture for an evening with Margo.

Cordovan penny loafers, tan, cuffed Dockers, a white polo shirt and a gray tweed sports jacket, "Should be good enough for a fancy evening," I thought to myself. While combing my hair and grooming my beard, I had second thoughts about meeting with Margo for dinner. I knew nothing about her anymore. I lost touch with Margo after she moved to New York twenty-five years ago. She had worked as the Chief Financial Officer for a Los Angeles based development corporation before she moved to New York. Last I heard a savvy headhunter had arranged an interview for Margo as Controller for a Wall Street International brokerage firm. Undoubtedly, she clinched the position because of her looks, but I pitied any man who crossed her. Margo had perfected the term Ball-Buster deserving her new title amongst testosterone corporate America. I presume that she still lives in the Big Apple and is probably unmarried. Her last phone number entry in my directory now belongs to a coffee shop in Manhattan. Long distance information informed me some time ago, "Sorry sir, no forwarding number for a Margo Evans."

As I drove north on Pacific Coast Highway, the night light view of Laguna Beach drew me closer to Las Brisas. The restaurant, perched on a cliff bordering Pacific Coast Highway, lit the gentle surf from the dining rooms' chandeliers. The dimness of the crescent moon acquiesced to the city's evening lights. The valet, a sixteen-year-old kid parked my car. "Cool," he said, tossing my keys into the air and then retrieved them with Michael Jordan's finesse.

The aromas of grilled lobster, cilantro and handmade corn tortillas welcomed my senses before entering the pricey rendezvous. The hostess welcomed me as I stepped up to the reservation desk. She wore a basic black dress that clung suggestively to her curvaceous figure. "Good evening, sir," she said, "have you a reservation?"

"Actually, no," I replied. "I'm supposed to meet someone here. The reservation would be under her name, Evans, Margo Evans."

The hostess glanced at the list of names in the reservation book for that evening and then said to me, "Yes, she has already been seated. Please follow me." She turned and with a flirtatious glance over her shoulder escorted me to Margo's table.

A forty-foot bank of bay windows framed a panoramic view of the Pacific Ocean from one of the three dining rooms. Each dining room was a shrine to pretentious extravagance. Red brocade upholstered high back chairs complimented the crisp white linen tablecloths. Waterford goblets accented the gold-rimmed bone china and silver flatware. Perched in a crystal vase, a Bird of Paradise crowded the center of the intimate table for two.

Margo stood and then edged slowly toward me. "Thank you for coming, Jack," she said, pressing her silky cheek against my beard, her Bordeaux painted lips near my ear.

"Thank you for inviting me," I said and offered my other cheek to hers with cautioned affection.

Margo clasped my nervous hands. Her slender fingers and gentle touch reminded me of Annie. She leaned away from me, refused to let go of my hands, and checked me out from head to toe.

Blushing, I asked, "What are you doing?"

"Taking you all in," she said. "And you haven't changed a bit, except for the little touches of gray around the edges," she blushed while brushing the hair from my temples with her fingertips.

I waited for Margo to sit. The hostess presented the menus but offered me the wine list. Margo smoothed the linen napkin across her knee and rested her elbows on the leather bound menu. I loosened the Band-Aid around my index finger to ease the circulation and browsed the list for a Cabernet.

"What happened to your finger, Jack?"

"Paper cut while opening your letter," I responded, and continued to search for an appropriate wine to suggest.

Margo pressed her fingers to her lips. A diamond ring adorned her right hand. "I'm sorry," she offered apologetically.

"Don't be."

She folded her hands beneath her chin and asked, "Jack, where do we begin?"

"How about why you left Annie and me and never called."

"That far back, huh?" she teased. "Just kidding, Jack. How about a bottle of wine to ease into the evening?" she asked as she gestured to our waiter. She clapped her fingers against the heel of her hand like a single castanet which delivered him to our table pronto, a gesture she must have learned from dining in New York City restaurants.

"Are you and the gentleman ready to order?" the waiter asked politely.

"We'll begin with a '95 Jordan Cabernet Sauvignon," I said.

"Excellent choice, sir."

"Jordan? And I thought you were all about running shorts and Big Macs," Margo said.

"'95 was a good year and its Breakfast Jacks not Big Macs," I corrected her.

"My error, Jack; wrong drive-thru."

"You look fabulous, Margo. Not having raised children suits you."

She moved her salad fork slightly to the right of her plate. "Your bitterness surprises me," she said then closed her menu.

"It shouldn't," I said coldly.

"Jesus, let it go, Jack. You had the joy of raising our daughter, not me."

"And whose choice was that?"

"Mine. All mine. When I told you that I was pregnant I also told you that I did not want to have a baby."

"I remember. I remember your whole confession. I have made peace with that. I have a problem with your disappearance, Margo. You wrote in your letter that you would call. Why didn't you?"

"Annie was baggage. During the seventies, corporate America prohibited women from infiltrating their good old boy network. An unmarried woman with a child competing with the good old boys, I would have kissed my career goodbye."

"Baggage. That fits, you threw us away."

"That's not fair."

"That's not good enough."

"Goddamn you, Jack. You begged me not to have an abortion. I gave to you my baby! What do you want to hear from me, that I'm a bitch, that I'm selfish? I'm sorry that I didn't call."

That was the Margo I remembered. Grab you by the balls and bring you to your knees.

Four couples surrounding our table glared at us.

"Margo, I was scared and broke. I was just a fucking kid. It was the seventies. A single father, gay, with his infant daughter, alone, not easy."

"Back then nothing was easy, for any of us," she said in her defense.

A voice in the back of my head begged me to leave the restaurant, but I remained seated, my eyes focused on the windows just beyond her shoulders. Margo waved her hand to penetrate my blank stare and asked me, "Jack, you in there?"

I put the voice in the back of my head on hold. Clinking the gaudy wineglasses, Margo and I toasted an unspoken truce.

"Jack, let's put this behind us, start over?"

"Yes, let's."

"What are you having for dinner, Jack?"

"I haven't even looked at the menu yet."

"You decide. I'll be back in a bit." Margo excused herself to touch up her lipstick, fuss her hair, and stretch her nylons or whatever women do whenever they visit the powder room.

At $90.00 a bottle I topped off the crystal wineglasses finishing the high priced vintage and asked the waiter to bring another, same vintage, same vintner.

Heads turned as Margo returned to the dining room. Our waiter pulled her chair away from the table assisting her to sit and offered her a fresh napkin. He corked the wine, raised an eyebrow, and glanced my way as my stomach growled. I hadn't eaten since that morning following a five-mile run. I politely excused myself and asked for a few more minutes before ordering dinner.

The waiter attended to an elderly couple seated nearest the bay windows which allowed me a full view of his physique. His expanded waistline stressed the buttons on his black, silk vest. He had a build like a married old man, no ass, legs up to his waist, and a beer gut. I didn't notice any wedding ring, not that I cared.

Margo returned her napkin to her knee. "You ordered another bottle," she said. "Good. Sorry I was so long, I promised Peg Fitzpatrick that I would call her this evening."

"Peg? Jamey's grandmother?"

"Uh, huh."

"How do you know her?"

"I met her yesterday. A girlfriend from college invited me to have lunch with her at the Balboa Bay Club. She asked me why I was in California. I filled her in about Annie, the funeral, and when I mentioned your name this stunning woman sitting directly behind me tapped my shoulder and asked me how did I know Jack Turner? She nearly spilled her gin and tonic when I introduced myself as Annie's mother."

"I'll bet she did."

"She's delightful. Her husband was having lunch with her; isn't he a prize!" she said with playful sarcasm.

"Only to Peg."

"She asked for my address. Rob handed me his business card and offered, "Call anytime." Evidently, Peg has several photographs of Jamey and Annie that she wants to send to me."

"You should stick around a while longer. My bet is that you and Rob would become real chummy."

"I doubt it," she said begrudgingly.

"Margo," I said, placing my menu backside up to the right of the crowded table. "Why are you really here?"

"There's no play with you is there, Jack?"

"Not anymore."

"Ten years ago I was engaged to be married. It was the happiest time of my life, Jack. You would have liked Kyle. We found a house in the Hampton's that we both fell in love with. It's not what you think. It was a cozy 1500 square foot summer cottage, the backyard a sandy beach. I was seven months pregnant with his baby. We agreed to wait until the baby arrived before making an offer. Then Jonathan arrived, my six-pound, blue-eyed, bushy-haired son. Kyle left me two days before Jonathan was born. I haven't a clue of where he is; frankly, I don't give a shit. Jonathan lived only two weeks. It was a Saturday morning around 7:00 o'clock, time for my baby's breakfast. I went to his crib; I'd warmed his bottle and tested it on my wrist. I thought Jonathan was still asleep. The coroner's report determined the cause of death was SIDS. I lost my baby, Jack."

"I lost my baby too, Margo."

For several moments we didn't speak as we shared our common grief.

"Jack, I'm 52. I haven't any family. After William called me about Annie, I booked the first flight available to California. You and Jamey are my only family. Please, allow me the opportunity to be a part of my grandson's life," she implored with heartfelt sincerity I had not expected from her.

"Margo, Jamey may not be a part of my life within the next few months. The Fitzpatricks have filed a legal action against me to take him from me. I can't predict how this will play out."

"How can I help, Jack?"

"There's nothing you can do." I glanced down at the fluorescent arms of my Mickey Mouse watch. "Six a.m. rolls around early at my house. My grandson wags his sleepy face into my bedroom every morning before the alarm goes off. He throws my robe over my lazy head and orders me to "Get up Grampa!" We ride together every school day morning and share a Breakfast Jack on the way. Before he runs across the school lawn, we high-five and look forward to the day's end together. You're twenty-five years too late. Have a nice flight back to New York. Thanks for dinner, it's been swell." Leaving Margo to herself with her pricey wine, I walked out of the restaurant.

By 9:00 p.m. the cool coastal breezes off the ocean encouraged other leaving guests to wrap in something warm. I draped my sport coat around my shoulders like a shroud to cool off from the warmth of my anger while I stood curbside. Rocking on the heels of my shoes, I waited for ten minutes for the valet to bring my car. Another five minutes passed so I strolled along Cliff Drive to locate my ride. It was wedged between a Lexus and a BMW.

The young valet repeatedly cranked the ignition, cursing, "What a piece of shit! It won't even start."

I tapped on the driver's window and scared the kid. His embarrassment flushed his pimply cheeks. "It's a temperamental piece of shit," I courteously informed him.

"I can't get your car to turn over, sir."

"She's on her last leg. I'll start her up."

Knowing the carburetor-flooding threshold, I pumped the throttle four times while holding the ignition on. The old piece-of-shit gave into my persistence and blew another cloud of black smoke into the night. I tipped the valet five bucks and turned onto Pacific Coast Highway.

I needed another drink.

Inside my car a gray foggy haze burned my eyes. I cranked open the driver's side wing window. The cigarette smoke trailed through the opening like billowing mist from dry ice. I butted my smoke in the heaped ashtray while waiting for a green light. The Little Shrimp was a block away. Two guys strolled arm in arm as they passed my car, oblivious to my envy. My eyes followed them to the sidewalk as I thought of William, arm in arm, next to me. The light turned green. I drove beyond the Little Shrimp and turned left onto Bluebird Canyon Road toward the house.

Sprawled out like lump, Willow waited for me on the front porch, snoring.

Chapter Six

S teinman, Steinman, and Becker occupied the entire top floor and part of the fifth of the seven-story glass office building facing Pacific Coast Highway. Ambitious attorneys practicing law in Orange County sought the prestigious Newport Beach address that Kevin had acquired after accepting the firm's invitation to join them.

Four years ago, Kevin's skillful litigation and confident courtroom presence triumphed, winning a child custody case setting a precedent in the state of Maine. He represented a divorced gay man who sought full legal custody of his five-year-old daughter and seven-year-old son. The defendant had been living with his male partner for two years. William told me that they were raising their family in Ogunquit and that the ex-wife remained in Portland to be near her children. Steinman, Steinman, and Becker followed Kevin's career after he had won the landmark case. One year later the State Legislature passed a Domestic Partner's bill into law giving gay men and lesbian women equal rights in the state of Maine.

The firm owned the new building that had an unobstructed view of Newport's Peninsula, the Rodeo Drive of Southern California's coast, and Corona del Mar, the West Coast Hamptons. The difference between the sister cities—pineapple palms substituted for East Coast pampas grass. I wanted nothing to do with the affluent, self-satisfied people of this community, but I needed Kevin. Rather than park in the firm's lot that was filled with BMWs, Porsches, and Land Rovers, I parked my Chevy on Pacific Coast Highway in front of the building.

Kevin shared the fifth floor with six of the firm's associates. He was the new kid on the floor but an old friend to me. I had some reservations about Kevin's firm even though Steinman, Steinman, and Becker reportedly had a liberal philosophy. I walked into the lobby, cleaned my glasses with my shirttail, and tried to restrain my fear of losing Jamey.

Polished mahogany paneling accented the thick industrial carpeting of the elevator. Piped in music from K-Earth 101, LA's oldies radio station, played songs from the 50's and 60's through a hidden speaker between the panel box and emergency telephone. The elevator opened onto matching carpeting that led to the fifth floor reception desk.

Imposing brass letters, spelling out the name of the firm, graced the wall behind the desk. A young woman, nineteen at best, sipped a Starbucks coffee and motioned with her index finger that she would be with me in a minute. I leaned against the desk and waited for her to finish her phone call. She wore a black bustier and mini-skirt and crossed her legs at just the right angle. I imagined some of the male clients and the firm's associates appreciating her allure. She hung up the phone and tugged at the bottom of her strapless blouse trying to get a little more cleavage between her tiny breasts. "Good morning," she said.

"Good morning. I'm Jack Turner. I have a ten o'clock appointment with Kevin Stevens."

"Please, have a seat. I'll let Mr. Steven's secretary know that you're here."

I sat down on the sofa, crossed my legs, and made every effort to suppress my anxiety.

Above the music, I overheard the receptionist speak to Kevin's secretary, "Sara, Mr. Turner is here to see Mr. Stevens." She paused for a moment. "Yes, I'll tell him." The receptionist scribbled a few notes. She peered over her desk and said, "Mr. Turner, Mr. Stevens is still in conference with a client. He'll be about ten minutes. May I bring you a cup of tea while you're waiting?"

"Thank you, de-caf please."

The reception room had been recently redecorated. The gray and burgundy striped chintz upholstery on the chairs and matching sofa showed no signs of wear. The glass sofa table was dust free except for the yellow pollen from the fresh bouquet of gladiolas. The smell of new wood from the white plantation shutters reminded me of new home construction, sterile and antiseptic, like a doctor's office minus the Phisohex.

Moments after the receptionist brought me a cup of tea Kevin entered the reception room accompanied by his client, Tim Higgins, an old friend of mine. They clapped each other on the back in camaraderie; they were laughing, probably having shared a good joke. I cleared my throat to get Tim's attention. He stretched over the arm of the sofa to hug me.

"Jack," he smiled. "Haven't seen you at the gym lately."

"Too busy right now," I said.

"Sorry about Annie. You okay?"

"Tying up some legal ends."

"Kevin's your man. Call me before the middle-age spread attacks your hard work," he said, then in a gesture of friendship, patted my waist.

"Will do. Say hi to Frank."

"I will. He asked about you the other day."

As he walked away I remembered the first time we met then the elevator chimed and Tim was gone.

Kevin Stevens was my age but looked ten years younger than me, no trace of gray hair, even in his sideburns. His dark brown straight hair sported a forty-five dollar haircut, tight above the ears, quarter inch sideburns, the top left just long enough to stand up, defined with a little gel. His dark eyelashes drew my attention to his restful blue eyes and tan complexion. He was clean-shaven except for a trim mustache that outlined his full upper lip. His build was similar to mine, tall and lean but more athletic and muscular. His charcoal Armani slacks hung well around his narrow hips. Below the cuffed trousers he wore tasseled Gucci loafers, not my style but they looked good on Kevin. He wasn't wearing a sport jacket; his white silk shirt defined his broad chest and shoulders. Kevin was a man's man, the type that caught my eye.

Feeling slightly underdressed in my Dockers walking shorts, polo shirt and tennis shoes, I sat up on the sofa and visually followed Kevin's long confident stride as he approached me. On some subliminal level I felt relieved that William had returned to the East Coast.

Sipping the hot tea, I choked, spraying the beverage all over the glass table. Kevin placed his hand between my shoulder blades and asked me, "Jack, you okay?"

After catching my breath, I said, "I'm fine. This always happens to me. Whenever I swallow liquids it predictably goes down the wrong pipe. Someday I'll get it fixed."

Unfolding my napkin to wipe up the mess was a challenge. I had clenched it in my fist and compressed it into a wad as I struggled to catch my breath.

I smeared the glass making the problem worse. Kevin said to me, "Leave it, Jack."

"What about the chair?" I asked.

"Forget about it; housekeeping will take care of it," he assured me.

The fifth floor view of the Balboa Bay Yacht Club and Newport Beach Peninsula's elite residential real estate mirrored Kevin's three-hundred-fifty-dollar an hour fee. Opposite the windows, cherry wood bookshelves spanned the entire wall from floor to ceiling. Kevin proudly displayed his personal law library, a Christmas gift from William a few years ago. I questioned him if he actually worked in his office; his desk was void of paper clutter, unlike mine at home. He laughed it off. "I have Sara." he said, "She does all the real work."

An extensive collection of Lalique' crystal swans and Lladro' porcelain figurines graced the opposite end of the lit bookshelves. The orchestra conductor and violinist were out of circulation and impossible to find, even for collectors. The fragile display softened the masculine overkill of Kevin's office. His tough guy image had a softer side.

I admired the mocha leather wingback chairs for clients, a smaller version of Kevin's throne. I ran my sweaty palms across the padded arms. "Three-hundred-fifty an hour, huh?" I said, still standing.

"Have a seat, Jack."

Kevin walked past my chair and sat down behind his desk. He leaned back and crossed his legs, left ankle balancing on his right knee, relaxed and in control. I breathed in the sweet fragrance of his Polo cologne; the tension in my neck began to relax.

"I don't set the fees, Jack. The big cheeses upstairs, that's their job."

"Nice office," I said.

He brushed off the compliment. "It's temporary. In two years I'll make partner and move upstairs. Bigger office, better view, bigger bucks."

I handed my folder to Kevin. He thumbed quickly through the documents. He cleared his throat and pinched the cleft in his chin between his thumb and forefinger. "You should have received an "*Order to Show Cause*" from Superior Court. Here it is," he mumbled to himself. He continued with his personal conversation, "Need that to file response to the allegation, "*Notice of Hearing*" for what, where, when, "*Nomination of Guardianship*", Annie's signature, "*Appointment of Guardianship*" signed off by the judge. Good start, Jack."

Kevin was all business.

"Jonas Simon is representing the Fitzpatricks," he informed me. "He is the best family law and probate attorney in Orange County. He's brutal, convincing, a real son-of-bitch. He and Fitzpatrick make the perfect couple. He won't consider your feelings, reputation as a nationally published columnist or good name, Jack. He'll grab you by the nuts; he hates to lose."

My patience ran thin listening to Kevin's personal courtroom drama. I slammed my fist on top of the closed folder. One of the Lladro' figurines toppled from the shelf and landed on the thick carpet; the violinist lay silent and unbroken. "Kevin, I need to know what's going to happen to my grandson, not about some arrogant lawyer who may or may not grab my crotch and smear my name."

He planted his elbows on his desk and folded his hands together like some deity calming the sinner. "Jack, I apologize. Sometimes I come across as cold and to the point. It comes with job. I really do know what you're going through."

"You do not know what I'm going through. I'm the one who takes care of my grandson, not Rob, not Peg, not you! I've read one of those legal books written for non-attorneys by attorneys like you. You must know the term Psychological Parent? I've been Jamey's psychological parent since Annie's diagnosis of depression four years ago. Four years Kevin. I see to his medical needs, take him to the pediatrician. I make certain that he eats breakfast, I pack his lunch; Maria usually prepared dinner that I delivered to Annie's most evenings. I drive him to school and pick him up every day. Last year I coached his soccer team. I spend two hours a week volunteering in his classroom. Before Annie died, Jamey spent a minimum of four nights each week at my house. Jamey stays with me. He's my boy. Fitzpatrick can go to hell!"

"You are absolutely right, Jack. But whether you agree or not we have to proceed according to probate dictated by California law. My job is to prepare you and this case for whatever Jonas will throw at us."

I sank back into the chair and wiped my forehead with my arm. "Alright, Kevin, what's next?"

"I need some history from you."

"I'm all yours."

"Have you ever solicited a male prostitute?"

I hesitated before responding to his cross-examination. Repressing my smoker's cough, I choked, "What!"

"A female perhaps?"

I raised my eyebrows and shook my head. "Not on a bet, Kevin."

"Jack, if it's out there Jonas will find it."

"About eight years ago United Press invited me to speak at their annual conference. Reno hosted the convention that year. After dinner three of my cronies egged me on to accompany them to the Moonlight Bunny Ranch, a brothel about thirty minutes outside of Reno. Prostitution is legal in Lyon County. I laughed it off. False eyelashes, red lipstick and fish net stockings didn't float my boat. They urged me to reconsider assuring me that there must be guys working the brothel. I bowed out; told them they were nuts and wandered downstairs to the casino."

Scribing my story in his indecipherable shorthand, he laid his pen aside. "Therefore you did not solicit a prostitute," he presumed continuing his battery of questions.

"I'm not finished," I said. "I gambled playing a quarter progressive slot machine, did well actually, won five hundred bucks. I had killed half a bottle of wine with dinner earlier so I was feeling pretty loose. This good-looking guy sat down and began playing the machine next to mine. He wore faded jeans, snug and suggestive, a fitted ribbed tank and flip-flops. It was July. He was hot; heated my libido a degree or two. He introduced himself; told me he lived in Dana Point and was in Reno for the weekend. He was a couple years younger than me. One thing led to another. For six months after we met we dated until he confessed his past to me. During his early twenties, he earned his living as a male escort for some pimp in Palm Springs and acted in several gay pornography films. I broke off my relationship with Tim. You know Tim; he just left your office. I regret my decision to this day; my fear of his past fucked me out of another relationship just the way I waited too long for William."

"My William?"

"Don't act so surprised."

"You're right. I've always suspected."

"Anyhow, will this be held against me in court?"

"It's unlikely. Dating Tim does not constitute gross immorality."

"Tim's a CPA now; owns his own business. His boyfriend Frank and he have been to my house several times for dinner. Jamey thinks Tim is pretty cool; he does chin-ups on Tim's biceps."

Kevin glanced momentarily at me in between his questions. He finished scribbling his hieroglyphics, loosened his tie and asked if I wanted a smoke. He plugged in the tabletop smokeless ashtray and joined me.

"Now it's your turn to jot some notes," he said then took another drag off his cigarette. "Place the parental lock on your on-line service. Protect

Jamey. Trash any pornography, magazines, and videos, mail solicitations pertaining to the same."

I attempted to keep up with Kevin's instructions but my hands began to shake.

"Do you frequent the gay bars in town?" he continued without letting up.

"Saturday nights, I have a drink at the Little Shrimp, sometimes dinner."

"Do not bring home a date, at least during the proceedings," he recommended emphatically.

"Christ, Kevin, you make it sound like I'm a whore."

"Not me, but Jonas will."

Kevin rang his secretary and asked her to bring copies of the parenting worksheets. Sara knocked before entering and quietly placed a folder onto Kevin's desk. She was middle-aged, wore her tinted hair in a French twist and carried her over weight frame gracefully.

Kevin offered me the folder and said, "Some homework for you, Jack. It only looks overwhelming; it'll take you about an hour to complete. The worksheets provide a profile of you and Jamey and your relationship, how you deal with parenting situations, etc., for the judge to review."

"I'll start on it this evening." I closed the folder and sank back into the chair. While running the assignment through my head, I asked Kevin, "Anything else?"

"Judge Marilyn Harcourt will be presiding over this case. We couldn't have asked for a fairer judge. Her daughter is an Assistant District Attorney for the City of Los Angeles who is open about her lesbian lifestyle; she has a seven-year-old daughter. That's not a guarantee that Judge Harcourt will favor our side. Because of the alleged reasons for guardianship termination she will appoint a court investigator and very likely order a psychological evaluation of Jamey."

"An investigation? For what?"

"Your neighbors will be interviewed. So will Maria, Jamey's teachers, school counselors, places you frequent together. Jamey plays soccer, correct?"

I nodded yes.

"The investigator will interview the parents of Jamey's soccer team as well."

"Eventually, I'll have to explain this to Jamey, but not now," I said.

"That's at your discretion, Jack. I've scheduled a briefing with Judge Harcourt for Monday morning. I'm presenting a preliminary motion requesting a closed courtroom during the hearings. Because you are nationally recognized I want to protect both you and Jamey from the media and public scrutiny."

"I had no idea that this was going to be so ugly, Kevin."

"Tell ya what. It doesn't all have to be doom and gloom. Come to my place for dinner Saturday. I make a killer pesto pizza. Red or white wine?"

"Red."

"Bring the worksheets. I'll have a stack of documents for you to sign. Don't concern yourself. The paper stream, that's how the legal system justifies its big salaries. We'll go over all of this in detail over dinner. I won't book the hours. The firm needn't know. Seven okay?"

"I'll ask Maria to watch Jamey."

"One suggestion, Jack. Dump the car. It isn't safe for Jamey to ride around in."

"Annie must have talked to you," I muttered.

"Huh?" he asked.

"Never mind," I said and glanced at my watch. "That was a quick three-hundred-fifty bucks."

Kevin stood up and motioned for me to do the same. With one arm he hugged my shoulders and pulled me close to his side. "We'll win this, Jack."

Before escorting me to the door he tugged at a frayed belt loop snagged at the back of my shorts. "Nice legs," he said. "But wear a suit and tie to court."

I owned one blue silk tie.

Chapter Seven

Captain Walt grinned from ear to ear after I signed over the pink slip and handed him the keys to my Chevy. His toothless smile had filled in; he had remembered to wear his bridge. The five thousand-dollar check that he paid me made a nice down payment on my new car.

I was chomping at the bit to surprise Jamey with my new wheels; I hadn't told him. Wednesday, 3:00 p.m. on the dot, I pulled into the driveway at Emerald Cove elementary.

Like a herd of leaping gazelle, grades one through six spilled out of their classrooms and onto the school lawn. The encroaching line-up of chauffeuring parents wedged my new car between a mini van and a school bus. To prevent the stampede from taking my life before its time I barricaded myself behind the steering wheel. I smiled to myself when I saw Jamey demonstrating a header for Johnny. With only one soccer season under his belt, Jamey bounced the ball off the principal's office window. Her parking space was empty, lucky kid. After breathing in the new car smell of my PT Cruiser, Chrysler's remake of the old Woodie, I waited curbside until the school bell rang. Two of Jamey's classmates stared in open admiration as they passed the red and yellow flames painted on the highly buffed plum fenders. I stepped away from the car and yelled, "Hey, Jamey!"

Leaving Johnny in the dust, Jamey flew toward the Cruiser.

"Cool car, Grampa!" He waved his right hand over the flames and pretended that the heat burned his skin.

"More like hot," I added. Jamey wrinkled his forehead and raised his eyes a notch when he looked at me. He didn't get it. Evidently saying hot wasn't cool anymore; it showed my age. I tweaked his chin and rubbed his head like Mo teasing Curly. "You like, huh?"

"It's way cool!" he exclaimed, accentuating "way".

"Way cool" was worth the thirty-six monthly payments.

"Can Johnny have a ride home in your new car, Grampa?"

"Not today. I need his parents' permission, Jamey."

Disappointed, he asked me, "Why?"

I hedged the truth and told him, "Johnny's mom called me this morning. She told me that she would pick him up after school today. They had to go somewhere this afternoon." Jamey's innocent request knocked the wind out of my sails. All I needed was to have Jonas accuse me of impropriety with one of Jamey's friends. I was becoming paranoid, fearful of even hugging my grandson in public.

On our way home we stopped by Captain Walt's place. He had washed the old clunker and parked in front of his café on Pacific Coast Highway, but the bath didn't help; the car still looked pretty bad. Walt made his promise good; Jamey and I snacked on a complimentary croissant, cinnamon-walnut drizzled with sugar glaze. Jamey ordered milk; I preferred my milk frothed in a latte. Both of us were so anxious to ride in the Cruiser again that Jamey had neglected to wipe the milk from his mouth. He rode home with me sporting a milk mustache.

I lived on Bluebird Canyon Road, a quiet street, restful and retired. The average age on the block teetered around seventy. Retirement's protocol predictably scheduled the evening's events on Bluebird Canyon Road, five o'clock cocktails, dinner by six, and lights out and in bed by seven, excluding my house. It was easy to find my house at night, the lights glowed until midnight most evenings. Staying up late and sleeping in until ten came to an end once Jamey began kindergarten. I kept to my late night routine but my nocturnal habit continued with one exception; at 7:00 a.m. Jamey ruled the mornings.

Even before Annie's death Jamey had been adopted by a slew of doting grandparents who lived in the neighborhood, with the exception of the old bastard who lived next door to me. Last Christmas, Jamey described Jarret as an old coot. I asked him where on Earth he had heard the word, coot.

"From you, Grampa," he informed me. "That's what you always call Mr. Thomas." I noticed Maria roll her eyes back in her head and bite her tongue because she and I had called Jarret much worse.

The Jarrets had been retired for several years before I bought my house. Bicycles did not roam the block, nor did roller blades. A few garages still wore the signs of children's play from days past; rusted basketball hoops, minus the nets, hung above the garage doors. Those same kids have since grown and moved away to raise their own families. But during the holidays the neighbors' kids came home, usually for a long weekend. The grandchildren rode electric scooters rather than bikes; the basketball hoops were abandoned. Jamey missed the kids once they left; most of them lived out of state. Once they had gone, the neighborhood remained kid-free except for Jamey.

Maria met us at the front door. She wiped her runny nose with her apron. Tears rolled down her cheeks. "Nasty onion," she said, "you guys hungry for penne with meatballs and garlic bread?"

"We had a snack at Captain Walt's," Jamey replied. He grabbed her free hand. "Maria, come see Grampa's new car." Her short legs ran double time to keep up with him.

Maria's eyes widened. She searched her apron for a sauce free spot to clean her hands. "It's so . . . so . . . purple."

"Cool, huh, Maria?" he boasted as if the car were his own.

"Yes, Jamey, way cool!" she played up to his enthusiasm.

Beaming with pride, I stood beside the flaming fender of my new car. I planted my sneakers firmly on the moss covered driveway, crossed my arms like a proud father, and waited for Maria's reaction. She closed her eyes, shook her head and pinched my cheek. "Purple?" she questioned me.

Correcting her, I said, "It's plum."

"Purple," she insisted. "Excuse me, I have spaghetti sauce to finish." As she sauntered past my car, she smiled at her reflection in the hood. "Maybe you can take me for a ride after dinner?" she asked then disappeared into the house.

"You're on, Maria," I said.

I polished the finger smudges from the door handles. From the kitchen window I heard Maria chuckle under her breath, "Men and their toys!"

Jamey flew through the house, unloaded his schoolbooks and ran back outside to the car. "Grampa, I'm gonna go find Willow."

"Just follow the shoe trail," I said, "and stay in the yard, okay? Dinner will be ready pretty soon."

The pungent yet sweet aroma of roasted garlic made my stomach growl. Maria slapped my hand for dunking my finger into the sauce. She minced fresh Oregano and Thyme and then sprinkled the herbs into the simmering pot and on top of my head.

I thumbed through the daily mail that Maria had stacked on top of the kitchen table. "Edison bill, health insurance bill, Visa, a card from William. What's this? From Henry Parker?"

"Give me that," she said, reaching as far as her short arms allowed in order to steal the envelope from my hand.

I waved the envelope above my head and with peeked curiosity, questioned her, "Henry Parker? As in Santa Barbara rendezvous?"

Before ribbing Maria further about her romance, I peered through the kitchen window to check on Jamey. "No! Willow," I shouted loud enough for the neighbors to hear.

My distraction gave Maria the perfect opportunity to snatch the envelope from my hand. She accidentally crushed my right foot beneath her hard soled pumps and then quickly buried her mail in her skirt pocket. "Easy on the toes," I whined then grabbed my foot and hobbled to the pantry.

"Serves you right," she said and returned to her sauce. I opened a new package of cookies from the pantry and asked Maria to join me in a latte.

"Mr. Jack, espresso must run through your veins. I'll have a single."

Maria sipped; I sat. "So," I began, "tell me about Henry."

"This may take awhile," she said.

"I have all evening," I said and propped my legs on the chair next to me. I folded my arms and made myself comfortable and said, "Fire away."

My tease had turned into a coffee clotch confessional.

"I met Henry and Mrs. Parker thirty-five years ago when I lived in Genoa. During summer holidays from the university, I worked for vacationing American families as a companion for their children, you call a nanny. I adored their two children. Melissa was eight years old, a darling. Red hair, freckles covered her button nose. She was terribly self-conscious of them. I told her that they were kisses from angels. In one of her letters to me after her son was about five she wrote about his freckles and the angels. The Parker's son, Tommy, was fifteen, a handful, rebellious, cocky. His father couldn't see it coming. He excused Tommy's behavior as just a stage. But Tommy had confided in me; he told me that he was gay. I honored his confidence and never said a word about it to his father. Henry's business kept him too busy to even ask Tommy about his adolescent struggles. Henry's business consumed him; he flew all over the US and Europe promoting his wines while building his empire. Even so, his children have grown into adults who are so dear to me." She paused for just a moment and then continued, "I'll ask Henry to send us a case of his wine; his Zinfandel, bellisima!" She reached for a package of penne pasta from the cupboard. "You've already met Tommy Parker."

"Tommy . . . Tommy . . . Richard's Tommy . . . back in West Hollywood?" Maria nodded.

"Tommy saw me leave your apartment in Los Angeles after our interview. He was nineteen then, a handsome boy, so happy about his new relationship. He promised to keep my secret, even from you."

The froth on our espressos began to melt away and cool off. I lit a cigarette; Maria cracked open the kitchen window. I urged her, "Tell me more."

"At summer's end Henry and Mrs. Parker offered me a full-time position as nanny. I accepted. Papa disapproved. Mama had passed away two years earlier; Papa begged me to reconsider, but my brothers, Marcos and Lucas persuaded him to let me go. I bid my family ciao', and moved to the United States."

"You've never said a word about this to me."

"The less I talked about it, the less it hurt," she confessed.

"I know that one. You and I have more in common than I thought."

"Maybe it's because we have lived together for so many years now," she said affectionately.

"Alright, tell me more about Henry," I said anxiously.

"Henry traveled ten months out of the year," she continued. "He'd be away three and four weeks at a time, home for a week then off again. It strained his marriage. I'd watch different men arrive at the house; one young handsome fellow one month then someone else the next month. They would always leave in the morning. I protected Tommy and Melissa the best I could, but they knew. Mrs. Parker asked Henry for a divorce. I overheard one of their arguments one evening. "Why divorce me?" he asked her. "You have all of this and your boyfriends too. It's too expensive to divorce you, Nancy." Henry moved into the downstairs' bedroom near my apartment off the kitchen. We'd stay up late into the evening just talking."

"About what?"

"His wine business, his children, and Mrs. Parker. She turned her nose up at his wine. She preferred vodka, straight up in a martini glass with a green olive stuffed with a pimento. She began drinking alone in her bedroom every night. I felt sorry for her and for the loneliness she felt as she wandered from room to room in her Malibu mansion."

"Did they ever divorce?"

"Henry finally asked me out, a dinner date. He wouldn't tell me where we were going, only that the restaurant was in Marina Del Rey. It made me nervous; I didn't want anyone to find out about us. We hid our romance for six months, but Tommy suspected. I gave my notice to quit. Henry was married; I did not want to embarrass the children. The angels guided me to you and Annie and now to Henry again. Mr. Jack, I am so much in love with him. I remember my interview, a year ago at the battered women's shelter. He was the executive director, but I knew that before I arrived that morning. Henry moved slowly to stand from his desk, his eyes moistened, so did mine. He spoke first. "I divorced Nancy," he confessed. There wasn't an interview, only his embrace and my love for him exploding in my chest."

At that moment Jamey bolted through the living room, knocked over an end table by the recliner, and screamed out, "Grampa! Grampa! Something's wrong with Willow. Hurry!"

Maria and I ran behind Jamey and followed him to the clothesline behind the garage. Willow lay on the sparse grass. I placed my ear near her mouth and nose. She wasn't breathing. Petting her still head, Jamey began to cry. Maria ran next door to find Mrs. Jarret while Jamey and I expressed our silent goodbyes to Willow.

Willow's golden silky head lay motionless across my forearms. In his hands, Jamey supported her quieted hind paws as we climbed the Jarrets' front porch steps. We caught up with Maria. She continued to knock at the front door. Willow's heart had stopped beating; another loss for my grandson. Mr. Jarret finally answered Maria's persistent rapping. Smoking a half-chewed cigar, he spoke through the screen door. His right hand choked a bottle of beer. His sweat stained T-shirt stretched around his beer gut like a hand-me-down maternity frock. Slouching, he slurred, "What did you do to my dog, Turner?"

"My Grampa didn't do anything to Willow," Jamey butted in. "I found her in our backyard. Are you gonna take her to the doctor?"

"Yeah, I'll do that." He slammed the bottom half of his beer, belched a cloud of soured ale, then turned to Jamey and said, "Thanks for bringing her home."

"Is she gonna be okay?" Jamey asked.

"I'll let you know. Now run along, you, the old man, and the maid. All of you."

I laid Willow to rest on a chaise lounge covered in a damp beach towel. Holding onto my hand, Jamey led me away from the old drunk. His ninety-proof insult hurt Maria's pride. She walked away from the house and cursed under her breath, "Bebutto bastardo!"

If Jarret overheard her he made no response.

Before Jamey and I descended the steps I turned my head toward Jarret and said to him, "Now I understand why Willow slept on my front porch each night. Good afternoon. Come along Jamey."

For a little woman Maria was tall on pride. Grinding her teeth, she emptied the pasta into the boiling cauldron. I said to her, "I'm so sorry, Maria, about Jarret."

"No need. What is it you say? Consider the source?" she said and then continued to stir the boiling pasta.

She set the timer for twelve minutes. According to Maria, the pasta must be cooked aldente or down the garbage disposal it went. I dunked my finger into the sauce again. Nudging me away from the stove, Maria bumped my legs twice with her hip. But not far enough away from the simmering pot for me to steal one last dunk before I said to her, "I need to ask a favor."

"You're incorrigible," she scolded, slapping my hand. "If I can."

"Kevin asked me to have dinner at his place this Saturday. Sign a few documents; prep me for the impending trial. Will you watch Jamey?"

"Henry and I had planned to go to Palm Springs this weekend. But I'll cancel; we can plan our get away the following weekend."

"That's not necessary. I'll regret this, but I'll call Peg."

"Mr. Jack, at times you are so naïve and not too bright."

"She is Jamey's grandmother," I reminded her.

"Yes, and she and her husband have filed a lawsuit against you. Kevin would say that you are a fool. I will take care of Jamey this weekend."

"If you must make the sacrifice then I insist that you invite Henry for dinner Saturday afternoon and introduce him to me."

"I'll do that," she said, delighted.

*   *   *

I honored one of Annie's rules for Jamey, bedtime at 8:00 p.m. I filled the bathtub with mounds of Mr. Bubble bubbles and molded white foamy horns on top of his head. He reciprocated by drenching my pants and shoes. I rinsed the bubbles off his skin, still tender with the sweetness of childhood, and dried him off. The bath sheet wrapped his body like a toga dwarfing his slight build. Sitting on the john, I dried his hair with the blow dryer. Jamey pulled on his Spiderman pajama bottoms; I buttoned his nightshirt and sloshed my wet socks down the hallway leaving perfect impressions of my size eleven feet and long toes along the hardwood floor.

After I put him to bed, Jamey snuggled Pooh next to his pillow. I tucked the comforter around his sides like a cocoon and tugged its edge just beneath his chin. A photograph of Annie, pregnant with Jamey while hugging Derek belly to belly, faced Jamey's bed. Standing lens side down, Jamey's flashlight remained on throughout the night. I stored an arsenal of "C" batteries in the kitchen junk drawer.

"Okay, Tiger, it's time to go to sleep."

"Grampa?"

"Hmm?"

"I'm gonna say a prayer for Willow and my mom and dad."

"You want to say it now?" I asked.

"No, I'll wait."

"Okay."

Jamey squirmed and pulled at the comforter then settled in for the night. He reached for the flashlight and drew figure eights on the ceiling. He asked me, "Why is Mr. Jarret so mean to you?"

I sat down at the edge of his bed, fumbled with the flashlight, mesmerized by its reflection on the window. I reached for Pooh and held him in my lap fearful of how much a six-year-old could comprehend.

"Sometimes, Jamey, people can be mean to others for reasons we're not sure of. Being afraid of things that they don't understand can make them react in a mean way. I remember during one of your soccer games when one of your new teammates didn't understand some of the rules and you got on his case because he didn't know what to do. At times what we don't know makes us angry until someone explains it to us. Am I making sense to you?"

Jamey sunk his head bottoming out his pillow all the way to the mattress. The sides of the puffy goose down wrapped his cheeks like a soft taco. Bored with my lame explanation, he sighed, rolled his eyes, sat straight up and said to me, "I know why Mr. Jarret is mean to you."

"You do?"

"It's 'cause you're gay. Mom told me."

"What did she tell you?" I asked, surprised that Annie had discussed this with him.

"Gay means you don't have a wife, just like Uncle Tommy and Uncle Richard. I heard Mr. Jarret say mean things about 'em. You can be gay Grampa, it's okay with me. You don't need a wife. We have Maria."

"That we do," I said, relieved.

Society's bigotry hadn't poisoned Jamey's childhood innocence. At six years old his compassion had left me humbled from admiration and envy.

I kissed Jamey's forehead and mussed his hair. "I love you so much, Jamey."

"I love you too, Grampa. Don't turn off my flashlight."

"Never, ever. Sleep tight."

Jamey tickled my ribs. Finishing the rhyme, he echoed, "Don't let the bed bugs bite."

Jamey turned off the nightlight but left his flashlight on. He set it on the nightstand so that it pointed to the ceiling. I slowly closed his bedroom door leaving it cracked just a smidgen which allowed me to hear his clucking noises throughout the night.

Before our final goodnights our special tradition played out the who-would-get-the-last-teasing-jab-of-the-day in before the other. Jamey won the previous night. Nestled between his clean carpenter jeans and folded underwear on top of the dresser a perfect ball of crew socks waited for my pitch. I bounced them off his head before he could blind me with his flashlight. He giggled the same way he would if he played with the dogs, found the socks and missed me by a mile.

"Ha, ha! I won! See ya in the morning."

"Grampa?"

"Yes Jamey."

"Cool car."

"Goodnight, Jamey."

At 8:30 p.m. Maria wished me good night. "Sleep well, Mr. Jack."

"What about your ride in the Cruiser?"

"Tomorrow," she replied. She paused at the doorway and cocked her head over her shoulder. "Purple?" she asked and then closed her bedroom door.

"It's plum. Good night, Maria," I said then headed for my office.

Chilling my bare feet, the cold evening air seeped through the glass slider. Maria had opened it earlier to freshen the smoky room but hadn't closed it tightly. I switched on the fluorescent light illuminating only my desktop, poured myself a glass of wine, opened a fresh pack of cigarettes and started on my homework for Kevin.

Chapter Eight

J amey Robert Fitzpatrick had blown me away that night. It is a father's prerogative to be proud of his child. Annie had made me proud and her son's insightful definition of my lifestyle had lifted my spirits and boosted my confidence for the months that followed. To Jamey I was simply his Grampa.

By mid Saturday afternoon the parenting worksheets lay completed on my desk. I cut the grass, a seasonal task because a freeze seldom occurred at the beach. I trimmed back the rose bushes for winter, and reassured Maria for the tenth time how fabulous she looked. Henry had accepted her invitation. I parked the Cruiser safely in the garage and scoured the slick algae from the weathered cement driveway. Diluted from the flow of the pressure hose, bleach had pooled beneath the tires of a 1959 Mercedes 300 SL Gullwing that had pulled onto the driveway. Mr. Henry Parker, a caricature of the little old winemaker, cowboy style, stepped onto the slimy residue and introduced himself to me, "Howdy, I'm Henry. You must be Jack."

We shook hands as gentlemen do. His handshake was strong. His hand fit in my palm like a child's, yet thick and callused from years of working in vineyards.

"Nice to meet you Henry," I said. "Please watch your step. I've been trying to get in some winter clean up before it rains again; the driveway is a bit slippery."

"Huh," he said, looking up at me. "Not to worry, I'm built real close to the ground, I don't have far to fall," he said while balancing in his boots that were one full size larger than mine.

The heels of his Tony Llama boots added a deceiving three inches to his height. He hoisted up his wrangler jeans in spite of the leather belt that was wrapped snugly around his potbelly. He refastened his silver belt buckle, jeweled with turquoise, one more notch. An image of Maria wearing a knee skirt erupting atop three layers of crinolines, dosee doeing with Henry stayed with me most of the afternoon.

At 5'4" Henry's tall-in-the-saddle cowboy charm contradicted his genteel manner. His cheeks blushed from years of wine tasting. His salt and pepper hair betrayed his age. From the size of his waist, I assumed that he had spent his life enjoying good food and wine, but not getting much exercise. Henry's soft-spoken tenor voice was easy to listen to.

"Sweet car, Henry," I said.

"I bought her new back in '59. Two-hundred-fifty-thousand miles on her now. Help me out here, champ, I have something for you."

We stepped lightly along the edge of the concrete driveway being careful not to trip on the encroaching fescue. I had neglected to edge the lawn after mowing it the week before. Henry asked me to take a case of wine from the trunk and commented, "You're sure a tall drink of water, Jack. Just like my boy. He gets it from his mother's side of the family."

I tilted the case to read the vintage. "Tome' Winery and Vineyards, Estate Reserve, 1994 Zinfandel, Bella Maria, Sonoma. Bella Maria, my Maria?"

He nodded affirming my suspicion. "It was my way to honor my love for her," he said lovingly with pride.

"Tome'?"

"I named the winery after my kids, Tommy and Melissa. Melissa runs the operation now. The winery sets on a hundred acres in the Valley of the Moon near Kenwood, California. I visit every summer when I take a break from the shelter. Maria and I are gonna head on up in July. She insists on driving my Mercedes."

"I don't think that her Beetle has that many miles left in her."

Henry put his arm around my shoulder. Drawing my head near his, he said, "Just between you and me, I've purchased another Gullwing, a '62. A friend of mine is restoring it for Maria. She hasn't a clue. Her birthday's in September, ya know. It'll be a surprise."

Within fifteen minutes Henry had weaseled his way into my heart just as Maria had in 1974.

I balanced the case of Bella Maria forward on my hips. Henry strolled alongside me as we climbed the porch steps together. Maria swung open the screen door hard and wide nearly knocking me on my butt. Embracing Henry, she peeked over his shoulder, "Oh, sorry Mr. Jack."

Before I took another step I braced my hips against the banister to balance the box of wine and said to her, "Maybe you can get the door for me?"

My family shared a tradition common to households across the country. Friends and family gathered in the kitchen to visit, shoot the breeze and even hammer out solutions to the world's woes. Henry pulled up one of the red and silver metallic plastic upholstered chairs and rested one elbow on the white Formica tabletop.

"I haven't seen a kitchen set like this since the "Donna Reed Show," Henry said, scooting the chrome chair legs closer to the table.

"I have a thing for nostalgia. Picked it up in a thrift shop a couple years ago," I said.

"Your recliner in the living room, another nostalgic flashback?" he asked.

"I suppose it is. I bought it new when my daughter . . . ," my eyes focused on Maria, ". . . when she was six months old."

"Jack, I'm sorry to hear about your daughter."

My voice began to crack. I swallowed to soothe my throat and pressed my lips together attempting a smile. "Thanks," I said.

Maria sensed the wavering tone in my voice and intervened, "Mr. Jack, where's Jamey?" as she continued to rummage through the silverware drawer, searching for a paring knife.

"Haven't seen him," I said then excused myself. I checked his room but his bicycle and helmet were gone.

When I returned to the kitchen Maria held open the laundry room door and stood clear of the breezeway. "Henry, hold on to your seat," she warned him.

Jamey slammed the back screen door, pounded a drum roll against the washing machine and then leaped into the air to tap the door jam above his head. He missed and finished with a standing squat jump into the kitchen. How one little body could create a cacophony of sound in such a small space was beyond me. He ran past Maria, didn't notice Henry sitting at the table when I grabbed the back of Jamey's britches. Grass stains and mud packed the knees of his carpenter's jeans like soccer shin guards. A perfect mud trail outlined his spine all the way down to the crack of his ass. "Okay, Superman, where's the fire?" I asked.

The innocence of childhood has no shame. Jamey squeezed his privates to halt the pressure. Wriggling like a worm, he said, "Grampa, I have to go potty."

"Slow down, Tiger; we've got company." A grassy mudpack fell to the kitchen floor. "And change you britches before you come back."

Once I released my hold he disappeared down the hallway. I promised myself that I would install fenders on his bicycle before the week's end.

Maria served a platter of sliced Fuji apples, Brie and Triscuits. She added a cluster of Thompson seedless grapes for Jamey because he turned his nose up at Brie and crackers. A freshly pressed apron, free of spaghetti sauce stains, accented Maria's signature pleated wool skirt. Before too long, I suspected that she would teach me how to rid my shirts of similar stains and gift to me an apron much like her own, crisp, white, and tied at the waist. The glances between Maria and Henry assured me of the inevitable as I recalled William's suggestion that I learn to cook and clean.

Maria fawned over Henry like a schoolgirl romancing her first love. She had remained unmarried all the years that she lived with me. I don't recall her mooning over a lost beau whom she may have left behind in Italy, no broken hearts. She had been content to care for Annie, me, and now Jamey. Henry was her first love and last.

Jamey stood at attention inside the kitchen doorway while drying his hands on his clean trousers. He waited patiently for us grownups to cease our babble. Maria led him by the hand toward Mr. Parker. "Jamey, honey, I want you to meet Henry."

Henry reached out first to shake Jamey's hand. "Hey, pardner," he said to Jamey.

"Hi. What's a pardner?" Jamey asked.

"Buddies. Like old friends," Henry replied. "I remember a time when I could run as fast as you."

"Grampa taught me. We run on the beach. I can only go one mile. Grampa can go twenty miles."

"Twenty miles? Impressive considering you smoke," Henry said to me as he tapped my pack of cigarettes.

"Four or five cigarettes a day unless I'm training for an event then I quit," I confessed.

"You run 10K's?"

"Some. I prefer distance, marathons. I run mostly for exercise. You run?"

"Not anymore. Last time I ran it was on the heels of my son. I chased him down the Malibu pier when he was sixteen," he said, the tone in his voice was stern, but the expression in his eyes was fatherly and caring. Henry continued, "Before I had a chance to explain why I was so angry with him, Tommy ran away from me, but I finally caught up to him. Earlier that day he had confided in me about his lifestyle choice. I had laid into him, not because he had told me that he was gay, but because he had used my credit card without asking me." Henry paused for a moment. He looked as though he was remembering a pleasant thought, then without a word, he spread a healthy helping of Brie on a cracker. "Richard's a great guy except for the grub that he eats," Henry said as he licked the cheese from his fingertips.

Maria pulled a chair out for Jamey. "Henry is staying for dinner while your Grampa goes to a meeting tonight," she informed him.

Jamey scooted his chair nearer to Henry. "You'll like Maria's veal parma . . ."

". . . giana," Maria finished.

"Maria talks about you a lot," Jamey said, telling on her.

"She does, does she?" he asked and then smiled at Maria.

"You grow wine and drive a cool car. I saw it outside. My Grampa just got a new car."

"What did he get?"

"A plum," Jamey winked at me, "PT Cruiser. Come. I'll show it to you."

Henry raised his brow asking permission.

"Sure," I said and tossed him the keys.

While Superman and the Cowboy checked out my new car I took advantage of our privacy. "Maria, I like him. He's a good man."

"I know," Maria agreed and with a smile on her lips sliced another apple.

"You and Henry, you guys are serious about each other, I can tell."

"Mr. Jack, I don't know what will happen between us, but I do know that I love him."

"That's good enough for me, Maria," I said as Henry and Jamey walked into the kitchen. Henry held out his right hand to Jamey, each of them slapped their palms together as if to express victory; they must have overheard our conversation.

"Henry," Maria persuaded, "tell Jack about this coming July."

"Maria tells me that you and Jamey have birthdays in July."

"Yep, Jamey's the 14th; I'm the 4th."

"Bastille Day and Independence Day. Couple of firecrackers."

"More like a couple of cherry bombs," I said.

With a mouthful of apple Jamey proudly informed Henry, "I'm gonna be seven."

"Whew, you're almost as old as your Grampa," Henry teased him.

"Na uh, Grampa's way older than me."

I squeezed Jamey's knee to tickle his funny bone. He laughed and chewed simultaneously. "Watch it, buster," I warned him playfully.

"Maria is spending the Fourth of July with me this year at my summer place at the winery. I think you and Jamey should come along. How 'bout it?" Henry asked.

"Can we Grampa?"

"I don't see why not. We just need to be back in time for your birthday. Remember, Gramma Peg and Grampa Rob are taking you to Universal Studios," I told him and then thought to myself, "Unless the court takes you away from me."

Maria read my thoughts and then broke the silence of my stare when she said, "Henry, tell the guys about the pillow fights."

"Jamey, you'll like this. Every year on the Fourth of July, not far from my winery, the annual World Championship Pillow Fights take place. Guys and gals balance on logs above all this mud and smack each other with pillows trying to knock the other one into a slimey, muddy pond."

"Cool!"

"Way!" I added. Jamey grabbed my knee but his tiny hand failed to tweak my funny bone.

"Jack, it is *the* event in Sonoma County during July," Henry said. "The small town of Kenwood and the local Fire Department sponsor the fights and the Kenwood Foot Race, a 10K through the vineyards of the Valley of the Moon. You should sign up. It's an all day party, food, games, wine tasting. There's no place like the Sonoma valley during summer."

"You sold me. When do we pack?"

"Alright!" Jamey cheered.

I checked my watch and snatched a bottle of Henry's vintage Zinfandel. "It's almost 6:30. I'd better get going. You'll need to back your car out of the driveway, Henry."

Henry tossed me his keys and said, "No need, you take her."

"You serious?"

"Sure. Besides, we can take Maria's Beetle. The three of us are going to see *Harry Potter and the Chamber of Secrets*. I noticed that it's still playing at the theater in downtown Laguna."

"Jamey's already seen it twice," I said then gave my grandson the paternal stare down.

Gulping his glass of water, Jamey blurted out, "I could see it again, Grampa."

"And Maria says I'm incorrigible."

I tossed my keys to Henry. "You take the Cruiser. It'll be Maria's first ride."

From a man's point of view, driving a vintage Gullwing will raise a man's testosterone levels beyond its natural threshold. But for a woman, its body and style, is all about fashion and elegance. For me, driving the car was pure joy. I hadn't been that close to the pavement since Jamey and I went rollerblading in the parking lot surrounding Dana Point Harbor last summer.

The sun had set by 6:45 p.m. A gentle evening breeze had cleared any fog that dared to hover along the January coastline. Winter's full moon lit up the breaking surf along the three and a half mile undeveloped beach between Laguna and Corona del Mar. Back in the 80's the Irvine Company had contracted to develop the hills on the east side of Pacific Coast Highway and agreed to preserve the coastline and its beaches. But on the opposite side of the highway, imposing facades indicated private entrances to the multi-million dollar residences. Twenty-five foot date palms lined brick paved driveways leading to hidden villas. Lush bougainvillea, elephant ferns and lavender ice plant landscaped the rolling hills of planned extravagance. Sun bleached tiled rooftops peppered the twilight skyline. Across the highway, parking lots and blacktop buried the meandering horse-riding trails that had disappeared after the sixties; preservation of the beach must have been defined as, "no housing". Preserving the romance of this gentle coastline, pampas grass and aging driftwood painted the surviving landscape.

I turned onto Newport Boulevard from Pacific Coast Highway and drove across the Newport Bay Bridge leading to the Peninsula. The bridge catapulted the residents and wide-eyed tourists into the bay of conspicuous consumption. At dusk, the Newport Pavilion glimmered like a crystal carousel reflecting on the water; a post card waiting to be sent to families shoveling snow in Michigan. The light shining through portholes of docked sailboats and private yachts cast surreal images onto the incoming tide. This sort of extravagance wasn't my style. It was, however, Kevin's.

I circled the peninsula twice before finding Bayside Court, an address that suited Kevin's impeccable taste and lavish lifestyle. After I pulled into the driveway, I pressed the intercom button to the left of the locked iron gate and spoke into the intercom box, "Kevin, this is Jack. Where should I park?"

"Are you in the driveway?" he asked.

"Barely."

"I'm sure you're fine. Come on up."

The gate hummed, unlocked and opened the way to a courtyard that mimicked the tropics. Bird of Paradise that graced the stone walls appeared to be in flight above the lava rock fountain, a sanctuary for Koi. A softly lit walkway brightened the gray and black hues of slate tiles at the front door. Compelled to touch the enormous banana leaves opposite the pond, I knocked over a ceramic giraffe, lunged to save it from breaking and grabbed its neck in the process. A Phoenix Palm tangled with my hair. I brushed it aside and snapped one of its delicate stems. Embarrassed, I tossed the evidence over the fence and fished for my specs.

A five-foot iris, exquisitely etched in the center of the solid glass front door, made Kevin's silhouette gentler than he would admit. He opened the door before I knocked. "Hello, Jack. Seven on the dot. Come in."

I cocked my head toward the galley kitchen and took a deep breath. "Mmm, something smells good."

"Thanks, I took a shower."

"You must have showered with fresh basil and garlic then. Smells more like Maria's pesto."

"With a personal twist," he said. "I called her yesterday for her recipe."

I offered him the bottle of Zinfandel and said, "A gift to add to your wine collection."

He recognized the label and said, "Ah, Tome'. Enjoyed a wine tasting at Tome' in Kenwood, beautiful country. Make yourself comfortable. I'll open the wine."

I draped my jacket over a teak bench setting in the entry and followed the terra cotta floor into the condo's great room. Offering an unobstructed nocturnal view of the bay, ten-foot windows scaled the eighteen-foot vaulted ceiling. A limestone fireplace warmed the hard lines of wood and glass and leather furniture, a Xerox copy of his law office, uncluttered and precise. Psychologists would have had a field day analyzing Kevin's type-A, anal retentive personality, not a thing out of place in his home. My unprofessional analysis concluded, not uptight, just compulsive and orderly.

Poised with two glasses of wine, Kevin reappeared from the kitchen. "Cheers! Here's to Jamey's future," Kevin toasted.

He removed my jacket from the bench and hung it in a closet hidden behind mirrored doors. He sipped his wine and insisted, "Make yourself at home."

I pulled up a barstool at the center-island in the kitchen. I didn't want to risk spilling wine on the new Berber carpet in the living room; I figured the bleached oak hardwood floors in the kitchen were the lesser of two evils.

Although, watching Kevin prepare our dinner, I wasn't so sure. He twirled the pizza dough into the air and caught it with his knuckles then stretched the herb-speckled crust and tossed it into the air again. With each toss came a perfect catch. He slid the dressed pizza into an open-faced brick oven and within minutes the air was filled with the aromas of fresh basil, oregano and roasted garlic.

Impressed, I said, "I always use a Boboli."

"In a pinch, me too," he confessed. "Wait until you bite into this. Your taste buds will dance."

Kevin was easy on the eye, a looker, and he knew it. Without his lawyer uniform of an Armani suit, his creased-from-the-cleaner's blue jeans, leather sandals and loose shirt made him far warmer and more approachable. His edge of arrogance was a product of environment, money, and William spoiling him for twenty-five years.

"Grab your wine, Jack," he said and opened the double French doors leading to a patio off the kitchen. "Let's have a smoke."

Outside speakers played an unfamiliar voice. "Who is that?" I asked.

"Enya. Her voice is like a massage melting away the day's tension." Kevin eased into his chair. With his hips balancing on the edge and his arms dangling near the ground, he said, "Think of *The Lord of the Rings*; you'll recognize her voice." Kevin closed his eyes, propped his feet on a chair and cradled his wineglass. "Sweet, huh?"

"I may have to add her to my Carpenter's collection."

Sinking into the music, sharing good wine and gazing at a star filled evening sky made me momentarily forget my reason for coming to dinner. I had held onto the parenting worksheets since my arrival. I offered them to Kevin and asked, "Shouldn't we talk about the hearing?"

"After dinner," he said. "Listen to this next track." Kevin reached across the table to light my cigarette. I eased back into the swivel chair, sipped my wine, and thought about the void William must have felt when Kevin left him. But my impatience hadn't been soothed by the music or Kevin's postponement of a discussion about the hearing.

Breaking the silence, I said, "Annie's house sold this week for two and a half million dollars. The trustee at the bank called me yesterday to tell me that Fitzpatrick gave him a visit."

"You needn't be concerned. Jamey is the heir to the trust. Fitzpatrick can't touch it. Nor can you except for Jamey's needs."

Unlike William, Kevin did not have a knack for calming me down.

"You said you had some documents for me to sign?"

Irritated by my persistence, he grabbed his wine and flipped his hand toward the kitchen. "Come inside. I'm sure the pizza is done."

The Brie and crackers I had snacked on earlier had metabolized. The familiar smell of pesto baking with sun dried tomatoes and roasted garlic blanketed under shredded Parmesan cheese appealed to my hunger. I had hardly touched my wine. Kevin offered to top off my glass. "Thank you, but no," I said, "I'm driving Henry's car."

We sat in the dining room. Kevin offered me the seat with an unobstructed view of the bay. "China, crystal and linen napkins, awfully fancy for pizza," I said. I hadn't eaten pizza with a fork until that night.

He lit candles and dimmed the chandelier. "I do this every night," he said. "It's a tradition that William started after our first date."

"You miss him, don't you?"

"Not anymore." The tone in his voice let me know that our discussion about William was over.

"Kevin, let's talk about the hearing," I interrupted and handed him the worksheets.

"I'll forward these worksheets to Judge Harcourt's office Monday morning. Copies of any documents or subpoenas that Jonas may present will be forwarded to me. Nothing has crossed my desk yet, but when it does I'll call you."

I licked the pesto from my fingertips and stole another clove of roasted garlic from the empty pizza stone. "That's it?"

"Jack, if you're still hungry I can fix you something else."

"I meant regarding the hearing; anything else you need to tell me."

"You'll need to send me a list of your close friends, their names, addresses, and phone numbers. I may subpoena them to testify on your behalf."

"There's Richard and Tommy, Mr. Thomas, and of course Mrs. Zucker, although she's in her eighties now, traveling is difficult for her."

"Any friends in the community, businesses you patronize, restaurants or stores you frequent, places that you and Jamey hang out together?"

"There's Walt. He owns an espresso café in Laguna."

Kevin jotted the information in a spiral notebook.

"I'll want Margo's address as well."

"Not a good idea." I stepped away from the table, caught my shoe on the edge of the Sisal rug, and dropped my empty wineglass onto the hardwood floor. "Clumsy," I said, cursing myself. "Where's a broom, Kevin?"

"Relax, will you. I'll clean it up. I can't believe after all these years that Margo can still affect you this way."

"After confronting her at my house, I suppose she does. You were at the house. You must have overheard our conversation."

"Bits and pieces."

"That was just the beginning. A few days later, she invited me to dinner. I accepted and met her at Las Brisas. She fed me a sob story about losing her baby several years ago. She begged me to allow her to begin a relationship with Jamey. I said no. In my crass way I basically told her to go to hell."

"Sometimes your charm is overwhelming. Consider an apology, make amends with her," he recommended, his tone professional and to the point.

"I won't do that."

"It may back-fire on you," he warned me.

"I'll take that risk."

"As your attorney, I strongly urge you to reconsider, Jack."

"No, I'm hell bent on this one."

"Well, she has been out of the picture for what, twenty-five years or so?"

"Or so." I took Kevin's advice to heart, but it sunk into my gut. "What about Jonas? What's he like?"

"He's British, you know, the accent, the thirty-five-hundred-dollar tailored suits. He graduated second in his class at Harvard Law. He's currently the senior partner for his law firm, Simon and Lutz. He tried to recruit me when he heard about my work in Maine, but his firm is too conservative for my venue so I turned down his offer. He seldom works the courtroom these days. He and Fitzpatrick are tight. Jonas probably owes him a favor."

"Have we anything to fear going into this?"

"Jack, the burden of proof falls on Jonas and Fitzpatrick. There's no way they can prevail. Look at you, Mr. Morality, everybody's Grampa. It doesn't fly. They're up to something. I cannot figure out why Jonas agreed to represent the Fitzpatricks, unless it's for money. That pompous Brit would sell his mother down the river for a nickel."

"And Rob is so tight he'd squeeze the nickel until the bull shits. So what's their game?" I asked.

"Beats me, except they do share one thing in common."

"Two hour lunches, too many martinis, attorney privileges?" I asked, amused.

"They hate faggots."

"They deserve each other," I said.

"Maybe. But now they have you, me and a weak case to contend with. Unless there's some aces up their sleeves, they'll lose this case, Jack."

I helped Kevin clear the table and carry the dinner plates into the kitchen. "I'm banking on it," I said.

"What's Peg's motivation in all this?" Kevin asked. "She doesn't strike me as vindictive."

"She's not. You need to know Peg to understand her. She moved here during the early seventies from Port Angeles, Washington, worked as a waitress at Coco's, your favorite hangout on West Cliff Drive and 17th. Rob also hung out there; it must be a lawyer thing because I see your car in the parking lot most Sunday mornings. Anyway, they began dating, Rob introduced her to his lavish lifestyle, and then they married."

"If she married the guy just for his money, she's nothing more than a prostitute."

"That's cruel. She's Rob's wife and genuinely loves her husband," I said in her defense. "Peg also loved Annie like her own daughter and she dotes on Jamey every chance she gets. You saw Peg at the funeral, how she was with Jamey."

"You're right, Jack, my apologies. I remember the hurt in her eyes after Jamey told her he had to get your permission to spend the night with her and Rob."

"Now that Annie's gone and Jamey's with me she doesn't come around much. I suspect that Rob put the kibosh on her visits with us until this is resolved. They've been married for nearly thirty years. Peg will stand by him. Something hard to find nowadays."

"Is that a jab at me and William?"

"Not a place I want to go to."

"William hooked up with Joey, an adolescent wanna be. It doesn't matter now anyway. It's over. What about you Jack?"

"What about me?"

"You know. A little romance. Forever after?"

"Shit, I don't know. When it happens I guess."

"You wanna go out?"

"Go out where?"

"You really don't get out much do you? Go out . . . on a date . . . with me."

"Wouldn't that be a conflict of interest?"

"Depends on who's interested."

"I'll think about it."

"Please do."

"I'd better get back to the house. Henry will want his car. Jamey will be wound up from seeing *Harry Potter* again and I have a deadline to meet. Our meeting here has helped me to focus on an idea for next week's column. I'll send the information about my friends to your office tomorrow afternoon. Thanks for the pizza."

"Show me the winemaker's car before you go." We walked through the courtyard together. Kevin decided to feed the Koi before checking out Henry's car. "Hmm," he said, "the cleaning lady moved the giraffe again."

Guilt forced me to own up so I confessed about the giraffe's demise.

"Will you consider?" Kevin asked.

"Moving the giraffe?" I asked, confused.

"Leave the giraffe out of this. Going out with me?"

"Like I said, I'll think about it."

I lifted the Gullwing's door. With only the driver's side door open it reminded me of a big, maimed bird. Running his hand along the hood, Kevin was awed by the car's timeless style. "Maybe you should trade up," he suggested.

"Nah, too high maintenance. Besides, Maria will let me borrow hers when Henry has it delivered. I'm afraid he's wooing my Maria out from under me."

When I closed the door I was enveloped in a dense, luxurious silence. Nestled inside the cockpit, I pressed the power button and watched the window glide down. Like my new car, the fuel injection turned over the engine without pumping the throttle, a ritual from days past that I didn't miss one bit. Before backing out of the driveway I asked Kevin, "Do me a favor?"

"Sure."

"Leave Margo out of this."

Chapter Nine

I kept telling myself that today was Saturday; after all, Jamey hadn't roused me. I lay across my bed, half-asleep, my right arm hanging off the edge of the mattress, my left leg exposed to the morning chill. The digital alarm clock said it was 8:30 a.m. My subconscious had lost; it was Wednesday, February 27th. Court was scheduled for 9:30 that morning and my human alarm clock had overslept. And announcing another school day at Emerald Cove Elementary, the bell had already rung. We were running late.

After staggering out of bed I dragged the comforter behind me with the satin edging wedged between my toes. I had slept wearing only my skivvies. I rushed to wake Jamey, pulled my pajama bottoms on ass backwards, tripped on one of the torn cuffs and stumbled headfirst into the closet door. The cold air in my bedroom raised goose bumps on my bare shoulders and chest; the furnace hadn't kicked on. Cloud cover dimmed the morning light from the new skylight that normally brightened the dark hallway. Out of habit I switched the hall light on and then yelled, "Jamey, time to get up. We're gonna be late for school."

Whether it is a school day or the weekend Maria seldom woke before nine. She opened her bedroom door. Thoroughly annoyed by the racket, she waited inside the doorway, cinched the waist of her chenille robe and cocked her head in my direction. She scuffled across the floor in her slippers, tucked her hair under a turban and then asked me, "What is going on out here?"

My palms went up in my defense. "I overslept. So did my alarm clock."

She cupped one hand to her mouth to cover her yawn and cinched the waist of her robe again to tighten its fit. She poked fun at my pajamas when said to me, "I see Jamey's taught you how to dress yourself."

Rubbing his eyes while taking his sweet time, Jamey sauntered out of his room. "Come on pardner, let's get you dressed," I said then directed his shoulders toward the bathroom. Still groggy, I stepped on the cuff of his green plaid pajama bottoms. I broke his fall, wrapped my arms around his little body and hugged on him like a papa bear having a tender moment with a cub.

While he went potty I spread a dollop of toothpaste onto his Spiderman toothbrush, a reward from his dentist for having a cavity-free check-up. Above his sleepy face, Jamey raised his arms to assist me as I peeled his shirt over his head. After he stepped into his britches; I pulled his crew socks onto his bony, narrow feet. His straight hair seldom needed combing which saved me a few minutes. Maria had packed his lunch, cooked a breakfast sandwich with eggs and sausage for all three of us while I dressed. I threw on a button down print shirt, a pair of shorts and tennis shoes and scuttled Jamey to the car. I honked good bye to Maria as we tore ass down Pacific Coast Highway. A latte to go would have been nice.

Morning coastal fog had reduced visibility to two car lengths, so we crawled along Pacific Coast Highway. I fought to keep my cool while Jamey surfed for a radio station that played only heavy metal music. By 8:55 a.m. we sprinted across the school lawn until we reached the corridor that led to the principal's office. Jamey yanked my hand and warned me, "Grampa, no running in the hallways."

"Yes, sir." We walked extremely fast instead.

Dressed for a winter snowstorm, bundled up in a turtle neck sweater and a jacket, the school secretary stepped away from her desk. "Good morning Jamey, Mr. Turner."

"Good morning, Tammy. Is Mrs. Radcliffe in this morning?" I asked.

With her arms folded beneath a pink cardigan sweater, Mrs. Radcliffe, the principal, leaned against the door jam of her office. With a stern but welcome tone, she said, "Good morning, Jamey, Jack."

Standing before the principal with my tail between my legs, I felt like I was back in grammar school. Jamey held onto my hand for mutual moral support.

"I apologize for being late . . ."

Jamey interrupted, "Mrs. Radcliffe, I slept in."

"We both slept in, sorry," I offered apologetically. Above Tammy's desk hung a school clock, perfectly round, solid white background with bold black numbers. "9:00 o'clock; I have to run. I'll pick you up after school, Jamey."

Mrs. Radcliffe's warm smile let me know that she knew about my day ahead. I followed them outside to the corridor. "Thanks, Mary," I said, then excused myself, ignored Jamey's warning, and ran to the car. Mrs. Radcliffe escorted Jamey down the hallway to his classroom.

The fog had thinned clearing visibility to a quarter mile. I made good time until I entered the Superior Court House parking lot. At the entrance, a "Parking Lot Full" sign directed cars to a side street. Two-hour parking warnings lined the curb for two blocks. By 9:20 I had passed through security and scaled the stairway three steps at a time to the second floor. Rob and Peg were huddled with Jonas outside Courtroom J-202. Signs were posted on the cream stucco walls of the vacant waiting room. Kevin hadn't arrived yet. I read one of the signs that hung on the wall directly across from me. It read, "Shorts and tank tops are inappropriate attire for the courtroom." My bare legs developed a chill.

From a side door the bailiff entered the waiting room. Until he introduced himself I suspected that he was a police officer; his uniform and badge reminded me of Hank. "Sir," he said, "shorts are not allowed inside the courtroom."

"I apologize," I begged, tugging at the knee length cuffs. "My grandson was late for school this morning. I ran over the speed limit to get here on time; maybe you can make an exception?"

"Judge Harcourt makes no exceptions. She will ask you to leave her courtroom."

"But I have to be here, in court, at 9:30," I argued. I checked my watch; I had five minutes.

"Sir, go downstairs to the Public Defender's office, room J-100; they'll loan you a pair of long pants to wear."

"Thank you, sir." I ran past Peg and Rob and their attorney. Kevin had described Jonas well, nice suit.

I felt that I had let Jamey down as I rushed into the Public Defender's Office. I was Jamey's grandfather, not one of his playmates running through the courthouse corridors in shorts. I realized how ridiculous I looked as I stood in front of a glass partition. A young man in his early twenties asked me, "Can I help you, sir."

"Hopefully," I said, "the bailiff sent me. I need to borrow a pair of slacks."

He pointed to a metal wardrobe closet near the entrance to the room. "Pick a pair. You'll need to leave your driver's license with me until you return them."

Swimming in a pinstriped, size thirty-eight pair of slacks, I surrendered my driver's license to the clerk. I wore my walking shorts under the baggy britches which filled out the generously cut pleats. I passed through security one last time, ran up the stairs while tripping on the baggy cuffs of my borrowed trousers.

Looking up and down the corridor, Kevin checked his watch repeatedly as he tapped his polished wingtips against the worn linoleum floor. He cocked his head and raised his eyebrows when he saw me turn the corner. He rushed me through the waiting room and asked me, "Where is your suit and tie?"

"I'll tell you later," I gasped.

Rob and Peg had settled into their seats to our right. As I walked past them, Peg lowered her head; Fitzpatrick nodded once to acknowledge Kevin and me. Jonas shook Kevin's hand. They exchanged professional good mornings to one another. Kevin pulled the heavy wooden chair away from the defendant's desk and told me to take a seat. Both attorneys approached the judge's clerk and offered their business cards; I assumed to type the exact spelling of their names.

I felt my heart pounding, either from running upstairs, or maybe from rushing to take Jamey to school, or maybe I was just apprehensive about the trial. Kevin put his hand over my wrist to reassure me. I took a deep breath when the bailiff stepped away from his desk to address the court. "All rise," he instructed.

Judge Harcourt's petite frame moved gracefully as she stepped up to the bench. The official black robe of authority hid her tiny frame, her delicate arms hidden beneath the Kimono-like sleeves. Her red hair cropped short, lay smooth against her scalp. Her diamond earrings reflected the fluorescent lighting. She laid a thick folder on her desk and sat in the only upholstered, cushioned chair in the courtroom. The jury box was empty. The judge is the jury in a family law case.

"Everyone please be seated," she said. Judge Harcourt reviewed papers from her folder then handed copies to her clerk. She addressed the court, "Good morning, I'm Judge Harcourt. Would counsel from both parties please stand and introduce themselves."

"Good morning, Your Honor. My name is Jonas Simon representing the plaintiffs, Mr. and Mrs. Fitzpatrick."

"Good morning, Your Honor, I'm Kevin Stevens representing defendant, Mr. Jack Turner."

"Thank you, counselors. We're here this morning for the guardianship issue over minor child, Jamey Fitzpatrick. Let me remind all parties that this court hearing is closed; therefore, be reminded that what goes on in this courtroom remains in this courtroom."

I elbowed Kevin and said to him, "She's certainly to the point."

Shaking his head, Kevin urged me to shut up.

Judge Harcourt asked me, "Mr. Turner, is there something you wish to say to the court?"

Embarrassed, I replied, "No, Your Honor."

She continued, "I agreed to close this hearing; let's keep it closed. The first thing on our calendar is the Plaintiff's motion for recusal. "Counselor," she said to Jonas, "I'm giving you the opportunity to tell the court why I'm not fit to sit in this chair today or wear this robe."

"Thank you, Your Honor. It is common knowledge in the legal community that your daughter leads an alternative lifestyle which might bias Your Honor in favor of the defendant."

"So counselor, what's your point?"

"Your Honor, your daughter, Assistant District Attorney for the City of Los Angeles is gay and is raising a daughter as a single parent."

"Counselor, I am so proud of my daughter and of her work as Assistant District Attorney and for raising my granddaughter on her own. I also have a son, who is not gay, raising his son as a single parent. Never in the years that I have sat on the bench have I been challenged for bias. My decision will not be influenced by sexuality or gender. I will rule what is best for the child. Your motion is denied. Have you anything else to add?"

"No, Your Honor." Hiding his chagrin, Jonas tapped the neatly stacked edges of his documents. His Southern California lifestyle had modulated his British accent only slightly. He remained standing. "Thank you, Your Honor," he said, smoothing the back of his trousers before he sat down.

"Let's get on with this," Judge Harcourt ordered. She clasped her hands together and rested them beneath her chin; her elbows planted firmly on the top of the bench then addressed Jonas, "State your case, Counselor."

"Your Honor, it is not our intention to question Mr. Turner's sexuality. We will seek to prove that his behavior, not his lifestyle, places the minor child at risk."

The judge remained quite still as she considered what Jonas had said. Her eyes skimmed across the ceiling then came to rest on Jonas. "What do you believe is gross immorality, Counselor?"

"Not conforming to accepted sexual standards, Your Honor," Jonas replied.

Kevin did not flinch. I expected him to object; I would have objected but Kevin had instructed me to say nothing unless spoken to.

"By whose standards?" Harcourt probed.

"Those standards scripted by Mosaic Law, Your Honor."

"Help me out here, counselor. Are you talking Moses or tile?"

Her sarcasm made me smile; I covered my grin with my hand.

"With all due respect Your Honor, I refer to the Great Commandments, Love your neighbor as thyself. Put no one in harm's way . . ."

"Counselor, I am aware of the Commandments," she interrupted him. "Do you believe that under Mosaic Law that oral sex between consenting adults constitutes gross immorality?"

Jonas hedged, "No, Your Honor, unless such blatant sexual behavior is exposed to a minor, in this case a six-year-old boy. Without due consideration and responsible parenting for the child's psychological welfare, Mr. Turner's behavior does place the child at risk. We urge the court to grant temporary guardianship of the minor child to his grandparents, Mr. and Mrs. Fitzpatrick until this case is resolved."

To my relief, Kevin stood to address the judge. "Your Honor, if I may?"

"Enlighten me, counselor."

"Your Honor, Plaintiff's counsel has stated that he has no intention of questioning Mr. Turner's sexuality; however, he seems to be saying that being a homosexual makes Mr. Turner immoral. No facts that they will ever present to this court will show Mr. Turner as anything but moral, kind, caring and a wonderful parent figure for his grandson. I ask the court to end these proceedings now and permit the minor to remain under guardianship of his grandfather, Mr. Turner."

"Because we're interested in the welfare and safety of the child I am not willing to dismiss this case. I need to hear both sides as well as get independent evaluations."

Jonas addressed the bench. "Your Honor, until such hearings and evaluations be done I move, again, to grant temporary guardianship of the minor child to his grandparents, Mr. and Mrs. Fitzpatrick."

"All parties present seem overly anxious to end these proceedings," Judge Harcourt said then continued, "Counselor, you have not presented any evidence to warrant moving the child from his present home. Is there any concrete reason other than Mr. Turner's sexual preference why the minor child is at risk to remain in the Defendant's care?"

"Thank you, Your Honor. I would add that Mr. and Mrs. Fitzpatrick have known the defendant for a number of years. Mr. Turner has a pattern disturbing to my clients. He consistently frequents a notorious gay bar located in Laguna Beach. By Mr. Turner's own admission, every Saturday night. Equally disturbing is the bar's location, only four blocks from his residence. God knows what goes on with him and the men inside the bar."

"Objection, Your Honor. Opinion and conjecture from counsel."

"Sustained."

"Thank you, Your Honor," Kevin said.

"Your Honor," Jonas went on, "we will prove that Mr. Turner picks up men from this establishment and lures these men home with him placing the minor child at psychological and physical risk. Engaging in such lewd behavior is unsuitable for any minor child to witness and places him in harms way. Furthermore, we will prove that Mr. Turner frequently seeks sexual favors from a male prostitute."

I erupted from my chair and jammed my right hip against the hard edge of the table. The desk placard designating, "Defendant", tumbled across the floor and finally rested near the court reporter's feet. "You son-of-a-bitch! None of that is true!" I swore out uncontrollably.

"Sit down, Jack," Kevin ordered.

"I will not. This whole thing is bullshit!"

"Mr. Turner," Judge Harcourt interrupted, "your behavior is not helping your case. That kind of language will not be tolerated in my courtroom. Another outburst like that, I will hold you in contempt. Sit down, Mr. Turner."

"My apologies, Your Honor," I said. My cheeks were flushed, my heart rate over the top.

"I have before me a *Nomination of Guardianship*, signed by the minor's mother and approved by this court to award guardianship of the minor to Mr. Turner. The allegations need to be proven in my court. I will allow the minor to remain with Mr. Turner until such allegations be proved or disproved. This court will appoint an investigator and recommend a psychological evaluation of the child. Are there any further issues that need be discussed prior to adjourning and setting our next court date?"

Jonas and Kevin spoke simultaneously, "No, Your Honor."

Judge Harcourt asked the court clerk, "Judy, what do we have eight weeks from now?"

"Wednesday, April 24th at 1:30 p.m., Your Honor."

"Counselors, does that suit your calendars?" Judge Harcourt asked.

Kevin checked his Palm Pilot. "I'm open that afternoon, Your Honor."

"We'll be here, your Honor," Jonas assured her.

"Good. We have a tentative calendar for Wednesday, April 24th. Hopefully, we'll all have our taxes paid by then. Thank you everyone, court is adjourned."

I overheard Judge Harcourt instruct the court clerk to send the referral to a Dr. Michael Aldrich. She dictated, "Request a psychological evaluation of the minor, Jamey Fitzpatrick regarding: Currently, would the grandfather's lifestyle be detrimental to the minor presently or in the future? Also, what would be the impact on the minor losing his grandfather as his primary caregiver?"

Kevin tapped me on the shoulder. "Jack, are you coming?"

"In a minute. I'll meet you at the stairway."

Constant foot traffic had worn down the courtroom's faded green commercial carpet. A wall-mounted clock hung above the bailiff's station. Its ticking was the only sound in the deserted courtroom. It was 11:05 a.m. Above the clerk's desk, one fluorescent tube flickered.

The faint smell of cologne and after shave hung in the chamber's stale, recycled air. Jonas followed Kevin out; Rob stayed behind. I knelt down on my hands and knees to retrieve the defendant desk placard. Behind me, Rob parked his middle age spread on the edge of the plaintiff's desk, crossed his legs at the ankle and supported his portly build on the heels of his hands.

He didn't notice Peg's effort to avoid me. She remained seated, her left hand on her left shoulder, her right hand picking lint from her tailored suit. Crows feet showed her age, but her elegant clothing, creamy complexion and cosmetically bobbed nose softened the wear of time. A far cry from a coffee shop waitress in a uniform saving her tips to pay for a ten-dollar haircut.

Peg clutched her purse and stood up. She smoothed the wrinkles from the front of her skirt and repositioned the shoulders of her jacket. Hoping they would leave, I centered the placard on the table. Rob uncrossed his legs and planted the soles of his loafers on the carpet. He folded his arms stressing the seams of his sport jacket. As he pushed up from the table he grunted like an old man. The table creaked when he pushed off from its edge. With his left hand buried in his trouser pocket, he jangled his keys and said to me, "Jack, old man, one word of advice. Start packing my grandson's things."

"This isn't over yet, Rob," I shot back.

Peg took her husband's hand in hers. "Let's go, honey."

I stayed behind until they left. Kevin waited for me near the stairway. My eyes followed the Fitzpatrick's until the elevator doors closed behind them. "Kevin," I called out. After I caught up with him I asked, "What just happened in there? They're blowing smoke up their ass. Lies! All lies!"

"Jack, you and I know that they cannot prove any of it. All three of them know that they haven't a case against you. Jonas accomplished what he set out to do today. He had you by the nuts and you fell for it. I could kick you right in your ass for what you pulled in there, but Judge Harcourt had the pleasure instead."

I felt bad enough as it was; Kevin's reprimand stung. I stopped at the landing of the stairway; Kevin continued on his way down.

"Kevin . . ." I shouted, his name echoed in the stairwell.

He turned toward me and then leaned against the railing. He raised one eyebrow and asked in a parental tone, "What is it, Jack?"

"They'll investigate Tim."

"Let them. That was eight years ago. Besides, when Tim confided in you about his past, you broke off the relationship. Jonas is bluffing."

"He convinced me."

"That's his job." We walked down the steps together. Kevin continued, "They're hiding something. There's more to Jonas than a little theater."

"And we don't have a copy of their script," I added.

"Jack, relax, go home, be with your grandson, but before you do I suggest you return those dapper slacks to their rightful owner."

Defending myself in a public forum had forced me to summon up all my resolve. I couldn't recall slugging another kid or being slugged back in grade school. Wimp, the kids called me; I wasn't worth beating up. Reacting to Jonas' slander may not have been appropriate, but I felt better for it. The last two hours stuck in my craw the rest of the day. And when I emerged from the courthouse I found another reason to be pissed off-there was a parking ticket stuck to my windshield.

I dialed the house on my cell phone from the car. The machine answered; forty-five seconds passed before the beep signaled, speak. I made a mental note to shorten the drawn-out message. I asked Maria to pick Jamey up after school and to call me back on my cell phone; I needed to go for a run. I shoved the parking ticket in the glove compartment then slammed it shut.

Noon traffic near the courthouse had slowed to a crawl. I scarped down a Power Bar and drove back to Laguna Beach.

The cramped rear bucket seats of the PT Cruiser doubled as a dressing room, a private spot for me to change into my running gear. Tinted windows blocked the inside view from any curious onlookers. My knees indented the leather back of the front passenger seat as I attempted to undress. The new micro fiber running shorts and tank slid onto my body like silky loungewear, but, the hair on my chest poked through the shirt like a pincushion. The manufacturer claimed that the new fabric was state-of-the-art, guaranteed to draw sweat away from the skin, allowing evaporation, thus helping to maintain a consistent body temperature. They also claimed that the fabric is weightless on the skin, breathes and prevents wind chill. My personal opinion, the stuff works. Not working as well was the back seat of my Cruiser; the manufacturer of the car had skimped on legroom in the back seats. I had to crunch into a ball in order to change into my running gear. A lack of flexibility which came with age had cramped my hips. I scooted my butt forward, peeled my running shorts over my quads and jumped out of the car to relieve the pain. The cold, damp pavement shot through my bare feet, warning me to grab my socks, Nikes and warm up before my run.

I strapped my cell phone to my waist and secured my keys in a pouch, too close to the crotch for a runner's comfort. Five hundred miles of pounding the pavement and trudging the coastline had worn out my favorite pair of running digs. I prepared to give them one last run before tossing them away. I dug the soles of my tattered shoes into the sand, parked my left heel on the Boardwalk and stretched my hamstrings to tame the Charlie Horse in my leg.

Earlier that morning, Laguna Beach Parks and Recreation had groomed the sand along Main Beach, a quiet, protected cove in the middle of town. Perfect rows and valleys had been plowed horizontally; all the cigarette butts and gum wrappers were gone. The beach awaited spring's renewal of tan bodies, bikinis and Speedos. Whenever the Santa Ana winds blew, Santa Catalina Island could be seen through binoculars, a view for those not interested in the carpet of beautiful bodies.

I massaged sport cream into my calves to expedite the warming up process. With each kick of my heel grains of sand stuck to my skin as I jogged past the abandoned lifeguard station. Perched on wooden stilts, it towered above the beach like a sentinel warding off the distant fog bank. White and gray seagulls challenged the pippins that were perched on the tower's weathered rooftop. Puffing out their chests, the gulls extended their wings to intimidate the smaller birds. The pippins screeched and cawed at the gulls; they finally yielded to their persistence and flew away.

I bid the courageous pippins goodbye, checked to make sure that my cell phone was on, and ran south along the beach toward Monarch Bay.

Five hundred yards beyond Aliso Pier, unmarked property lines of private beaches and rocky coastline brought me to a halt. I moved over to the bike lane of Pacific Coast Highway which gave me a straight shot south of Laguna, a two-mile detour to Annie's house.

After a couple of miles, runners experience a psychological high, a self induced dreamlike rhythm. Hamstring pain, carbo depletion, and pre-exhaustion is overcome by the freedom of pounding the pavement. Running was my release, my escape, but it failed me that day. The dreamlike high played like a bad movie in my head, the actors rewrote the script to suit their parts. Directing the nightmare, Annie sat motionless behind the judge's desk. Crimson tears rolled down her cheeks as she scolded me for running late that morning. Her bullet shattered face was recognizable only to me. The bailiff was wearing shorts and a badge. Rob and Peg warned me not to bother with Jamey; they'd pick him up after school. Annie ordered them to remain seated; she would decide who picked up her son. Rob cursed her to go to hell. When I lunged for the son-of-a-bitch I tripped on the curb at the entrance to Monarch Bay.

Behind me, Tim Higgins shouted, "Jack, wait up. I've been chasing you for a mile. You're sprinting like a jack rabbit."

Winded, I bent forward and clasped my knees. My lungs ached, my breathing labored, and my back muscles cramped with each contraction. Smoking had caught up with my aerobic endurance. My forearms slid against my shorts. Soaked with sweat the micro fabric clung to my legs like peeled onionskin. "Tim," I said, still bent forward, "where did you come from?"

"You didn't hear me calling you?"

"Sorry, man, my head's been somewhere else."

Demanding that we move out of her way, an impatient teenager leaned on the horn of her BMW. In order to let her pass, we moved beyond the bike lane then onto the sidewalk of Crown Valley Parkway, avenue of the nouveau rich and gateway to Laguna's urban sprawl. Once she was gone, Tim and I continued our visit.

Tim had a runner's build, lean, graceful legs like a thoroughbred, his chest, aerobically thin and cut. Dismissing the current athletic trend, he refused to shave his legs, arms, and chest. Quoting him, "They all look like a bunch of salamanders running down the road." At 5'11" he weighed one-hundred-fifty pounds soaking wet. His running shorts accentuated his tight, boyish butt and twenty-nine inch waist. By all accounts he was pretty cute, looked thirty-five not fifty-five. He wore his personal time warp without inhibition; the wet tresses of his blond sixties surfer style hair clung to his tan, youthful face with its three day stubble. Behind his brown eyes there was an unspoken caution. We had remained friends despite his past and my once naïve fear that ended our sweet, short-lived romance.

"For an old man you can still kick ass," Tim teased me.

"Look who's calling the kettle black, Gramps."

"Gramps? That's your job. I was gonna call you tonight. I'm throwing a surprise 50th birthday party for Frank, April first."

"April Fool's Day?"

"Say yes. Frank will love it. You know all the guys on the guest list. No presents, BYOB."

"Add my name to the list. You'll need to call and remind me; I don't know if I'm pitchin' or catchin' these days. I'm involved in a family dispute right now."

"Is that why you were at the law office?"

"I'm not supposed to discuss it."

"Fair enough."

"I was surprised to see you there, though," I said.

"My sister, what a bitch. She's contesting the disbursement of our father's trust. Lives in Nebraska; Queen of the Bible Belt. Wears her Baptist preacher husband around her neck like a crucifix."

"She sounds charming," I said with reservation.

"To her husband I suppose." Tim continued to run in place. I pulled my ankle toward my butt to stretch my quads.

"Business must be good; Kevin's not cheap," I said and then stretched my other leg.

"His fees are definitely over the top; but one of my clients recommended him; swears by him."

"William swore by him too," I said bent forward while clasping my ankles with both hands in order to stretch my hamstrings.

"Who's William?"

"An old friend," I said, brushing it off.

Maybe I was jealous; maybe I missed the six months that Tim and I had shared together; or maybe I was just lonely. I waved my arm above my head to say goodbye to Tim and jogged toward the entrance gate to the private community. The guard flagged me through, "Nice to see you Mr. Turner. New family bought the house, two kids, nice folks."

I sat on the curb opposite Annie's house. The new owners had planted pansies, winter's annuals, along the walkway. Crisp white drapes replaced the plantation shutters upstairs. Annie's bedroom faced the driveway. Turned on its side, a kid's Big Wheel blocked the sidewalk. Steam from the kitchen vent billowed above the rooftop, spilling the familiar aroma of beef stew throughout the neighborhood. The house had come back to life.

The silhouette of a woman peered through the drapes. Our eyes met and then she disappeared.

"Damn you, Annie!"

Chapter Ten

S omewhere between Laguna Beach and Crown Valley Parkway, a four mile stretch along Pacific Coast Highway, I had accidentally turned off my cell phone. Maria did leave a voice mail, "Mr. Jack, I'll pick Jamey up from school. Please bring home a gallon of skim milk and a pound of espresso beans. Dinner's at 6:00. William called, wanted to know how today went. Me too. Ciao."

Risking a one thousand dollar fine, I tossed my last pack of smokes from the car window, certain that a reformed smoker would crush them beneath his tires. It made Maria happy when, in recent months, I had made efforts to stop smoking. She stopped ragging on me about stinking up the house. Lysol consumption had fallen to one can every two months instead of one can a week. I stashed cases of sugarless chewing gum in the pantry, my home office, my bedroom and the glove compartment in my car. Once again, I decided to give up cigarettes.

Late that evening, I fidgeted at my desk, craving one. I chewed gum incessantly until my tongue burned from spearmint overload. Spearmint and Cabernet did not mix well, so I spit the gum out. Pages in my books had yellowed from nicotine; the stale musk of cigarette smoke lingered in my office.

With my life on trial, work had become a nuisance, neglected, my stories trite and contrived. Nicotine withdrawal fueled my pen while fleeting hallucinations colored my syndicated weekly column. My daily schedule remained on track as well, mundane and foretold. Tucked in for the night, Maria and Jamey snoozed by 10:00 p.m. I changed my routine to confuse the neighbors. Before midnight, I started turning off the lights, beginning in the kitchen. The house was dark except for my office. Once that was done I called William.

"Hey, handsome," I said, knowing that I woke him up.

"Jack, it's one o'clock in the morning. I hope this is earth shaking."

"No, Maria said you called. This is the first time I've sat down today other than parking my derrière in that damned courtroom this morning."

William's yawn breathed through the receiver. "How did it go?" he asked.

"Not well. I've been accused of soliciting a male prostitute, whoring at a gay bar, and performing lewd explicit sex in front of my grandson."

"Fitzpatrick is really scraping the bottom," William yawned into the phone again.

"The judge has ordered an investigation of the allegations and a psychological evaluation of Jamey."

"Jack, a psychological evaluation is a fairly ordinary procedure. For the psychologically unsophisticated it only sounds difficult."

"What do you mean, unsophisticated?" I asked, taking his lawyer babble personally.

"Oh, get over yourself, Jack," he jabbed playfully. After a moment of dead silence he reassured me, "Hang in there, you'll win this."

"Maybe, if I survive the repercussions of my own temper. I lost my cool in court this morning. I thought you lawyers objected at the drop of a hat. Not Kevin. He allowed their fabricated allegations to continue. You know me, my mouth overloaded my ass, I called Fitzpatrick's attorney a son-of-a-bitch. The judge threatened to hold me in contempt."

"Oh, Jack," he said with a sigh, "what am I gonna do with you?"

"Get a load of this. Fitzpatrick's attorney urged the court to grant temporary guardianship of Jamey to Rob and Peg. The judge denied their motion pending the investigation and evaluation."

"Excellent. Sounds like you and Kevin moved your case forward today."

"I'm not so sure, it's too soon to predict the judge's call. By the way, I gave up the smokes today."

"It's about time. Maybe I can have you around awhile longer."

"The desire to light up is killing me. Chewing gum helps the cravings though."

"At least the gum won't kill you off. Speaking of cravings, my mother is flying out next week. I haven't seen her in over a year. She'll spend a couple of months with me organizing my life and re-arranging my kitchen. I'll take her to New York. "Chicago" is still running on Broadway. Saw the movie. Have you seen it yet?"

"I haven't."

"Mr. Razzle Dazzle. He was fabulous."

"Maybe you'll run into Margo."

"Have you heard from her?" he asked.

"Not since the funeral. Kevin suggested I make amends with her. That is not going happen," I said with a vengeful tone.

"If I run into her, I'll be sure to send her your love," he added; his sarcastic timing on cue.

"You jackass," I came back at him with playful intent.

"Love you too."

"How's Joey?"

"Gone, I don't know what was I thinking? He's young enough to be my son. I suggested to him, no, let me retract; I insisted that he get a job. A houseboy I don't need. He moved back home with his parents who live in Florida. How's Kevin?" he asked subtly changing the subject.

"He's got the world by the ass. I suspect he's a bit of a playboy. Wants me to go out with him."

"He does?" William's jealous undertone let me know that he still cared for Kevin.

"Kevin's not my type, William."

"Hmm, I'll have to call him tomorrow. I'll tell him to back off."

"Don't. Don't bust his ego. I need his full co-operation and attention during the hearings. I'll continue making excuses until the hearings are over."

"Sounds like you've got Kevin's number."

"I don't know about that, but I do trust him."

"He is a top-notch lawyer, Jack."

"Say hi to your mom. Go back to bed, William. That's where I'm headed."

*   *   *

Customarily, March meant springtime, longer days, Easter break, surfing and impossible-to-get restaurant reservations. For the entire month I changed hats, taking on the roles of nursemaid and housekeeper. Jamey had managed to come down with the mumps. The glands on both sides of his neck swelled making him look like a chipmunk foraging nuts for winter; unfortunately, the disease can play havoc in adult males. But to my benefit, I had the mumps when I was seven so I was immune to its adult consequence. Jamey and I hung together, housebound, baching it while Maria and Henry vacationed in Palm Springs among date palms, day spas and golf courses.

Jamey's teacher sent home lessons and homework so he wouldn't fall behind. Creating excuses, he procrastinated, leaving the work to another day, a behavior too much like my own. I threatened him: no homework, no TV, so he finished his lessons.

During Jamey's illness the court had scheduled the psychological evaluation, but Judge Harcourt agreed to postpone the appointment until Jamey recovered. By the end of the month Jamey had bounced back. Kevin re-scheduled the evaluation for the last Friday in March.

The morning of Jamey's appointment with Dr. Aldrich proceeded as any other morning around my house, except that Willow was not on the front porch napping. Transformer cartoons battled across the television screen. Eating cinnamon-raisin oatmeal and sourdough toast smothered in strawberry preserves, Jamey sat at the kitchen table, Indian style. Maria soaked the sticky oatmeal pan in the sink while I sat on the couch, put my socks and shoes on and eavesdropped on their conversation.

"Maria, what's a psyhco-cologist?" Jamey asked.

"A psychologist? That's someone who listens to our special thoughts."

"That's what God does," Jamey replied with a mouth full of toast and preserves. "Is a psycho-cologist like God?" Jamey asked.

"Not quite, Jamey. We can see a psychologist; we can only talk to God."

"Grampa said I'm gonna see a psyc . . . cologist today. She's gonna ask me questions. God doesn't ask questions."

"Did your Grampa tell you about the psychologist?"

"Yes. Grampa told me she's a lady doctor. She's gonna ask me questions about Grampa and my mom. Grampa told me just to say," he pointed to his chest, "what's in here."

I walked into the kitchen while buckling my belt and pretended that I hadn't heard a word. "Okay, guys, are we about ready to go?"

Smearing strawberry preserves on his shirtsleeve, Jamey wiped his mouth without thinking. "I guess not, buster, not until you change your shirt," I said, and then tossed him a paper towel.

Jamey wiped the preserves off his shirt with the towel, which only made matters worse, then tossed it onto the table. He huffed and rolled his eyes back and said to me, "There, it's all gone now."

I began to lose my patience with him. "Jamey, go to your bedroom and change your shirt, now," I said, "we're gonna be late." He didn't budge; instead, he sunk into the chair and rolled his shirt sleeve up to cover the stain.

Maria intervened, "Jamey, take your shirt off and give it to me. There's a clean shirt in the top drawer of your dresser. Do what your Grampa says."

Jamey peeled off his shirt, handed it to Maria, and in a huff went to his bedroom without speaking a word to me.

"Maria, what the hell was that all about?" I asked.

"Mr. Jack, it's been a long time since you were a father to a young child. Think back to when Annie was his age."

"I'm not certain I can remember that far back. Just ten minutes ago he was telling you about meeting the psychologist and being fine with it. And then the attitude change."

"He's lost his mother. Jamey is going to act out. Let him."

"Maria, all of us feel the loss of Annie."

"Yes, we do. But you need to show Jamey how much you love him. Reassure him, that's what he needs from you right now."

The thought of relinquishing guardianship of my grandson to Rob and Peg scared me, not because they wouldn't love and care for him as their own child, but because Jamey was the only family I had left.

I took it upon myself to do what I thought was right and challenged Kevin's persistence to request another psychologist so I contacted Dr. Aldrich myself. Judge Harcourt's referral of Dr. Aldrich stood fast with me.

The sixties had spawned the era of "nurturing your inner being", "finding yourself", EST, Eschalon, Pearle, and Dr. Michael Aldrich. Dr. Aldrich earned her Bachelor of Science degree in 1969 from Sonoma State University, a California State campus, a sanctuary in the middle of a small cow town north of San Francisco. The Psychology Department, an experimental, non-Freudian, touchy-feely mecca for Rogerian groupies enticed students searching for nirvana. She bypassed her master's and launched into UCLA's Ph.D. program in Child Psychology an honor bestowed to an exceptional few. Dr. Aldrich made a name for herself during the McMartin preschool molestation trial back in the mid eighties. She shook up the news media with her uncensored organic psychobabble and professional witness testimony. I allowed Kevin full range decisions regarding the hearing with one exception, Judge Harcourt's referral of Dr. Aldrich. Kevin's pretentious, over-the-top self-esteem viewed relaxed, earthy lifestyles as unproductive, tax evading and wasteful. I challenged his self-opinionated prejudice. Kevin challenged my challenge. In retaliation he e-mailed me a *Los Angeles Times* clipping of Dr. Aldrich from 1984. He captioned, "Re-consider."

I downloaded her organic, ethereal Stevie Nick's impersonation which transcended time on-line. Lyrics from Fleetwood Mac hummed in my memory as her image filled my computer screen. Sheer, black gauze skirted her willowy figure, her shoulders shrouded beneath a lace shawl, ebony and delicate. Capped underneath a floppy, knit chapeau, her fine, straight blonde hair traveled to her waist. Captioned beneath the news clipping were quotes from Dr. Aldrich: "*After exhaustive analysis of all the records and individual assessments of all parties involved, the clinical evidence that would support these allegations of abuse left me unconvinced. However, only time can truly determine how these events will impact the lives of these children.*" Her statement following the word, *however*, concerned Kevin.

Dr. Aldrich was a seasoned professional and two years older than I was. I felt certain that Jamey would feel comfortable with her because he lived amongst a bunch of gray haired old fogies. Jamey related to my generation. I did not want some young, ambitious, newly licensed upstart Marriage Family Therapist to question my grandson's emotional stability and when we stepped into Dr. Aldrich's office I knew that I had made the right decision.

In the Cruiser, Jamey and I followed Kevin and Maria to Dr. Aldrich's office. Jamey sang out-of-tune to some heavy metal headache while I tried to keep up with Kevin's heavy foot. My world had been shaken before I met Dr. Aldrich, but that Friday morning she welcomed us into her world.

Because my life had been ensconced in the establishment for twenty some odd years, die-hard hippies who had sold out oftentimes inspired my sense of reminiscence. They traded in their VW busses for BMW's, sported trendy haircuts and sought style makeovers seen in *Vogue*. Dr. Aldrich had golden blond streaks that minimized the natural silver in her bobbed hair. She was wearing a creamy, pastel blouse tucked casually into gray gabardine slacks and understated two-inch heel pumps. Since she confined her practice to treating children, her reception room was a playground of primary colors, enormous beanbag chairs, and Lego Land tables.

Sipping a cup of coffee, Dr. Aldrich stood at the reception desk. The moment we entered her office she greeted us, "Good morning, I'm Michael Aldrich." She reached out to shake Jamey's hand. "You must be Jamey."

He shyly responded, "Michael is a boy's name."

"Sometimes, Jamey, boys and girls have the same name, like Geri and Bobbie, even my name, Michael, that's what my daddy named me."

Her inviting smile met with Jamey's approval. I trusted his intuitive judgment. Dr. Aldrich set her coffee cup on the reception desk and said to me, "Mr. Turner, Mr. and Mrs. Fitzpatrick will not be attending this morning. They have been called out of town. They extend their apologies, but assured me that they will attend the second session next Friday." She then extended her hand to Jamey and said to him, "Let's you and I get acquainted."

Her years of experience and ability to connect with children were reflected in her warm smile; the fine lines around her hazel eyes had deepened with wisdom. Jamey turned to me; his eyes searched mine for reassurance. "Are you staying, Grampa?"

"I'll be right here, Jamey."

A two-way window allowed Maria, Kevin and I to view the interview from the hallway. Dr. Aldrich invited Jamey to sit at a small knotty pine table in the center of the room and observed his curiosity as he visually explored every inch of his surroundings. Her slender figure had crunched effortlessly into one of the miniature chairs opposite Jamey. Not one exterior window interrupted the freshly painted walls, the color like a new leather car chamois. Grounding the play land, wall-to-wall carpet in faded hues of forest green, periwinkle blue and banana yellow accented the knotty pine table, the therapist couch for children. I hung on to their every word as they proceeded.

"Jamey, have you been told about why you have come to talk to me today?" Dr. Aldrich began.

"You're gonna ask me questions about my Grampa Jack," he replied. Jamey tapped his chest above his heart as he had shown Maria earlier that morning. "Grampa told me say what's in here." Jamey scanned the room. I watched him struggling to remain seated but his manners won out. "This is like at school," he said. "Are we gonna do tests? I'm learning to print in school. I'll show you."

A brand new box of crayons lay next to a stack of primary grades school paper, gray and triple lined for printing lessons. Jamey printed his name for Dr. Aldrich and composed a sentence. They sat far enough from the window to prevent me from seeing Jamey's composition.

"You print very well, Jamey." Jamey's shit-eatin' grin brought a smile to my lips. "Does your Grampa help you with your schoolwork?" Dr. Aldrich asked.

"Oh, yeah. My Grampa's a writer. I'm gonna be a writer."

"What kind of things do you like to write about?"

"Stuff. Sometimes sad stuff. But mostly fun stuff." Anxious to share with her, he boasted, "This is my most excellent story. It's really sad. I wrote about Willow and Grampa."

"Would you like to tell me about your story?"

Contemplating how to begin, Jamey rolled his eyes upward. "Okay," he agreed. "Willow died. Willow was a Golden Retriever. She was twelve years old. Grampa said that Willow was eighty-four in people years. That's really old. Willow lived with Mr. Jarret. Mr. Jarret lives next door. He's an old coot. My Grampa said so."

Waiting for Dr. Aldrich's response, I cringed before the two-way mirror. She cupped her hand to her mouth to conceal her amusement from Jamey's response.

"Grampa and me took Willow home. Mr. Jarret didn't cry. Sometimes my Grampa cries. I told him it's okay to cry. Mr. Jarret smells bad. He drinks a lot of beer. He was mean to my Grampa. Mr. Jarret hurt Maria's feelings. I heard Maria tell Grampa, "Consider the source". My Grampa tucks me in at night when I go to bed. He told me a story that night when Willow died. My mom and dad are in heaven. Willow went to visit them. I say my prayers by myself. I like to do that. I said a prayer for Willow. I asked Willow to tell Mom I was doing good in school. The End."

Whenever Jamey told a story his pause for a breath occurred only when he finished.

"Thank you, Jamey, I enjoyed your story."

"You did? I know lots of stuff. I can write you a story if you want me to. It will take me more than one day because I have homework for school. My Grampa can mail it to you. He has lots of stamps."

"I would like that, Jamey, but first tell me about why you think your Grampa felt bad."

"Because Mr. Jarret doesn't like my Grampa. He calls my Grampa names. I hear Mr. Jarret when I play in the backyard. He called my Grampa gay. Mrs. Jarret told him to shut-up, the neighbor's will hear. One time, I was riding my bike and I told Mr. Jarret to stop calling my Grampa names. He was drunk and yelled at me to go home. My Mom told me not to call people names because it hurts their feelings."

"I think it is important not to hurt people's feelings too, Jamey. Tell me what you think the word gay means."

"Gay means you don't have a wife. My Mom told me Grampa is gay. My Grampa is my Mom's dad. I told him it's okay not to have a wife because we have Maria. I don't like it when my Grampa is sad. He's my very best friend in the whole world."

When I listened to Jamey's innocent rambling I hoped that Annie was listening.

Jamey continued to share, "Johnny is my other best friend. He lives next door to my old house. I miss my mom. She took pills. Grampa said she was sad when my Dad died. Guess what?"

"I don't know, tell me," she said with her undivided attention.

"My Grampa is a psyco-cologist."

"He is?"

"Yeah. I tell Grampa my special thoughts. One time I didn't tell him Grampa Rob said mean things."

"What did Grampa Rob say?"

"Sometimes I have sleepovers at my other Grampa and Gramma's house. Once I heard Grampa Rob being mad. He yelled at Gramma. He called my Grampa Jack a faggot. I don't know what that means. Is it bad?"

"Jamey, I am going to answer your question. But first I want you to say what you think it means."

"I think it's bad. Kids at school say it when they make fun of weird kids."

"I think it's bad to make other kids feel bad too, Jamey. I'm going to answer your question about the word faggot. When men and women grow up they sometimes fall in love. Then, like your mom and dad they get married and have kids, which is how you came to be. Sometimes, however, men fall in love with men or women fall in love with women. Even though it's the love that is important, and love is good, some people think that men should only fall in love with women and women should only fall in love with men. They feel that love between two men is bad, and they call a man who loves men instead of women a faggot."

"I think it's mean. I'll ask my Grampa. Sometimes when he talks to Uncle William on the phone he tells him he loves him. My Grampa is not a faggot and Uncle William is not a faggot."

"How do you feel about talking to your Grampa about this?"

"Good. We talk about everything."

Dr. Aldrich jotted down notes while listening to Jamey's responses.

"Jamey, I want to ask you about the men who come to visit your Grampa."

"Okay," he replied as he underlined the sentence he had written.

"Do these men have sleepovers at your Grampa's house?"

"That's silly," Jamey chuckled. "Grampa's don't have sleepovers, only kids do that. Sometimes Uncle William comes to visit. He sleeps at a hotel. Uncle William isn't my real uncle. He's Grampa's best friend just like my best friend, Johnny at school. I'm Grampa's best friend too."

"Jamey, would you like to talk about your mom today?"

Jamey's body language moved quickly from gregarious and open to contemplative and inward.

Dr. Aldrich asked, "Is talking about your mom sad for you?"

"Yes. I miss my Mom. My Mom isn't ever coming back. I know I'll never have another Mom. Maria isn't my real mom. She does a good job." Jamey stared at the tabletop; he rolled a crayon beneath his forefinger, quiet, thinking. "I know my Grampa won't ever marry a wife." He sat straight up in the chair and glanced toward the door. He folded his hands together, placed them on the table and looked up at Dr. Aldrich. "Can I go now?"

"Yes, this is a good time for us to stop. Before you and I say goodbye can you tell me how you feel about our talk we had today?"

"It was good. I like your hair. It looks like my Mom's hair. Can I go now?"

Kevin, Maria and I exited the hallway before Dr. Aldrich opened the door. I plopped down on a red beanbag chair. Jamey ran into the reception room, launched a half turn in midair and flopped in the purple beanbag chair next to mine.

"Jamey, go with Maria." I said. "I'll be right there."

To be in the presence of Dr. Aldrich felt like being under the calming influence of a mild sedative. She's just what one would hope for in a child psychologist.

Dr. Aldrich wrapped her arms around her notebook and clutched it to her chest as she and I walked back to the therapy room together. "Mr. Turner, Jamey is intelligent, adaptable and shows a high level of comfort with a stranger. It's unusual for a child to be so open but it indicates security rather than indiscriminate attachments and poor boundaries."

Digesting her comments, I agreed, "He can be a charmer."

She offered me her business card. "When Jamey is finished writing his story, I would love it if you could mail it to me."

I tucked her card in my wallet. "Happy to," I said.

"I've scheduled Jamey's second meeting with me for next Friday at 10:00 a.m. I encourage you to be here."

"Yes, M'am. Jamey's my sidekick."

"Mr. and Mrs. Fitzpatrick assured me that they will also attend. I look forward to meeting them. Have a good weekend, Mr. Turner."

"You too, Dr. Aldrich."

Kevin walked with me to the car. "Jack," he said, "I was wrong about Dr. Aldrich."

I just grinned back at him and kept my opinions to myself. Kevin waved good bye to Maria and Jamey then drove away in one of two BMW's parked on the lot.

As soon as we entered the house, Jamey bypassed his bicycle and headed straight for my desk to write his story for Dr. Aldrich. Maria brewed two espressos and brought Jamey a glass of orange juice. I balanced my big feet on one of the kitchen chairs; Maria sipped her coffee in silence. "Maria," I said, interrupting her reverie, "just fix dinner for you and Jamey tonight. I'm going out for a couple of hours. I'll grab a bite later. I need to filter through this day. I'll be back by 8:00."

*   *   *

On Friday nights the Little Shrimp's house special topped the menu. One-half pound of choice ground sirloin, hand patted, grilled to order, served with a side of Cajun spiced potato wedges and red cabbage coleslaw with sweet Maui onion dressing. Sitting in the half empty dining room were five couples, men I didn't know. Two of the couples had finished eating; the others were waiting to order. A breezeway passed the bar leading to a compact, stainless steel kitchen. The smell of grilled onions and sirloin filled the quiet dining room. I struck up a conversation with two guys sitting at the bar. They were obviously young and in their twenties. One of the fellas told me that he was visiting from Texas, the other guy said he was from Los Angeles; they both ordered a Bud Light. I pulled up a barstool next to the guy from Texas. He and Mr. LA were not interested in talking with me; they were into one another, not some gray haired old fart. By nine the restaurant and bar would be packed with locals overflowing the dining room and patio, all of them shouting to be heard over the loud music. At six, however, the light crowd, the gentle music, and a glass of wine eased some of the tension from my neck and mind. Smoking was prohibited in the dining room, so I carried a pack of gum in my pocket.

Gregory, the owner of the Little Shrimp, tapped my shoulder. "Jack, I saved your usual table." With a menu under his arm, a Rolex on his wrist, and a diamond stud on his left ear, he seated me at my favorite spot in the restaurant, a corner bay window with a view of the Pacific Ocean. Once the sun set the ocean became a black abyss. Spotlights illuminated lifeguard buoys that bobbed with the surf. "What'll it be tonight, Jack?" Gregory asked.

"The house special," I said.

"Well done?"

"Extra well done."

"Comin' right up."

"Easy on the Cajun spice, okay?"

"Sure thing, Jack."

Fixated on the lit buoys, I said, "Gregory, check this out. Pelicans perched on the buoys. I didn't think they flew this far north."

"They're vacationing from San Diego. Sea World probably doesn't feed them well enough." He finished jotting down my order. "Give the guys some time, extra well takes a bit longer. Another glass of wine?"

"Nah. But you can bring me a Coke. Thanks, Gregory."

I folded the gum wrapper until its minuteness rested on the tip of my finger. I slipped it into my pocket rather than leave it on the table and let my mind wander beyond the buoys.

A familiar voice broke my trance. "Is this seat taken?"

"Tim! What a nice surprise. I was just staring off into Never Neverland." I pulled the empty chair next to mine away from the table and invited him, "Please, join me."

"Never Neverland sounds pretty good right about now. That and a drink," he said.

"What'll you have? My treat."

"A margarita, no salt. Don't get up, Jack. I'll get it."

Tim looked like something the cat had dragged in, his jeans muddy and his sneakers untied. His blonde hair hadn't been washed for a few days. He was focused on his margarita. He spilled a third of his drink before he made it back to the table.

"Tim, what's going on with you? You look like hell."

"I moto-crossed with some guys today near Camp Pendleton. The mud was up to my ankles." He pulled his sweatshirt away from his skin and checked himself from chest to toe. "More like mud up to my eyebrows. I'm a mess."

"It's not your best look, Tim. Have you eaten?"

"I'm not hungry. Actually, I stopped by to see Gregory. I need to tell him to cancel catering Frank's party."

"Why? Are you hiring another caterer?"

"I wish it was that simple. Two days ago this investigator came to the house; introduced himself to Frank and me. Told me that he worked for the State of California, showed me his credentials, you know all his legal bullshit. He did explain that his questions would be regarding Mr. Jack Turner. Asked me if I knew him. Of course I know him, I said, I've known him for years. So I asked him, what's this about? Frank was sitting right next to me on the couch. The investigator asked me if I had ever accepted money for sexual favors. I knew right then where he was going with this. The court had sent an investigator to question my relationship I had with you. What a prick he was."

"What did you tell him?"

"I told him the truth. Frank freaked out. He stormed out of the house. He said to me, "Later, Tim." I haven't seen him for two days. I'm going nuts."

"Maybe he just needed some time to think this through," I tried to reassure him.

"I'm crazy about Frank. I never told him about Palm Springs. It was fucking twenty-five years ago. After I confided in you, you dumped me, now Frank. Fuck." He waved his hands and knocked his margarita glass onto its side; the remnants spilled on the tablecloth.

"Tim, calm down," I said and rolled up the corners of the tablecloth before his spilled drink ran onto the floor. "Frank is probably digesting this whole thing. I'll bet he's home right now waiting for you. I watch Frank when he's with you. He's all over you; you rock his world, man." A busboy removed the table linen and interrupted my attempt to reassure Tim. I shut up until the busboy was out of earshot. "Frank is nuts about you, Tim. I'm sure he just needs some time."

While I realized he was upset, I still had to ask him for a big favor and begged him, "Tim, I know that I'm out of line here, but would you consider testifying in court about our past relationship? I need you to testify in court that I didn't know about your past before we broke up."

"Jack, I'm trying to save my relationship with Frank. He would slam the door on me. I don't know, man. I have to think about it."

My cell phone rang. I hoped it wasn't Maria. "Hello, this is Jack," I said.

An unfamiliar voice answered, "No shit. What are you doing at the Shrimp, what are you thinking?"

"I'm having dinner. Who is this?" I demanded.

"It's Kevin, your attorney, remember? Meet me in my office in an hour."

"Kevin, I'm eating dinner," I said, annoyed with his intrusion. "And how did you know where to find me?"

"I drove past the bar on my way home from dinner and saw your car parked out front. Eat fast; we have a letter from Margo."

Chapter Eleven

It was Wednesday, April 24th, court day and Margo had remained in New York.

Tim had agreed to appear in court even though he was still distraught about Frank who hadn't turned up since the day he stormed out of the house. That morning Tim left a message with Maria; he cancelled Frank's surprise birthday party.

Waiting for Kevin and me, Tim paced the courthouse steps. He had arrived a half an hour before us. I envied his habitual punctuality; Annie had always hoped that I would develop that same trait. The ill-fitting, baggy suit he wore had belonged to his father. Tim's failed attempt to tie his silk tie left a gap between his Adam's apple and shirt collar.

Kevin had insisted that I buy a new suit. But even with me dressed in my version of respectable, there was no mistaking who was the defendant and who was the attorney.

The courtroom was like a stage; in this play everyone was expected to stick to the script. The court reporter sat below the judge's bench, her stare fixed on my shoes. The bailiff stood at his post and checked his watch. A wooden gate separated the chamber from seats reserved for spectators. The bailiff approached Tim to ask him if he was a witness. He jotted down Tim's name and handed it to the court clerk just as Judge Harcourt came out of her chambers. The bailiff asked everyone to rise.

In the eight weeks, since the last hearing, her red hair had grown longer softening her stern expression. A little gray peeked through at her temples. Her manner was all business, hurried and preoccupied. She removed her reading glasses and addressed the court. "Good afternoon, everyone. Please be seated, we have a full agenda to get through, so let's get started. Counselors, I trust you have received copies of the investigator's report, the psychological evaluation from Dr. Aldrich regarding the minor child and an affidavit from Ms. Margo Evans?"

"Yes, Your Honor," Jonas and Kevin responded in unison.

"Before I address Ms. Evans' affidavit we will hear from Mr. Edwards, the court investigator. Mr. Edwards, please tell the court your findings regarding the allegations made about the defendant, Mr. Turner."

"Thank you, Your Honor. After interviewing the defendant's neighbors, parents of the minor's schoolmates, friends and the owner of the Little Shrimp, a gay bar and restaurant on Pacific Coast Highway in Laguna Beach, I found no support for the plaintiff's allegations."

Rob erupted from his chair and slammed his clenched fists on the tabletop. His elbows brushed the side of Jonas Simon's head and pushed his lawyer's designer glasses away from the narrow bridge of his sloped nose. Peg stopped her husband cold from lunging at the investigator. Rob spurned Mr. Edwards, affronting, "You incompetent fool!"

Peg reproached Rob before the court and demanded that he sit down. "You're making a fool of yourself," she admonished.

"Sit down, Mr. Fitzpatrick," Judge Harcourt instructed him. "I will remind you and this court that outbursts will not be tolerated in my courtroom. I will hold you in contempt if it happens again. Counselor, I encourage you to control your client. Proceed, Mr. Edwards."

"Thank you, Your Honor. He was looking down at some papers he was holding. "His current neighbors, Mr. and Mrs. Jarret were forthright in their opinions regarding Mr. Turner's gay lifestyle. They expressed emphatic disapproval of homosexuality. However, when I asked them if they were aware of any men frequenting Mr. Turner's home, they replied and I quote, "Neither men nor women frequent Jack's house. He's pretty boring, sits up late at night alone, his house always lit up like a candle and listens to some song bird blaring on his stereo and types away at his computer. He feeds the damn blue jays in his back yard, rollerblades with his grandson, and sits on his front porch at midnight smoking alone now that our dog Willow is dead." Mrs. Jarret informed me that her kitchen window looks directly into Mr.

Turner's office. Quoting Mrs. Jarret, "Jack never closes the blind." A few days later, I questioned Mr. Higgins and his partner Mr. Frank Brown regarding the allegations of prostitution."

Tim rose from his seat and addressed the judge, "May I speak, Your Honor?"

"And you are?" the judge asked him.

"Tim Higgins, Your Honor."

The bailiff handed Tim's notes to Judge Harcourt. She glanced over them and said, "I will allow your testimony after Mr. Edwards concludes. Please be seated, Mr. Higgins. Continue Mr. Edwards."

"Thank you, Your Honor. I questioned Mr. Higgins regarding his association with prostitution. I asked him if he is currently involved with known prostitutes or engages in prostitution himself. At that point during the investigation he refused to cooperate. Mr. Brown left the room and did not return. Mr. Higgins argued that his days of prostitution were history. He said, "I'm sick of it following me around like a bad penny. No more questions." He then requested that I leave, Your Honor."

"Thank you, Mr. Edwards. You may present your recommendations concluding Mr. Higgins testimony." Judge Harcourt nodded to the bailiff. "Mr. Higgins, please approach the bench." The bailiff escorted Tim to the witness stand. "Let me remind you, Mr. Higgins, that you are under oath."

Tim cinched his tie; but there was still a gap between his collar and his neck. "Yes, Your Honor," he said.

"Defendant's counsel has informed me that you have a statement for this court regarding Mr. Turner's relationship with you?"

"I do, Your Honor."

"Proceed."

"When I met Jack eight years ago I had not escorted clients for more than twenty years. I was in Reno on a vacation. Went down to the casino to play the slots and sat down at a machine next to Jack. I didn't know him at the time. We chatted about, you know, the weather, the crowd, the good-looking guys. I just assumed he was gay. He told me that he lived in Laguna Beach. I told him I lived in Dana Point. "We're neighbors," I said. We shared a couple drinks, exchanged phone numbers. I asked him if I could call him sometime, he said he'd like that. We dated for six months; I thought we were pretty serious about each other. One night Jack was at my place for dinner, I was nervous and anxious about telling him about my past. I really cared for Jack and needed to let him know the truth first hand. I don't blame him for leaving. Prostitution is a heavy chain to toss away. My point, your Honor, is Jack had no idea that I had been a prostitute. I am grateful, though, that we have remained friends over these last eight years."

Judge Harcourt folded her hands and considered Tim's testimony silently. She addressed Jonas, "Have you any question for the witness, counselor?"

"Thank you, Your Honor." Jonas remained seated. "Mr. Higgins, I don't have to remind you that you are under oath. Are you in fact continuing to escort clients, as you put it?"

Tim responded, "I don't understand your question."

"Let me ask in terms someone of your background can understand."

Kevin interjected, "Objection, Your Honor, badgering the witness, false assumption."

"Sustained."

"Mr. Higgins, allow me to be direct. Do you currently exchange sexual favors for money?"

Tim stared right through Kevin, their eyes locked with hesitation. Tim shook his head denying the inference from Jonas's question and then sought me out for reassurance. Tim was like a brother to me, he confided in me whenever he was troubled.

"No, I do not," he replied. I could see just how much this ordeal had taken out of him when he looked at me.

Kevin sighed in silence. Jonas closed his notebook and peered over his glasses at Tim. "I have no further questions, Your Honor."

"Thank you, counselor. Mr. Stevens?"

"I have no questions for Mr. Higgins, Your Honor."

"You may step down," Judge Harcourt instructed Tim.

Tim hoisted his slacks, loosened his tie and whispered to me as he passed, "Frank called."

"Oh, good," I said in a low voice.

"He's not coming back home," he said; disappointment misted his eyes.

"Tim . . . I'll call you tonight. Thank you for being here today," I said, clasping his hand in mine.

"Mr. Edwards, is there anything else from your investigation you wish to add?" Judge Harcourt asked.

"I've concluded, Your Honor, that the allegations of gross immorality against the defendant are unfounded. All statements given to me by those I have interviewed lead me to believe that Mr. Turner provides a safe and loving environment for his grandson to live in."

Mr. Edwards respectfully remained standing.

"Thank you, Mr. Edwards." The court investigator took a seat in the jury box and filed his notes in his briefcase.

Judge Harcourt pursed her lips and focused on Jonas. "Mr. Simon, how do you respond to these conclusions?" she asked.

"Your Honor, my clients disagree with Mr. Edwards' conclusions; however, their only concern is for the well being of their grandson. We propose to the defendant and his counsel to agree to meet in a conference so that we may reach a compromise in order to serve the best interest of the minor."

"Mr. Turner, Mr. Stevens, is this agreeable to you?"

Kevin and I conferred and quickly reached a decision. "Yes, Your Honor, we will listen to what they have to say," Kevin said.

"Progress," the judge said cheerfully. "We will recess for an hour. When we return, we will proceed as compromise may dictate. Before we recess let me inform all parties about the psychological evaluation of the minor. Dr. Aldrich is unable to appear in court this afternoon. She extends her apologies. She will schedule appointments with the defendant and plaintiff in my chambers if there are any questions regarding her conclusions and recommendations. Counselors, contact my clerk, Judy Ramsey, to schedule times that fit your calendars. We will resume at 4:00 p.m." Jonas and Kevin compared calendars. They committed us to a meeting the following Wednesday morning at 9:30.

All parties remained seated as Judge Harcourt left the courtroom. I was relieved to stretch my legs but craved a cigarette so bad I could taste it.

Once we convened in the hallway, Peg seemed flustered and embarrassed. Rob sat furthest from me. Pomposity, Rob's personal antidote against decency and honor, served him well. He slouched in his chair, unmoved and picked his teeth. Kevin and Jonas rearranged the chairs to form a circle.

Peg took in a deep breath and spoke first. "Jack, where do we go from here?"

I folded my arms to steady my hands and crossed my legs. "You tell me."

"To begin with, Rob and I wish to express our apologies for this unfortunate mess we're all in. Our concerns are out of fear for Jamey's future."

"Out of fear? Fear of what?" I demanded.

"We've met some of your friends; Rob even met with you at that bar. Yours is a lifestyle we don't understand. Even though our fears seem less threatening now, Rob and I still want what is best for Jamey."

"Now? What about an hour and a half ago? Why the sudden change of heart?"

"It's all about our grandson, Jack. Jamey adores you, but Rob and I feel that he needs a balance in his life. We see in Jamey's behavior how much he needs and relies on you but he also needs a grandmother to help guide him. There is no woman in your life, Jack."

"You haven't any consideration for Maria?"

"Maria is not Jamey's grandmother. She is not family."

"She may not be Jamey's grandmother, but Maria is my family. She helped raise Annie," I said, my face burned with anger.

"Assess the results, old man," Rob said, insinuating that Maria had somehow failed Annie.

"Fuck you, Rob!" I stepped away, buried my hands in my trouser pockets and choked my keys rather than Rob's bulbous neck.

Jonas butted in, "We're not getting anywhere with this bickering. Mr. Turner, what is it going to take to come to a compromise?"

"Drop this ridiculous charade," I said. "Christ, the three of us are Jamey's grandparents. He should be with all of us, but I insist that he live with me."

Rob budged neither from his seat or his stubborn commitment to take Jamey. "Well old man, we'll let the court decide."

The bailiff ushered us back into the courtroom. Judge Harcourt resumed her seat. Jonas straightened his tie, cleared his throat and then addressed the bench. "Your Honor, the defendants and plaintiffs are unable to reach a compromise at this time."

"I suspected as much," the judge sighed. "My first inclination is to pass judgment in favor of the defendant." Judge Harcourt turned her head slowly toward Rob; her suspended pause wrenched my gut. I shrunk my toes inside my wingtips; the soles of my shoes gripped the carpet. "However," she resumed, "Ms. Evans's allegation needs further testimony. Counselors, as you know a document cannot be witness as evidence without testimony. Ms. Evans is unable to be here today to testify. Supporting her reason for not appearing today is a letter from her physician. Because of surgery, Ms. Evans will not be able to travel for another five weeks. She has agreed to testify to the allegations set forth in her own letter. I'll read it to the court:

"I am saddened for Mr. Turner's and Jamey's loss. I too share their loss. Jamey's mother was my daughter. It is true that I played a less than maternal role in Annie's life. Jack raised my daughter. Twenty-seven years ago I found out that I was pregnant with Annie; I made the decision to have an abortion. At the time, Jack and I were roommates in college. He persuaded me to have the child, that he would raise her as his own. I agreed to give birth to my daughter and to christen her Elizabeth Anne Turner, not Evans. It is not my intention to hurt Mr. Turner; it is my obligation as the child's grandmother to do what is best for him. Mr. Turner is not the biological father of my daughter; nor is he

Jamey's biological grandfather. It is my recommendation to this court that guardianship be awarded to his biological grandparents, Mr. and Mrs. Robert Fitzpatrick."

Rob muttered to Jonas, "Now we're getting somewhere with this hearing."

Kevin cleared his throat, tilted his chin forward and straightened his tie. "Your Honor, I would like to address the allegations set forth in Ms. Evans's letter."

"Proceed, Counselor."

"It is unfortunate that Ms. Evans is unable to appear in court today. I am certain that I express the sentiments of this court that we wish Ms. Evans a speedy and healthy recovery. Until we all have the opportunity to hear and to cross-examine her testimony, my client is confident that Ms. Evans's allegations are false and are motivated out of anger and revenge. Mr. Turner has agreed to voluntarily submit to a DNA test."

For more than an hour I had listened and refrained from speaking my mind. Without thinking, I raised my hand like a first grader asking his teacher permission to speak.

"Mr. Turner?" Judge Harcourt said quietly.

"Thank you, Your Honor. I would like to add something here."

"I'll allow it."

"Margo, Ms. Evans, attended Annie's funeral this past January. She made no attempt to contact me before her arrival. Prior to that day I hadn't heard from her for over twenty-five years. She just showed up. Margo sat in her limousine parked near the cemetery entrance. Once she drove away I was convinced that the woman in the limo was Margo. She pulled up in front of my house later that afternoon. Jamey stood on the front porch near my side. Margo's face lit up when she realized Jamey was her grandson. I have battled with a demon in my head for years. I cannot forgive her to this day for abandoning Annie and me when our daughter was only five months old."

Jonas interrupted, "Your Honor, maybe Mr. Turner can get to the point."

"What are you getting at, Mr. Turner?" Judge Harcourt asked.

"The reason for Margo's letter, Your Honor."

"Continue. I'd like to hear the rest of this myself."

"I agreed to meet her for dinner before she flew back to New York. I was nervous about it, but seeing her again was bittersweet. She pleaded with me to allow her to acquaint herself with Jamey. I denied her that opportunity. I'm afraid that my emotions and memories clouded my judgment. I presume this is her reaction to my refusal."

"My, my, my. So many layers involved in this case. Mr. Turner, I appreciate your forthright admission of regret. The conclusions to this hearing remain to be judged from Ms. Evans's testimony and the results from your DNA test."

"Your Honor, may I have permission to speak with my client?"

"I'll allow it."

"Jack, the coroner's office will need your permission to exhume Annie's body, are you alright with that?"

"I suppose; I have no choice."

"Actually, you do. Jamey can be tested for DNA matching."

"Absolutely not. He's been through enough. I'll pay to have Annie's body exhumed."

Kevin turned to the judge and said, "Thank you, Your Honor. We will proceed with the DNA test."

"Very well. I have personally contacted Ms. Evans. She has agreed to testify in June. Judy, what have we on the calendar for mid June?"

"Wednesday, June 15th, 9:30 a.m., your Honor."

"Counselors, does that agree with your calendars?" Judge Harcourt asked.

Before Kevin and Jonas replied another bailiff entered the courtroom. He carried a memo and handed it to the court bailiff who then delivered it to Judge Harcourt.

She read it in silence. When she finished, she addressed the courtroom, "Everyone, before I read this note aloud, please consider today's hearing adjourned. However, I must ask all of you to remain seated. I have a note here from Maria Ibletto who claims to be the minor's nanny. Is that correct?"

My heart began to race. "She is, Your Honor," I replied. "Is there something wrong?"

"She says that Jamey is missing. She has called the police. A neighbor witnessed the child entering a vehicle . . ."

I bolted through the courtroom, knocked over two chairs and bruised my knees against the swinging gate. Kevin chased me to the parking lot. Peg called the police on her cell phone while Rob hurried ahead of her to bring the car.

"Jack, wait up," Kevin shouted.

I scrambled through the courthouse parking lot maze. I backed out from the parking space unaware of an oncoming car. Blasting his horn, the driver slammed on his brakes. Kevin's words were lost in the screech of my tires as I headed back to Laguna Beach.

Chapter Twelve

Daylight Savings Time was four days away. I had two and half-hours before sunset to find Jamey.

I rang Tim's house. Surprised to hear Frank's voice, I left a message for Tim. Frank's Georgian drawl hadn't been erased from the answering machine. Not five minutes later, my cell phone lit up. It was Tim. "Jack, your message, you sound like you've lost your best friend."

"I have. Jamey's missing. I need your help to find him," I said, panicked.

"What do you mean, he's missing? Did he run away?"

"Mrs. Jarret saw Jamey get into a parked car in front of my house this afternoon. God! I can only hope . . ." I went silent on Tim; my thoughts were focused on places where Jamey might be found.

"Jack, you there?"

"Jamey's wearing blue jeans, you know, his carpenter pants and his Spiderman T-shirt. He's not wearing a jacket. If I we don't find him before the sun goes down he'll catch his death of cold. He's such a skinny little guy. Whoever abducted him, if he lays one fucking hand on my grandson, I'll kill the son-of-bitch!"

"Jack, cool down. We're gonna find Jamey. Where are you?"

"Aliso Beach. Jamey and I have whiled away hours here solving the world's problems together."

"Do you want me to meet you there?"

"No. There's not enough time. Just start hunting for my boy, Tim."

"Is there a description of the car, the driver?"

"Old. An old car, that's all we have to go on. Mrs. Jarret was probably half looped when the police questioned her. She gave no description of the driver, male or female, we don't know. She did remember the license plate, black and gold. You know California plates from a hundred years ago?"

"Don't worry, Jamey's easy to spot, especially in his Spiderman T-shirt; he'll stand out like Mickey Mouse in a crowd of Munchkins. I'm on it, Jack. I'm out'a here."

"Thanks, Tim. I'm gonna get back on the road. I'll leave my cell phone on. Call me if you find or see anything, anything."

I later found out that Maria had e-mailed a recent photograph of Jamey to Hank Beyers. He printed reams of flyers for the Laguna Beach Police Department and for the volunteers who swarmed Walt's café. With Hank's help, Walt organized teams of merchants to saturate the local businesses, residential neighborhoods, joggers on the beach and people browsing the streets and local shops.

I scoured every side street and every alley in Laguna Beach within a five-mile radius of my house. I screamed out Jamey's name until I was hoarse. I checked every gas station, every cove along the coast and the parking lots of every restaurant, every doughnut joint, and every friggin' hamburger drive-thru. I refused to give into fear; guilt haunted my conscience. I had let Annie down. She had entrusted her son to me.

Maria waited at the house for Richard and Tommy to arrive from Los Angeles; they were stuck in commuter traffic on Interstate 405 between Long Beach and Anaheim. Mrs. Zucker insisted on coming with them to support Maria and to stand by the telephone. Maria called Henry. He contacted an old crony from the Costa Mesa Police Department, a retired sergeant who assisted Henry whenever battered women needed protection from their abusive husbands. After three frustrating attempts, I finally got hold of Hank at the Sheriff's Department. He assured me that the department was on top of the search. He told me to go home.

I ignored his order. "Not until I have found my grandson!" I told him.

"If Jamey were my grandson, I wouldn't listen to my advice either," Hank admitted. "My shift is over in thirty minutes but I'm not clocking out. Write this number down, 385-6675. I gave the dispatcher your name. If you need to get hold of me she'll put you through to my patrol car."

"Hank, Jamey's a smart boy. He did not go with a stranger," I said.

"Jack, we will find Jamey. Give me your cell phone number so I can reach you."

New legislation had specified that law enforcement agencies dictated that Law Enforcement act immediately upon the first report of a missing child and not twenty-four hours after the fact.

Isolated by my fear, I drove by every street in Laguna Beach. Even knowing that the Police Department and my friends searched for Jamey, I tried to imagine where he might be and prayed that whoever snatched my boy not harm him. Jamey had been missing for two hours. After the first fifteen minutes of abduction the odds of finding him decreased exponentially. The possibility that Jamey might still be in Laguna was unlikely. California's Highway Patrol had triggered the Amber Alert System. Computerized, large illuminated freeway signs along Southern California freeways from Los Angeles to San Bernardino alerted commuters to Jamey's abduction.

None of this made any sense to me. Annie and I had instilled in Jamey, never to get into a car with anyone without our permission. I suspected that Jamey knew who the driver of the car was.

I was oblivious to the rush of traffic. My fear crowded out rational thought. Then the red glare from the LCD clock in the car stereo suddenly got my attention and saved me from rear ending a parked car. 7:00 p.m., thirty minutes remained before sunset. Casting a gloomy haze between linear cirrus clouds, a cold orange sun hovered above the west horizon. Dusk was only moments away; minute by minute the sun lowered until darkness buried its glow. "Jamey, where are you?" I whispered.

The police continued their search. According to the bulletins coming over the car's radio, sightings of a child matching Jamey's description flooded the Laguna Beach Police Department dispatcher's switchboard. Eyewitness reports described Jamey's abductor as an elderly gentleman, crew cut, smoking a cigar. From the description of the car I had a pretty good idea who had taken Jamey. The black and gold license plate belonged to a '49 Chrysler Imperial; black and gold were the colors of California license plates when the car was sold new.

Two hours had passed since I left the courthouse. It was 7:25 p.m. by the clock on the radio. Crawling southbound on Pacific Coast Highway, two miles north of Laguna, I scanned the deserted beach at Emerald Bay from my car. With dusk approaching, imaginary shadows of kids played amid mounds of seaweed and driftwood marooned by the incoming tide. Desperation momentarily tricked me into thinking that I saw my grandson romping on the beach, a coastal playground he and I shared.

Tailgating my bumper, a frustrated driver honked her horn and flashed her high beams into my rear view mirror. Crowding the bike lane, I pulled to the side of the highway and waved from the window for her to pass. She pulled over and parked behind me. I recognized the Mercedes.

Peg kept a cautious eye on the stream of cars speeding past us as she walked toward my car. Teetering between the beach and commuter traffic, Peg balanced on the curb. She tapped her wedding ring against the passenger window. "Jack, I'm so glad I spotted your car. Have you heard any of the news?"

"Nothing's come over the radio."

"KTVU just telecast a special report describing the suspect's vehicle, an early model Chrysler or Dodge. The TV station showed a photograph of Jamey," she said as her voice faded. Tears welled in her exhausted eyes. Peg reached in her skirt pocket for a tissue. Her hand came up empty. Jamey had managed to deplete the box of tissue stored in my car's glove compartment. I retrieved a stash of napkins from the center console, leftovers from a recent school morning drive-thru and offered them to Peg.

"Jack, the photograph of Jamey, it was the one Annie took of him sitting near the Christmas Tree. That was only a few months ago . . ."

For the first time in eight years Peg let her guard down in front of me. Composure had always dictated her absolute presence no matter the cost. Her hands were trembling; she was exhausted. She suddenly broke down at the side of the car. I begged her, "Peg, please, get in. I think I know who has Jamey."

My instinct told me not to comfort her. Peg was the enemy, but when I put my hand on her shoulder she collapsed in my arms. Before the sun bid us good evening I persuaded her to come with me. "Peg, your car is fine where it's at. Let's get back to Laguna before the sun sets."

I remembered Peg sitting in Derek's library in the Monarch Bay house while she clutched a photograph of her son to her chest. Our sorrow had united us in the shared loss of our kids. Somehow, at that moment, the battle between the grandparents seemed petty and trivial.

Dabbing her smeared mascara, Peg asked, "Jack, do you think Jamey's okay?"

"I'm fairly certain at this point that he's unharmed. He might be a little cold; he wasn't wearing a jacket."

"You know this man who has Jamey, don't you?"

"He's an old friend, Peg. We met each other when Annie was just five months old."

"Have I met him?"

"No. If you had you would have remembered him. He's a crusty, retired military lifer. He loved Annie. He baby-sat her when she was still in diapers. I still have, stored away in a box in a closet, a Winnie-the-Pooh crib mobile, a gift from the old curmudgeon. He took to Jamey like he had with Annie. They've been buds for six and a half years now. My old friend was diagnosed with lymphoma eight months ago."

Peg's cell phone chimed interrupting our conversation. The advent of cellular phones had replaced Southern California freeway traffic as my personal peeve against technology, but I had ultimately given in; my cell phone came equipped with its own dashboard cradle.

"Rob," Peg answered, "I'm on Pacific Coast Highway . . . I ran into Jack. We're together in his car . . . No; I parked the Mercedes off the highway . . . Of course I set the alarm . . . Would you just shut-up for once. The Mercedes will survive. You should be here with us to help find your grandson!" Peg handed the phone to me, "Rob wants to talk to you."

"What is it, Rob?'

"Listen to me, old man. I suggest you rid your life of that incompetent housekeeper of yours. Her negligence placed my grandson at risk. Jamey better be found, unharmed, or I'll sling your faggot ass so far out over the coastline you'll wish you'd never met me."

Rob's ignorance and bigotry did not deserve a response. I flipped the phone back to Peg.

California Highway Patrol had set up a roadblock a mile and a half outside Laguna's city limits. Vehicles, twenty deep, idled in north and southbound lanes of Pacific Coast Highway. Officers searched the inside of vehicles, even the trunks, and questioned the inconvenienced drivers and passengers. I turned off the ignition, jumped out of the car and bolted past the line of vehicles toward the police barricade. An officer reached for his gun and ordered, "Stop right there, sir. Get back in your car."

I stopped but held my ground. "Officer," I pleaded, "Jamey Fitzpatrick is my grandson. I'm Jack Turner. His grandmother, Peg Fitzpatrick is in the car. I know who has him. I think I know where they are. I need to get to Main Beach."

One of the detained drivers rolled his window down; he was Johnny's father. "Jack," he yelled out, "what are you doing?"

"I need to get through this blockade. I know where Jamey is."

Johnny's dad asked the officer to come to his car. "Officer, I know this man, he is the boy's grandfather."

My hands were shaking, not from fear but from time wasted. I fumbled through my rear pocket for my wallet and then dropped it on the pavement.

Credit cards scattered beneath the line-up of cars. I crawled on my hands and knees scrambling to retrieve them. In my haste, I scraped the skin from my knuckles. I bandaged my hand with my shirttail to control the bleeding and gave my driver's license to the officer.

He glanced at the photo then at me and then returned my license. "Sir," he said, "please return to your vehicle. Sergeant Loomis will escort you back to Laguna."

The cop wrote hastily in his notebook as I described in detail the man who had Jamey. I pleaded with him to ask all law enforcement personnel searching not to storm Jamey or the old man. I didn't tell the officer, but I was certain that the man who had Jamey was Mr. Thomas.

The sun had dipped below the horizon. Houses on the densely populated hillside glowed with evening lights. The officer returned the American Express Card that I had overlooked and flagged Peg and me through the blockade. One patrol car escorted us back to town; its siren pierced through the chilly air. One mile from Main Beach, four additional patrol cars merged with the caravan. A police helicopter hovered above the beach. Its searchlight lit up the Boardwalk, the surrounding hotels and the lifeguard tower like Pac Bell Stadium during a night game. Converging sirens of patrol cars mixed with the battering rhythm of the helicopter's rotating blades. The noise drowned my plea to the police to stand back. I jumped from the car, planted my feet in the middle of the deserted parking lot and waved my arms imploring the cops to stay back.

The black and gold license plate stood out clearly in the high beams of my car. The Chrysler was parked facing the Boardwalk, but the headlights of my car faded under the helicopter's searchlight. The chopper's beam spotlighted Jamey. Snuggling up to Mr. Thomas to keep warm, Jamey lay still crouched on a bench on the boardwalk that faced the ocean.

The downward gust from the chopper's blades thrust debris three hundred sixty degrees. Plastic grocery bags that littered the beach had escaped by hitching a ride with the tide. Unearthed treasures of lost rings and gold trinkets lay exposed and unclaimed by metal detector junkies. Hungry seagulls, scattered and cried out, alarmed by the man-made storm. Grains of sand stung my bare arms. Jamey snuggled closer to Mr. Thomas to shelter his bare arms from the chopper's downwash.

A fence of aluminum cans weighted with sand encircled Jamey and Mr. Thomas. My voice competed with the screaming sirens, the helicopter and a voice from a bullhorn that ordered Mr. Thomas to "Release the boy and stay where you are."

The police closed in. My car was surrounded by black and whites and .48 caliber pistols aimed at an old dying man.

Peg struggled to hear me above the noise. She cupped her ear with her other hand as she tried to hear what I was saying. She started to get out of my car. I hollered above the racket, "Peg, stay there. I'm going after Jamey."

"I am not staying in the car. I'm going with you," she insisted.

Ignoring orders from the police to stay back, we dodged between the patrol cars.

Jamey peered over his shoulder. He leaped from the bench, shouting, "Grampa!"

Hearing his voice shouting my name and watching him run toward me hit me in my gut, reminding me of the feelings that had overwhelmed me after Annie's death.

Jamey was unharmed. His lanky, bare legs sprinted him across the Boardwalk. I caught him in mid-air; he wrapped his bare arms around my neck and locked his legs around my waist. Tears streaked his dirty cheeks smeared from a chocolate ice cream cone. I lost it when I hugged my boy tight against my chest and wrapped his shivering body in my coat. "Jamey, oh my Jamey, thank God you're okay!"

Jamey clung to me even tighter. The helicopter still hovered over us; the deafening noise from the rotating blades made conversation nearly impossible to hear. Jamey shouted near my ear, "Grampa, you have to hurry. Something is wrong with Mr. Thomas."

"Jamey, stay here with your Gramma. I'll go see what's wrong with Mr. Thomas." When I released Jamey he ran to Peg and nuzzled into her comforting arms. She knelt beside him, wiped his cheeks with a napkin and brushed his bangs from his forehead. Then Jamey brushed his Gramma's cheek and caught one of her tears with his finger. "It's okay to cry, Gramma," he said and hugged her close to him as his small body allowed.

Peg remained on her knees. She hugged her grandson to her bosom. Jamey peeked over her shoulder and kept his eyes on me as I approached Mr. Thomas.

The old man was staring at something beyond the sunset that had faded into the black horizon. I stood before him. "Mr. Thomas, it's Jack, Jack Turner." He continued to stare and didn't even blink when I touched him. I sat down next to him, draped my arm around his shoulder and pulled him close to me.

The sirens had stopped. The helicopter extinguished its lights and flew over Pacific Coast Highway toward Laguna Canyon. An Emergency Medical

Technician lifted Mr. Thomas' body onto a gurney. They shrouded his head and body with a wool blanket. The retired Marine, Annie's friend, had died while Jamey had been sitting next to him.

Before we left Main Beach, Jamey had fallen sound asleep in the back seat of the Cruiser. Peg and I remained silent as we drove back to her car. She clasped my hand as I came to a stop and whispered, "Jack, I'm sorry about what Rob said to you."

"Forget it," I said.

Peg caressed her grandson's sleepy head and gently closed the car door. I waited until she drove away toward Newport Beach then headed back to the house with my boy conked out in the back seat.

I dialed the house.

"Hello," Maria answered, her voice quavering.

"Maria, it's Jack. I have Jamey."

"Oh, thank God. We watched the whole thing on the news. How is he?"

"He's curled up in the backseat, out like a light. I think this day has done him in. I'm about ten minutes from the house. Are the fellas and Mrs. Zucker still there?"

"They are all here, waiting for you to bring Jamey home."

"Maria, ask them to wait in the kitchen. I don't want to wake Jamey. Please turn down his bed, we're almost home."

"I'll do it right away. Thank God he is safe and with you now."

"Maria?"

"Yes, Mr. Jack?"

"It was Mr. Thomas. He wanted to say goodbye to Jamey before he died."

Tommy, Richard and Mrs. Zucker had ignored my request to wait in the kitchen; except for Maria, they were all huddled together on the front lawn as I pulled into the driveway. Anxious to see Jamey, Maria met us at the curb and in silence welcomed us home. I tucked Jamey into bed. He squeezed my finger and then buried his head into his down pillow.

The mantel clock chimed 8:30 p.m.; however, it seemed more like midnight. A peaceful hush had fallen over the house. Tommy looked in on Jamey and reported, "Snug as a bug in a rug."

"Tommy, thank you for being here today," I said to him with my deepest gratitude.

He opened his palms to the air. "We needed to be here. Jack, Maria's not coping well right now. Go talk to her."

I tapped at Maria's bedroom door. "Maria, can I come in?"

"Wait, just a minute, Mr. Jack."

I heard the faint sound of Maria blowing her nose. After giving her a few moments to compose herself, I opened the door and went in. Hugging Pooh beneath her chin, she sat at the edge of her bed. She clutched a tissue in her fist; the wanting expression in her eyes begged me to sit down beside her. "Maria, why so sad? Our boy is home now."

"I was here, here in the kitchen. It's my fault. Nothing, I heard nothing. Gone. No sound, no scream, gone. Mr. Jack, I am so sorry," she sobbed deeply from a place I found difficult to console.

"Maria, no one is to blame. Not even Mr. Thomas." I cocked my head until we were face to face then nose to nose. I gently suggested, "Maria, I'll bet Jamey would love to have Pooh near his pillow."

Maria smiled, wiped her fallen tears from Pooh's stitched grin and then carried Pooh to Jamey's bedside.

Outside, Richard hobbled alongside Mrs. Zucker as he helped her down the walkway. "I might be an old woman, Richard, but I can certainly walk to the car on my own," she admonished.

"I know, Mrs. Zucker," Richard said, but retained a firm grip on her arm.

I yelled out across the lawn, "Mrs. Zucker. I should look and feel so fabulous when I'm your age!"

"Jack," she yelled back in a shaky voice, "you flatter yourself. Mr. Zucker, God rest his soul, would agree with you."

Tommy stayed with me on the porch. "Jack, are you gonna be okay?"

"I'll be fine. Never been better."

"I left a little gift for you on the coffee table. Don't tell Mrs. Zucker; she'll kill me."

"My lips are sealed. What is it?"

He only shook his head; no response. I felt cared for, like a child, when Tommy kissed me goodbye on the forehead even though the lummox was ten years younger than I was. Before he closed the door of his car, I asked him, "Tommy, call me when you're all home safe, okay?"

"Okay, Papa."

Tommy had left an unopened pack of cigarettes on top of an *Architectural Digest* magazine. Menthol Lights. I didn't smoke menthol cigarettes.

The first drag damned near choked me. The nicotine rush reminded me of dancing and inhaling poppers at a disco back in the seventies. My lungs had been spared for two months from carbon monoxide, carcinogens and the addictive pleasure of relaxing with a smoke. A glass of Henry's vintage Zin soothed the raspy burn in my throat.

Thanks to the alcohol and the tannins in the wine, I slowly relaxed and let the day's tension drain out of me. I stretched out on the chaise lounge, crickets and bullfrogs performed a spring evening concerto, background music to compliment a smoke and a vintage red. A calm feeling of reassurance filled me.

Whatever would happen in the days to come, my grandson and I would stay together.

Chapter Thirteen

Earlier that evening, sometime between Tommy's kiss and Mrs. Zucker's, "God rest his soul", the old coot next door and his wife had delivered a gift for Jamey and left it unwrapped on the front porch. Their gift was a ten-week-old Golden Retriever puppy who kept me awake all night, whining.

After just one week, Pooh had taken up residence on top of Jamey's dresser. He appeared no worse for wear except for a missing nose. Jamey came down with a case of the sniffles, an allergy caused from dog dander. Christened Willow, the puppy slept by Jamey's side cuddled up on the down pillow next to his new best friend.

Jamey turned over his job as my alarm clock to Willow; the trouble with a puppy, no snooze button. The entire household rose at 5:30 a.m. every morning including Sundays. My nocturnal lifestyle was no more. I collapsed in bed by 10:30 every night.

Early the next morning, Jamey and I huddled around the kitchen table, hungry for Maria's Saturday morning breakfast. Willow ignored the puppy chow in his bowl. The smell of pork sausage sizzling in a frying pan drove him crazy. Maria snatched him up from the floor and tucked him under one arm. "Willow," she said with a grin, "you're going to learn some rules around this house." She glared at Jamey and me as we sat at the kitchen table; we both wore innocent expressions. "Listen up you guys," she continued, "you are not exempt." Willow got the message and licked her hand. She pointed her finger at Willow and informed him, "Number one rule, sausage is people food." Willow squirmed and wriggled, begging Maria to free him, so she lowered him gently to the floor. He sat at attention, cocked his head back and forth and listened to Maria's every word. More likely his attention was focused on her fingertips that were coated with a tad of pork drippings.

It may have been over excitement, but the puppy lost it. Willow squatted, as puppies do, and piddled on the linoleum floor.

Maria laid down the law. "Mr. Jack, I am not potty training the puppy, nor am I on poop patrol. I suggest you and Jamey begin training this morning," she recommended with absolute conviction.

"Jamey," I said, "another new rule for you in this house. Good boys go potty outside."

"Me too?" he asked, giggling under his breath.

"You doof. Go on now. Take Willow outside to the back yard. Explain to him about the importance of keeping Maria's house clean."

Maria trailed behind the mutt and his buddy, tossed the towel she had used to clean Willow's accident into the laundry basket and held the back door open for them. "Stay in the back yard, Jamey, and close the gate," she hollered from the back door.

She wrapped her hands in the fold of her apron and returned to the kitchen counter. I read the paper and wedged a cigarette atop my ear while Maria rummaged through the junk drawer. She found one of my treasures, a souvenir ashtray from the Disneyland Hotel and then slammed it onto the table.

"Maria, I promise not to smoke in the house," I said begrudgingly and slid the ashtray away.

She removed temptation from the table and returned my souvenir to its original hiding place. She then informed me, "Good. It stinks up the house."

I snapped the newspaper to release the crease. "This coming Wednesday," I told her, "the attorneys have scheduled a meeting with Dr. Aldrich in Judge Harcourt's chambers. Rob and Peg expressed concerns regarding the doctor's evaluation and recommendations. Frankly, I have too. I think she crossed the line when she questioned Jamey about Annie."

"You think so?"

"Yes I do. Jamey has been crying at night after he says his prayers. He misses his mom."

"Time, Mr. Jack, it will take time. Speaking of time, what time is the meeting?" Maria asked then moved the ashtray to another hiding spot so I couldn't find it.

"9:30, I will be indebted to you for the rest of my life if you will take Jamey to school that morning."

"I'll just add that to your ongoing debt," she replied with a playful jab. "Of course I'll do that. Oh, before I forget, the lab called. You have an appointment Monday afternoon for the DNA test."

"I'll let Kevin know. He wanted to come along for the ride." The Home and Garden section of the newspaper fell to the floor. The Business section stared me right in the face. The Dow had dropped another two-hundred-fifty points. The headlines across the front page read: **President Bush threatens Saddam Hussein, linking him to the Al Queida terrorists, 9/11 and the attack on the World Trade Center.** Preoccupied by my own battle, I set the paper aside.

"Mr. Jack, what if the DNA results prove Margo's allegation?" Maria asked.

"That's ridiculous. She's lying!"

"My point exactly."

"Fuck the DNA test and Margo! I am Jamey's grandfather!"

"Lower your voice; Jamey will hear you. Of course you're his grandfather and Annie was your baby."

"Damn straight, Annie was my baby. What is Margo trying to prove? Crazy bitch. It's not about money. She can buy and sell the lot of us with her pocket change." Out of habit I raised a cigarette to my lips and dug in my pocket for a lighter. "What if I'm not Jamey's Grampa after all? Maybe the universe is trying to tell me something . . ."

"Mr. Jack, I've watched you grow up from a wide-eyed, bumbling new papa and mature into a seasoned dear friend to me and to your grandson. I love you too much to allow you to give in now. And besides, if Annie could hear you carrying on like this she would kick you right in your ass," she said, mimicking a phrase I used much too often.

"Well, my baby isn't here anymore," I said mournfully.

"No she is not, so I may have to do it for her."

Right on cue, Jamey leaped into the kitchen with Willow at his heels. "Grampa, we need a pooper scooper."

I folded my paper under my arm, cupped my latte in my hands and said to Maria, "Add a pooper scooper to the grocery list."

"Grampa, don't go away. I have to give you my letter." Jamey disappeared down the hallway with Willow tearing at his pant leg.

Willow glommed onto Jamey's leg and performed the vicious growling head twitch. Egging Willow on to chase him, Jamey dragged his muddy sneakers across the hardwood floor. Like hooking a fish Willow went for the bait. He locked his jaws onto Jamey's denim pants while his master bellowed with laughter throughout the house under the puppy's relentless grip.

Once Jamey freed himself from Willow's grip, he proudly handed me the letter he had written to Dr. Aldrich. In the left hand corner of the envelope he had printed: From Jamey, and in the middle of the envelope: To Dokter Aldrich. A smudge of fingerprints trailed the back of the envelope, pressed, gooey and sealed. I printed her address on it, affixed the postage and later mailed his letter, unread.

I excused myself and retired to the front porch, the designated smoking section. I wanted to read my column, so I scanned beyond the byline and settled into the chaise lounge. Before I finished the first sentence I heard footsteps coming up the walkway. I peered over my paper only to find my neighbors standing at the foot of the porch. "Mr. and Mrs. Jarret, good morning," I said to them.

"Jack, good morning to you," Mrs. Jarret greeted me. Mr. Jarret nodded politely.

"To what do I owe this morning visit?" I asked as I leaned forward on the chaise lounge.

"How are Jamey and the puppy getting along?" Mrs. Jarret asked.

"Like two peas in a pod. There is no separating them. You could not have given Jamey a nicer gift," I assured them.

"Every little boy needs a puppy. What has he named him?" Mrs. Jarret asked.

"Willow."

"I should have known," she said with approval. She looked up at her husband and prodded him to speak. "Jack, Mr. Jarret has something he wants to tell you." She elbowed her husband. "Go on, tell him, George."

Mr. Jarret cautiously stepped forward, stopped at the foot of the steps and began by saying, "Myrna . . . Mrs. Jarret and I want to tell you how glad we are . . ."

Mrs. Jarret butted in, "How glad George and I are that Jamey is home safe."

Mr. Jarret butted back in, "Hush, old woman, I was talkin' to Jack. Anyway, if there is anything that we . . ."

Mrs. Jarret butted in again, "If there is anything we can do to help out?"

"You guys have done more than enough," I told her. "Jamey has all but forgotten the ordeal thanks to you two and the puppy."

"Well, we knew how much he loved our old girl. Even you did, Jack," Mrs. Jarret said, inviting a response.

"Yeah, she and I became pretty good friends."

In step, Mr. and Mrs. Jarret turned to go home. "Before I forget," Mrs. Jarret added, "I'm baking peanut butter cookies this afternoon."

"Mmm, my favorite. Maria seldom bakes these days."

"I'll bring them by this afternoon, but you have to promise to share with Jamey and Maria."

"With Jamey around, no contest. Thank you for . . . you know."

Mr. Jarret waved once for goodbye. I overheard Mrs. Jarret telling him, "See, that wasn't so hard, you old fool."

Their bickering reminded me that being unmarried wasn't such a bad thing. Even so, the old coot and his wife made me smile. I hid behind the newspaper and thought, "How nice of them to care."

The mailman came up to the front porch and delivered a stack of bills, two home improvement catalogues and a bubble pack envelope from William. I handed him Jamey's letter. He looked at the envelope, "Impressive, in Jamey's handwriting. Must be important stuff sealed in here," he said then tucked Jamey's letter into his mailbag.

"Top secret," I said. "He sealed it before I had a chance to read it."

"I'll handle it with care, Jack. How's Jamey doing?"

"He's hanging in there. Jamey's gonna be fine."

"Where is the little guy? You and he are usually joined at the hip."

"We have a new addition to the family, a puppy, so now I'm chopped liver."

The mailman adjusted his mailbag over his shoulder, shook his head and grinned. "Things are finally getting back to normal around your place. See ya Monday, Jack."

I leaned back on the chaise lounge and opened the bubble pack from William. Inside the package I found a video of New England's changing seasons, the fall colors of October through the Christmas Prelude celebration, exclusive to Kennebunkport, Maine. In a separate envelope I found three round trip airline tickets, LAX to Boston for December 20th and a note, "Pack warm clothing!"

If I had had my way, that Saturday morning in March that I spent lounging on the front porch would have bridged time until Jamey graduated from college. But reality forced me to focus on Wednesday and the meeting with Dr. Aldrich in Judge Harcourt's chambers.

I was on a dead run. Maria took Jamey to school that morning. While rummaging through my closet to find my tie I discovered that my suit needed pressing, but that would have to wait. I got dressed quickly and backed the car out by 8:45 a.m.

I parked the car at the courthouse lot with fifteen minutes to spare, progress.

The parking lot was packed and people were streaming into the courthouse. Teenagers dressed in hip-hop garb, baggy ass jeans that drooped below their knees, moped alongside their parents as they walked toward the juvenile court. One boy smoked a cigarette while his dad scowled at him; his oversized cotton shirt had been starched as crisp as the crease in his jeans, grunge at its best. They kept an arms distance from one another. I wondered if the boy had a mom. The young man, probably sixteen, repositioned his baseball cap to cover his shaved head. His left eyebrow was pierced and adorned with a paper clip, his right ear was pierced from top to lobe. I overheard his dad growl at him, "Keep the cap on, you look like a fucking idiot." He held the door open for his son; the boy cocked his cap to the side of his head. A bailiff passed them and ordered, "Remove the cap, young man."

Directly across from the juvenile center the Superior Court Building stood like a fortress. I entered the courthouse. Only a few feet from me waited two security guards. One of them instructed me, "Remove all items in your pockets including change and keys please," the security guard instructed me. The second guard scanned my body with an electronic wand. I passed their inspection unscathed without a "good morning" from either of them.

Dr. Aldrich had not arrived yet. Sipping coffee from styrofoam cups, Rob and Peg paced the corridor outside the courtroom. Rob nibbled at a croissant and dropped buttery crumbs on the floor. Jonas stood near a window that overlooked the parking lot and reviewed Dr. Aldrich's recommendations. Peg said to her husband, "Rob, I'll be back in a minute," and then headed off to the ladies room. She was looking down at the floor when she bumped into me, head on. She spilled some of the coffee on her blouse.

"Sorry, Peg . . . Can I get you a paper towel from the men's room?"

"No, it's fine, Jack, I wasn't looking where I was going" she said. Peg's attempt to sop up the stain with a tissue only made the stain worse. She said to me, "The dry cleaners will get the stain out. Don't bother." She paused, brushed her bangs from her eyes and looked up at me. "How is Jamey feeling?" she asked.

"Better . . . he told me last night he wants to stay over at your place this weekend."

"I'll call him tonight. It's been awhile since he's had a sleep over. I miss seeing him."

"He misses seeing you, too." I looked beyond her shoulders to see if Rob or Jonas were nearby. "Peg?"

"Yes, Jack"

"No matter how this whole thing plays out . . . thanks . . . thanks for being with me when we found Jamey."

"Jack, we need to talk . . ."

At that precise moment Kevin arrived. "Jack, Peg, good morning to you both. You look lovely, Peg," he said and then turned to me, "nice suit."

Kevin seemed uncharacteristically flustered; his cheeks were flushed, his hands fumbling with a sheaf of legal size paper. "What's the problem? I've never seen you like this," I said.

"I'll fill you in later," Kevin replied. "I've been on the phone all morning with . . . we'll discuss this after the meeting. I just saw Dr. Aldrich speaking to Judge Harcourt in the parking lot. They're on their way up. I suggest we proceed to her chambers and check in with her clerk. Are you coming?"

"Be right there."

Peg started to walk away. "Peg, wait up," I hollered to get her attention.

She turned away from her husband who stood only a few feet from her. She looked at me and said, "We need to gather in the judge's chambers."

"Peg?" I asked nervously. "What did you want to talk to me about?"

"Another time, Jack, it's not important," she finished then joined her husband and Jonas.

With everyone gathered in the judge's office, I closed the door behind us.

The clerk stepped away from her desk. "Good morning," she greeted us cheerfully. "I'm Judy. If you need anything before we enter the chambers, water, coffee, maybe tea, please let me know. Judge Harcourt asks that we wait a few minutes before going inside." Her phone rang. "Excuse me," she said and answered it. ". . . Yes, I'll bring them in. Yes, uh huh, everyone is here." She hung up the receiver. "Please, follow me."

Judge Harcourt remained seated as we entered the room. Dr. Aldrich was standing near the edge of the desk. Judge Harcourt welcomed us. "Good morning," she said. "I am pleased to see that everyone could attend. Thank you, Judy, I'll have a cup of coffee, please. Ladies and gentlemen, anything for you?"

None of us wanted coffee or anything else; we were all anxious to move ahead with the meeting.

"At Mr. Stevens' request a court reporter will be present this morning. Please speak clearly and not out of turn," Judge Harcourt added.

Judge Harcourt's chambers were not at all like those depicted in film and television. One wall, a gallery of her family, one, a picture of her daughter, which made my mind flash back to Jonas's motion of recusal. A faux finish of pale yellow with a caramel background warmed the walls and softened the emotional climate building in the room. Arranged with a florist's flare a bouquet of apricot and lavender iris graced one corner of Judge Harcourt's desk. White crown molding framed the Palladian window behind her desk chair. Selected photographs of her grandchildren, framed in pewter, were displayed on the same shelves that supported the books of her law library. Instead of her robe of authority Judge Harcourt wore a tailored, gray pinstriped suit and lavender blouse that was unbuttoned at the neck. I noticed a tiny gold Lambda, a symbol of gay pride and unity, hanging on a delicate gold chain that lay gently on her chest. I assumed it was a gift from her daughter. Judge Harcourt's demeanor seemed more relaxed than days past in the courtroom which tempered the anxiety building in her chambers. Judy ushered the court reporter into the chambers, the same woman who had recorded the proceedings in the initial hearing. She set up her steno machine on its stand and sat on a chair she provided that appeared to be less than comfortable. Judge Harcourt made her opening remarks. "I have called you all together this morning at the request of Dr. Aldrich. Before I turn the meeting over to Dr. Aldrich I wish to express to Mr. Turner and Mr. and Mrs. Fitzpatrick my relief that Jamey was found safe and unharmed. How is he doing?"

Peg and I spoke simultaneously, "He . . ."

"You go ahead, Jack," Peg said.

"Well, Jamey's back at school, playing soccer with his teammates and potty training a new puppy. He's quite the kid."

"A new puppy? I'll bet your house is up early every morning. She smiled and then turned to the business at hand. "I will turn this meeting over to you, Dr. Aldrich."

"Thank you, Your Honor." Judge Harcourt relinquished her chair to Aldrich and sat down on a small, upholstered sofa, crossed her legs and arms and listened. Dr. Aldrich continued, "I understand at the last hearing questions came up regarding my evaluation and recommendations of Jamey. Mr. Fitzpatrick, your concern is?"

"My issue is quite to the point regarding the matters involved in this hearing. I do not believe that it is your job to promote the virtues of homosexuality to my grandson. I disagree with your painting a permissive picture of a lifestyle that my wife and I find detrimental to our grandson."

"Mr. Fitzpatrick, we need to remember that Jamey loves all of the people involved in this hearing. It is important for Jamey's feelings to be validated."

"Validated, not shoved down his throat."

Jonas interrupted, "Rob, let her finish."

"Thank you, Mr. Simon. Jamey is an intelligent, emotionally well-balanced, articulate and expressive six-year-old eager to engage his listener. He understands right from wrong and is concerned about events that he sees as harmful to those he loves. Mr. Fitzpatrick, when you refer to Mr. Turner as a faggot in front of your grandson, you run the danger of making Jamey wonder if something is wrong with his grandfather, the person he lives with. You need to realize that when you are negative about Mr. Turner, that Jamey takes it personally. It is detrimental to Jamey to make him feel shame about living with his grandfather. We can all learn from this child and his perception of the world he lives in."

"Sorry, Dr. Aldrich, I don't buy it."

"Dr. Aldrich, may I say something at this point?" Jonas said quickly.

"Please do."

"Rob, regardless of the outcome of these hearings, Jack will still be Jamey's grandfather," Jonas reminded him.

"Whose side are you on? The DNA test will determine that."

Kevin cleared his throat and spoke. "Even though we await the DNA results, they are not a measure of the impact of Jack's role as the psychological parent to Jamey. Am I correct, Dr. Aldrich?"

"It is not my role to be the judge in this hearing but only to offer my recommendations. From my observations of the child and interviews with all the grandparents I see two distinct relationships. Mr. and Mrs. Fitzpatrick are the child's grandparents. Because both of Jamey's parents are deceased Mr. Turner has assumed the role as the child's parent, the caregiver that keeps Jamey psychologically safe. To answer your question, I am not aware of any research indicating that blood relationship is necessary to giving a child a safe holding environment, as Mr. Turner has done for some time."

Judge Harcourt had remained silent until Dr. Aldrich paused. She re-crossed her legs and unfolded her arms, "Dr. Aldrich, if I may interject here. Are you indicating that the Fitzpatricks do not provide a psychologically safe environment for the child?"

"To the contrary, Your Honor. My point is that the emotional tie between Mr. Turner and Jamey has created a secure attachment for the child. Jamey is given permission to say what he feels; he has the freedom to have his feelings heard. He strongly identifies with his Grampa Jack; they dress alike, Jamey aspires to be a writer. Jamey has lived with Mr. Turner for the last four years and sees his grandfather as a parent figure. Whereas, even though the Fitzpatricks provide a loving environment for him to visit, safe as it may be, it lacks the emotional and secure attachment he has developed with Mr. Turner. Children need to be allowed to love who they love."

Peg pursed her lips and gently nodded in agreement. Rob continued scribbling notes on a legal pad, his concentration focused on Dr. Aldrich.

"Mr. Fitzpatrick, have you other concerns you wish to discuss?" Dr. Aldrich asked.

"Not at this time. I may, however, call you to speak with you personally."

"Please do," she replied.

I didn't trust Rob as far as I could throw him. He sat back in his chair with an air of satisfaction.

Dr. Aldrich then turned to me. "Mr. Turner, I understand that you have concerns regarding Jamey's recent reaction to the loss of his mother."

"Jamey has been crying at night after he's gone to bed. When I ask him, "why the tears?" his first response is, "Nothing". After we talk a bit more he tells me that he misses his mom. My fear, Dr. Aldrich, is that you dug too deep with him when you discussed the death of his mother. He was coping just fine until then."

"Mr. Turner, Jamey is mourning the loss of his mother and is dealing with issues of unfinished business in his mind."

"What do you mean by unfinished business?" I asked.

"Let me explain." She leaned forward from the chair, rested her elbows on the desktop and folded her hands. Her eyes paused for only a moment on each of us. She pulled her hands to her chin and took in a deep breath. "This brings up the issue of attachment. Even though Jamey was only a year old when his father died he recognizes his loss. It was clear to me during the interview of Jamey's real sense of detachment from his nuclear family. Not only did he lose his father, he psychologically lost his mother. Before her death, Jamey had already developed an insecure attachment to his mother, the initial stage of his mourning. Drug therapy and her depression widened the gap of insecurity for Jamey. You, Mr. Turner, have become Jamey's emotional and psychological attachment. I am confident that Jamey's reaction will sort itself through because of the emotional shield and secure environment you provide for him."

"I'll keep an eye on him. If his crying continues, we'll make an appointment with you and go from there."

"I will be glad to meet with any one of you. Before we end this meeting I want to leave you with this thought. Jamey is the reason we are here this morning. Allow him to love and be loved by *all* of his grandparents. It is my recommendation to this court that Jamey remain in the care of his grandfather, Mr. Turner."

Judge Harcourt remained seated on the sofa. Rob tore off two pages from his yellow legal pad and filed his handwritten notes in his jacket. Jonas politely stood up and reached out to shake Dr. Aldrich's hand. "Thank you for coming today. I will be in touch."

"If you will all excuse me, I have a session with a young lady at 11:00. I wish you all the very best." She closed her briefcase, ran her fingers once through her hair and leaned forward to smell the iris. "Thank you, Judge Harcourt. Good day, everyone."

Judge Harcourt pushed her chair back under the desk and gripped the sides of the leather-upholstered arms. "Before you leave," she said, "let me remind you of our calendar date for June 15th. Until then, have a good day."

Kevin held the door open for Jonas, Rob and Peg. They headed down the corridor. Kevin waited at the door for me. I wanted to get the hell out of the building. I had had enough of Superior Court for one day.

"Jack, slow down, let them get ahead of us," Kevin said.

"So what's the deal?" I asked Kevin. "Why the frantic arrival earlier?"

"The lab contacted me this morning regarding the DNA test results. Annie was your biological daughter."

Chapter Fourteen

Wednesday, June 15, 9:30 a.m. The bailiff unlocked the courtroom doors.

Jonas filed in behind Rob and Peg; Kevin held the door open. Margo paused before going inside. She thumbed through her billfold and removed an old Kodak color print, the edges were frayed; the colors had faded to brown from years of being stored away in a box somewhere.

Margo hesitated, then took one step toward me and stopped at a cordial distance.

"Jack . . ."

"Why, Margo . . . why did you lie?" I confronted her.

She handed the photograph to me. Without saying anything she walked past Kevin. Maybe she didn't recognize him; she hadn't seen him for twenty-five years when he sported a full beard and wore glasses.

Margo entered the courtroom and chose a seat near the jury box. I stayed outside for just a moment. I looked deeply into the photograph and remembered the day it was taken. Margo was five months pregnant then. In the photograph I was standing behind Margo, my hands were supporting her big belly. William stood next to me, Kevin next to Margo. William was waving the peace sign above my head. We were friends. That was then.

Judge Harcourt entered the courtroom. The bailiff addressed the court, "All rise."

"Please be seated," the judge said. "Good morning, everyone." She unfolded her hands and rubbed her right palm with her thumb. "It is important for us not to lose sight of the purpose of these hearings. Today, I will award sole guardianship of Jamey Fitzpatrick to one of his grandparents. It would be against the interest of the child to disallow visitation with any of his grandparents. The three of you are all he has now. In all of the years that I have sat on this bench I have awarded guardianship and custody of children to whom I believed would provide the most loving, emotionally protected and nurturing environment for the child. Jamey is an exceptional little boy, not because he is bright and articulate, but because he is insightful and wise. At the close of this hearing, I have something from Jamey that I will share will all of you."

"Your Honor, if I may?" Kevin asked.

"Proceed, Counselor."

"I trust that the plaintiffs and their counsel have received copies of the DNA test results?"

"Yes we have," Jonas confirmed.

"It is clear from the results of the test," Kevin paused then looked directly at Rob and then to Judge Harcourt, "that Mr. Turner is indeed the biological father of Annie Fitzpatrick, leaving no doubt that he is also the biological grandfather of Jamey Fiztpatrick. I move to disallow Ms. Evans' testimony on the grounds that she knowingly presented false documents to this court."

"Objection, Your Honor, assumption," Jonas interrupted.

"Sustained. Mr. Stevens, your motion is well taken. However, I met with Ms. Evans yesterday in my chambers. I am going to deny your motion, Counselor, and allow Ms. Evans to present her testimony to this court."

"Your Honor, in light of the seriousness of these hearings, I urge you to reconsider your decision," Kevin insisted.

"Counselor, this is my court. My decision stands. I will allow Ms. Evans' testimony."

"Thank you, Your Honor." Kevin made a note on a document in front of him, hoisted his slacks and sunk back into his chair.

"Ms. Evans, please approach the bench," Judge Harcourt instructed. She nodded to the bailiff to proceed. He assisted Margo to the stand; she hadn't fully recovered from her hip replacement surgery and was using a cane, teak, crowned with a sea gull sculpted from speckled white marble.

"Thank you," she said to the bailiff, "I can manage from here." Margo gripped the banister with her left hand to steady her balance. She smoothed her skirt before she sat; a frown closed her eyes revealing her pain then propped her cane against the judge's bench.

"Ms. Evans, I will remind you that you are under oath," Judge Harcourt warned her.

"Of course, Your Honor." Margo's voice, raspy from years of smoking had mellowed. Its sharp edge no longer cut you to your knees with its bitchy inflection.

Margo's eyes locked onto mine.

"Ms. Evans," Jonas began, "thank you for being here today. I know that traveling has been a hardship on you, but your testimony today will put to rest the uncertainty surrounding your allegations. So let us begin. Ms. Evans, please describe to the court your relationship with Mr. Turner."

"At one time Jack and I were best friends, roommates in college."

"And today?"

"After I moved to New York in 1975 we lost touch with one another."

"So, during the last twenty-six, twenty-seven years, you and Mr. Turner have not communicated with each other."

"No, not until Annie's funeral."

"You were living in New York; you and Mr. Turner have not had any kind of relationship for twenty-six years, a long time. How then, Ms. Evans did you find out that your daughter had died?"

"William Broderick, a mutual friend of ours called me. William has been my connection to Jack all of these years."

I stared at her with disbelief. William never told me that he and Margo had stayed in touch with each other.

"Were you aware that you had a grandson?" Jonas continued.

"No, William never mentioned a word about Jamey to me."

Somehow I felt relieved by her admission, but did not trust her, even under oath.

"Is it true, Ms. Evans, that Mr. Turner has denied you any opportunity to participate in your grandson's life?" Jonas asked.

"Yes, that's true."

"Not exactly a loving, fatherly thing to do."

"Objection, Your Honor," Kevin immediately interjected.

"Sustained," Judge Harcourt said. "Mr. Simon, we can do without the personal theatrics."

"My apologies, Your Honor. Ms. Evans, did Mr. Turner give you a reason or offer an explanation as to why he has denied you the opportunity to get to know your grandson?"

"Yes. A few days following Annie's funeral I invited him to have dinner with me. My hope was to make amends for my years of absence from his and Annie's life. The evening began on a sweet note. I actually thought that Jack was glad to see me again. But I sensed that he was troubled. He seemed nervous; the tone in his voice, edgy, but my heart went out to him. Before that evening I had no knowledge of the guardianship hearings regarding Jamey."

"Ms. Evans, how did your evening end with Mr. Turner?"

"On a sour note. Our evening ended before we ordered dinner. Jack told me to go back to New York and to stay out of his and Jamey's lives."

"Ms. Evans, why did you walk away from your infant child and Mr. Turner?"

"There was no room in my life for a child. My focus was on my career; I had my sights and resumes set on Wall Street. Back then penetrating the male dominated egos that powered New York's financial district was impossible for a woman, let alone a single woman with an infant. I stayed with Jack and Annie for five months. I began suffering from anxiety attacks when the baby was three months old. I tried to hide it from Jack. I refused to take medication because I was breast feeding the baby. I knew that I couldn't stay; I packed my things and left. Jack and the baby had gone to Newport Beach to celebrate his college graduation with his friends. One of those friends is sitting in this courtroom. Without his beard and glasses, I didn't recognize Mr. Stevens right off. But then I remembered; he was an old friend of Jack's, someone I met briefly when Annie was an infant. Jack was unaware of my plans. He found the note that I left in the baby's crib. In my letter I promised Jack that I would call. I never did. Jack cannot forgive me for abandoning them. I can't blame him for that. Because I wasn't there for Annie, Jack believes I do not deserve to be there for my grandson."

"Ms. Evans, is Jack Turner the father of your deceased daughter, Annie Fitzpatrick?"

"To my surprise, I suppose he is."

"Surprised? In your letter to this court, you alleged that Mr. Turner was not the father of your child. Were you certain beyond any doubt that these allegations were true?"

"As certain as I could be."

"You had some doubts?"

"It was the seventies when I was in college. I slept with a few men during the time that Jack and I were roommates. Jack and I had returned to the apartment from dancing at a disco one night. It was late, two or three in the morning. Jack was pretty drunk. I was a little high from smoking too much pot. I seduced him. The next morning he had no memory of our having sex."

"Ms. Evans, were you in love with Mr. Turner."

"I think every woman has been in love with a gay man at least once in her life."

"So you were in love with him?"

"Yes, I was."

"If you doubted who the father of your child was, why did you tell Mr. Turner that he was the father?"

"Jack begged me not to have an abortion. He told me that he would adopt the baby. I knew that Jack would never have the opportunity again to have a child, so rather than subject him to the legal paper shuffle of adoption I told him that he was the father."

"You lied to him."

"It wasn't a lie. I just wasn't sure."

"You weren't sure. Yet you sit in this court today convinced that Jamey should be taken away from Mr. Turner. Why?"

"I wanted to hurt Jack the way he hurt me. I wanted him to lose what he loved the most, his grandson."

I struggled with my feelings. I wanted to believe her, but I distrusted every word she had rehearsed. I listened to Margo spill her guts. Jamey was not hers to lose. She had no right to him.

"During the week that I spent in Laguna," Margo continued, "purely by chance, I had the opportunity to meet Mr. and Mrs. Fitzpatrick."

"Had you met them prior to your dinner date with Mr. Turner?"

"Yes. I met up with an old girlfriend from college while I was in town. We had lunch at the Balboa Bay Club. Mrs. Fitzpatrick was sitting directly behind me. We hadn't met before then. She overheard my conversation regarding Annie's funeral. Mrs. Fitzpatrick introduced me to her husband. I've kept in touch with both of them since that afternoon. Mrs. Fitzpatrick has been kind enough to send photographs of Annie and Jamey to me. They've welcomed me into their family. I regret the years of my not knowing my daughter or her pain or her struggle."

I had heard enough. "Oh, please," I said, mocking her.

"Mr. Turner, do not interrupt this court," Judge Harcourt said in a sharp tone.

I sat back in the chair, folded my arms and told myself to keep my mouth shut.

"Ms. Evans," Jonas said, "if I may speak for the court, your testimony leaves one issue unanswered. DNA proves Mr. Turner's paternity. From the results of the investigation and the psychological evaluation of Jamey Fitzpatrick and as the Fitzpatricks' attorney, at this point I see no other recourse but to award the child to his grandfather, Mr. Turner."

Rob looked at his lawyer with an expression of astonishment and anger and said, "What the hell are you doing?"

Jonas ignored Rob and continued his questioning. "Please tell the court why you believe that Mr. and Mrs. Fitzpatrick should have guardianship of your grandson."

"This is exactly why I am here today. I do not believe that Mr. and Mrs. Fitzpatrick should be awarded guardianship of Jamey."

Rob erupted from his chair. "What?" he screamed at Margo. "That is not what you told me on the telephone."

"Mr. Fitzpatrick, sit down," Judge Harcourt ordered.

Jonas whispered to Fitzpatrick, "What is this about?"

"The bitch is lying! She and I have never had a conversation," he said to Jonas loud enough for the court to hear.

"Mr. Fitzpatrick, I will not warn you again," Judge Harcourt threatened. "Continue Ms. Evans."

"Rob is a smooth talking lawyer. He begged me to lie about Jack's paternity. He told me that it was the only way he could win this case."

"You lying bitch!" Rob shoved Jonas' notebook onto the floor; torn sheets from his legal pad peppered the carpet.

"Mr. Fitzpatrick, you have already been warned in my court. Sit down and shut up. You are in contempt of this court."

"The contempt in this court, Your Honor, is this mockery and conspiracy to permit my grandson to live among lying perversion. My wife agrees with me. He looked directly at Peg and said to her, "Tell the court that Ms. Evans is lying."

Peg shook her head refusing her husband.

"You're just like the rest of these pathetic morons," Rob groaned.

Anticipating Rob's intentions, the bailiff stood guard a few feet from where Jonas and Rob were sitting and waited for Judge Harcourt's decision.

Kevin remained silent. He panned the courtroom, glanced at Margo, then Rob and then Peg. He scribbled a note for me to read, "Hold onto your butt!"

"Bailiff, remove Mr. Fitzpatrick from this court and escort him to the holding cell," Judge Harcourt instructed him.

The bailiff grabbed Rob's arm. Rob jerked himself free from the bailiff's grip and ignored Judge Harcourt's order. Chastising Peg, he finished, "You'd sell me off to benefit your whining need for family."

Judge Harcourt rose abruptly from the bench. "Mr. Fitzpatrick, how many times must I tell you to shut your mouth?"

The bailiff paused at the door. Rob turned around to face Judge Harcourt. Repressing his heated anger, he listened to her. "When you believe, Mr. Fitzpatrick that you have calmed down and can apologize to this court for your behavior I will allow you to return to these proceedings. Until then, we have a testimony to consider."

The bailiff escorted Rob out of the courtroom. An immediate hush swarmed the chamber. The court reporter's keys had quieted. Peg held back the hurt that her husband had shared with the court. She raised her cupped hands to her lips; tears pooled in the corners of her eyes. She swallowed her husband's public insult and with one finger wiped the tears from her cheeks.

Rob's loathsome display toward his wife stifled the courtroom voices. The court reporter's eyes traced Rob's every move as he exited the chamber, her jaw, suspended, the memory in her fingers recorded every word. Margo brushed the long sides of her hair away from her face then shook her head until her hair rested again on her shoulders. Her hands began to tremble; she clasped them together to steady her shaking. Her expression, disquieted from the drama, left her vulnerable.

Margo addressed the bench. "Your Honor, I would like an opportunity to clear up this whole matter."

"I wish you would, Ms. Evans," Judge Harcourt sighed.

"After several conversations with Mr. Fitzpatrick it became clear to me that he was grasping at anything to prevent Jack from keeping Jamey. I saw him as my opportunity to make things right with Jack." She looked right at me. "It was never my intention to hurt you, Jack. I know how much Jamey means to you." Margo then turned her attention to Judge Harcourt. "I hid my intentions from Peg, Mrs. Fitzpatrick." She then turned her head and spoke directly to Peg. "Your husband fed right into my plan. There were no other men that I had been romantic with before Jack. I knew that he was the father of my baby. Convincing your husband of Jack's false paternity was too easy. Oh, Jack hurt my feelings all right, but Jack's loyalty and soul go deeper than his words or his actions. Peg, I set your husband up and perjured myself to prove to Jack how sorry I am for the pain and loss he has suffered because of me. It was the only way I knew to convince Jack to let me back into his life and to let me be a part of my grandson's life."

"Ms. Evans, perjury in a court of law is a punishable crime. Are you aware of that?" Judge Harcourt asked.

"Yes, Your Honor. My attorney in New York is aware of my intentions."

Peg rose slowly from her chair and addressed the judge, "Your Honor, I would like to speak on behalf of Ms. Evans."

"Mrs. Fitzpatrick, I will allow it."

"Thank you, Your Honor. Ms. Evans speaks the truth. Long before the court had received Ms. Evans' letter I had overheard my husband's telephone conversation with her. Rob thought that I had gone to the market. I listened in on their conversation from the phone in my office. For several weeks, prior to that day they had communicated with one another four or five times. She made it clear to my husband of her desire to have a relationship with her grandson, Jamey. I was not aware of Ms. Evans' intentions until I had eavesdropped onto their conversation. I sneaked out of the house before Rob hung up. I kept their little conspiracy to myself. My husband needs to learn that he cannot control all that he touches. I do love my husband and apologize for his behavior. But today, this is not about my husband, it's about my grandson."

Peg's stare fell on my eyes; her eyes were drained, her burden released. Jonas placed his hand on top of hers, a comforting gesture he hadn't expressed to her before then. Margo remained still. The court reporter paused from the stillness of unspoken words in the courtroom. Judge Harcourt interrupted the silence. "Before I announce my decision, I believe that we all could benefit from a recess. We'll break for lunch and resume at 1:30, an hour and a half from now. Let me remind you again that this is a closed hearing."

The bailiff assisted Margo from the witness stand. Wavering against her cane, she stepped forward and with her lips still poised said to me, "Jack, I am so sorry for everything."

"I am too, Margo."

"Take a good look at the photograph. There's something missing," she said.

Jonas assisted Margo out of the courtroom. Peg reached for my hand. "I'm glad this is over, Jack" she said.

The chambers had emptied. I tucked the photograph next to my pack of smokes in the breast pocket of my jacket. Kevin laid his hand on my shoulder. "Margo put herself on the line for you," he said.

I nodded my head and breathed a sigh. I needed a cigarette and some fresh air. "She put herself on the line because she's alone. Her little drama did not convince me. It's about her, not Jamey and me."

"God, you're a hard ass. Let it go, Jack. You're wrong about this. You need to let her back in."

"Why should I?"

"Whether you like it or not, Jack, she was Annie's mother. These hearings are about Jamey, not about your cross you bear. Margo is Jamey's grandmother as well; you cannot change that. You need to allow your grandson to know her."

His sermon preached the truth but to forgive Margo was hard for me.

Kevin and I strolled through the courthouse parking lot; my memories wandered. I tried to light a cigarette but with each flick of the disposable lighter a light breeze blew the flame out. "I'll have one of those," Kevin said and reached for my pack. His casual stride forced me to slow down. Much like the parking lot, my head had been fogged in. It was June at the coast where the sun hid above the morning fog until mid afternoon. But through the fog I noticed the teenage boy I had seen earlier dragging his feet behind his father; the bill of his cap was tucked into the rear pocket of his baggy jeans. The boy's earrings were missing. I watched as his father waved his arms in anger; his son slouched down in the front seat of the car. I imagined the father's disappointment he must have felt regarding his son as they drove off into the fog.

Side-by-side Kevin and I strolled along the sidewalk in front of the courthouse. As I drew the photograph that Margo had given to me from my pocket I remembered the unfettered friendship that Kevin, William, Margo and I had spawned years ago. But Margo's testimony that morning had cut through time and grabbed me right in the chest. She wanted to start over. Margo was right; we had had the world by the ass.

"Jack, can I buy you lunch?" Kevin generously offered.

"I'm not really hungry, Kevin."

"I am. Join me anyway."

Three-piece pinstriped suits crowded the café across the street from the courthouse. Martinis and green olives substituted hors d' oeuvres among the lawyer lunch mob. Beyond the dining room, female attorneys joined their male associates for a cigar while discussing litigation they had argued that morning in court. Dark oak framed the leather-upholstered banquettes and coordinating chairs which complimented the white linens that draped the dining room tables. Above each table dimmed lights competed with the glare from the filtered sunlight that beamed through the solid glass windows. Kevin stopped to bullshit with an associate from Steinman, Steinman and Becker, their attire cloned, even down to the Gucci loafers. Rubbing elbows with the legal elite took on new meaning for me as I wedged my way through the chatter being careful not to crush someone's open toed heels. The hostess seated me before Kevin finished his dissertation.

Kevin's 6' 3" build towered above the clique of hungry lawyers. Searching the busy tables to find me, he waded through the gossiping mass. "There you are," he said. "What do you think of this place?"

"Busy . . . lots of booze flying about."

"Lawyers, martinis, and lunch, a second year law school requirement."

"It's a wonder you guys even graduate," I said flippantly.

"We all managed, somehow."

"There aren't any waitresses in this place," I mused, changing the subject.

"You noticed. All the food servers are young, good-looking law students . . . all guys."

Our waiter finished taking the order at the table next to ours. He flipped his order pad to the next page and scooted past the crowded aisle to our table. "Mr. Stevens, nice to see you again," the waiter said.

"Good to see you too, Ethan. This is my friend, Jack Turner."

Ethan reached across the table to shake my hand. "Pleasure to meet you, sir. Would you gentlemen care for cocktails?"

"Not for me thanks," I said. "I'll have a raspberry iced tea, no lemon."

"Make that two, Ethan," Kevin added.

"Shall I bring your beverages first, or would you like to order?" the waiter asked.

"We'll go ahead and order now. We have to be back in court before 1:30. What are you having, Jack?" he asked.

"I'll have the Club, no onions, hold the fries, and be generous with the coleslaw."

"And for you, sir," the waiter asked ready to take Kevin's order.

"I'll have a Rueben sandwich. Nothing else, thank you."

"Gentlemen, I'll ask the kitchen to rush this. Anything else I can bring you?"

"I think we're good," Kevin said. "By the way, Ethan, how's law school going?"

"I graduated two weeks ago. I'm scheduled to take the Bar in November."

"Good for you. Good luck, man."

I lifted my glasses from the bridge of my nose and massaged the permanent indentations, a gift from my specs. I squinted through the bifocal lenses; Kevin's face became a blur. Ethan brought the iced teas and said to us, "Your order will be right up."

Kevin draped his napkin over his knee, rested his elbow on the table and pinched his bottom lip between his thumb and forefinger. He asked me, "Have you heard from William, lately?"

"I got a letter from him a couple days ago. He sent airfare for Jamey, Maria and me to spend Christmas with him this year. It may end up being just Jamey and me. I suspect Maria will be getting married soon."

"She's serious over this Henry," he said, surprised.

"She has been for a lot of years. She kept it a secret from me. And you? Have you heard from William?"

"Actually, I'm flying out in July to visit with him. I owe him one. I'm taking him to the Boston Pops Fourth of July concert on the Charles River."

"I understand that his mother is still there," I said.

"Oh yeah, she's a trip. However, I am not one of her favorite people," Kevin moaned.

"What did you do to piss her off?"

"I left her little boy."

I didn't say a word.

He continued, "The Fourth of July, that's your birthday, isn't it?"

"Fifty-three big ones! Henry has invited Jamey and me to his summer place up in the wine country. Jamey will have a blast. So will Maria; she'll be driving Henry's car. She doesn't know about this yet, but for her birthday in September, Henry is giving her a beautifully restored vintage Mercedes Gullwing. Fucking car will be awesome. I only have a single car garage so guess who will park in the driveway then?"

"Grampa?"

"You got it!" Jamey and his Spiderman T-shirt flashed through my head. 'Kevin, if Rob and Peg prevail today I'll need to ask for their permission to take Jamey on the trip."

"They are not going to prevail today," he assured me.

"We don't know that." I rearranged the salt and peppershakers for the fifth time. "I wish they'd hurry with our lunch. We've only forty minutes left."

* * *

Kevin and I passed through the court security at 1:25 p.m. The bailiff had unlocked the courtroom a few minutes early. Rob had returned from his temporary incarceration. Margo hobbled to her seat. Kevin and I resumed our seats as Judge Harcourt entered the chamber. "Welcome back," she said. "I see Mr. Fitzpatrick has returned to these proceedings. Have you anything to say to this court?"

Rob pushed his chair away from the desk and stood before the judge. He cleared his throat, then dangled the keys in his slack's pocket and addressed the judge, "Your Honor, thank you for allowing me to return. Not only do I owe this court an apology for my inappropriate behavior, but I want to applaud my wife for her integrity." He then turned to Margo. "Ms. Evans, please accept my apology for my outburst of foul disrespect."

Margo nodded and mouthed, "Thank you."

The tension in Judge Harcourt's face relaxed. "Thank you, Mr. Fitzpatrick, you may have a seat. Mr. Stevens, at this time do you wish to cross-examine the witness, Ms. Evans?"

"No, Your Honor, we rest our case."

"Very well then. I won't drag this out. My judgment is for the defendant. Mr. Stevens, I trust you will draft the order awarding sole guardianship of the minor to Mr. Turner."

"Yes, Your Honor. I will have these documents on your desk by tomorrow afternoon."

"Thank you, Mr. Stevens. Before we adjourn I have a letter from Jamey that all of you need to hear:

She read aloud:

> *Dear Dokter Mikel:*
>
> *I like our talks in yor ofus You are a nice dokter You say nice stuff about my Grampa Jack He is my best frend Wen I am sad Grampa Jack makes me laff Wen Grampa Jack is sad I make him laff Grampa Rob nevr laffs He needs a frend like my Grampa Jack Gramma Peg is like my mom She is smart and prity She makes good choklit chip cookies I love my Gramma I no all about cort The juj is the law We do wat she says I want to be with all my Grampas and Grammas I want to live with my Grampa Jack He noz my speshul thots. Your frend Jamey*

"Out of the mouth of babes comes the wisdom of innocence," Judge Harcourt said. She paused for a moment then continued, "Mr. Fitzpatrick and Ms. Evans, regarding your admitted perjuries, I will inform the DA's office this afternoon. They will determine which course of action to take with each of you. This court is adjourned."

Jonas reached across the table to shake Kevin's hand. "You prevailed again, Stevens."

"The judge made the right decision," Kevin replied. He gathered his notes, locked them in his briefcase and turned to me and said, "Jack, I'll wait for you outside."

Rob followed Jonas out of the courtroom. Peg and I stayed behind. Margo, troubled by her hip, paused a few feet from us. "Peg," she said, "thank you."

"I think all of us have some starting over to do," Peg admitted. "If you two will excuse me, I need to catch up with my husband."

Peg took the stairs to the first floor. Once she was out of sight Rob barged out of the men's room. Drying his hands on his trousers, he brushed against my shoulders as I walked passed him. "Turner," he called out to me like some high school thug getting ready to pounce.

I stopped, but refused to turn around to acknowledge the condescending tone in his voice.

"Watch your back, old man," he said.

Kevin's look told me to hold back my anger. He turned his head toward Rob and said to him, "Watch your mouth, Mr. Lawyer. I'll remember your little threat."

"You do that, hot shot," Rob fired back and then brushed against my shoulder again as he passed between the wall and me.

"He's just pissed off," I said to Kevin.

"Maybe. We'll see."

"Let it go, Kevin. He has Peg to contend with now."

Margo moved slowly toward me. "What was that all about?" she asked.

"Rob doesn't lose graciously," I said. With her free hand she hugged me, her cheek pressed to mine. "Congratulations, Jack. Jamey's a lucky boy."

"And I'm a lucky lawyer," Kevin boasted, butting in. "Jack, I'll meet you in the parking lot. Margo, nice to see you again."

"The pleasure was all mine, Kevin," Margo said and then reached out to shake his hand. Kevin tucked his briefcase under his arm because carrying it by the handle annoyed him.

"Margo, let me walk you to your car," I said.

"Jack, let's take the elevator, I'm not ready for stairs yet."

Once the elevator doors closed a hush enveloped us in the cramped space. I broke the silence and asked Margo, "How long will you be in town?"

"For as long as I need to be."

"Can you come to the house for dinner Saturday?"

"My calendar is open."

"Come early. You have a grandson to meet."

I caught up with Kevin in the parking lot. He was leaning against my Cruiser and smoking a cigarette. Margo drove off in a convertible with the top down.

"Where did you get a cigarette?" I asked Kevin.

"You left your pack at my house. Care for one?"

"I don't think so."

"You and I have much to celebrate. We prevailed over the Fitzpatricks, and the other good news . . . William and I are getting back together."

Chapter Fifteen

K evin's news had punched me right in the gut. I had no room left in my gut or my life for jealousy, but if William had been standing on my front porch that afternoon I would have begged him to spend the rest of his life with me. But I needed to let go of him. Jamey needed a grandfather, not an old man wallowing in his own pity.

Peg had hit it on the head. It wasn't about me or Rob or Peg or William or even Margo. It was all about Jamey. In fact, that Wednesday evening, Jamey had planned dinner, a take-out pepperoni pizza, heavy on the olives accompanied with a litre of crème soda; his choice; my heartburn.

Summer vacation had begun for the two of us. That first week Jamey and I broke in a new pair of six-dollar drugstore flip-flops, casual beach bum attire and a summer wardrobe necessity. After one stroll along the beach their stiff newness had aged to tacky chic. The combination of tromping through sun-bleached sand and salty tide pools had faded the black rubber soles and loosened the nylon straps to a comfortable fit, much to Willow's chagrin. Willow had traded flip-flops for sneakers, a chew toy he could really sink his teeth into. He snoozed in bed cuddled up next to Jamey until 7:30 in the morning. My body thanked him for the additional two hours of tranquility. As a result, I embraced an old habit; I stayed up until midnight burning every light in the house, hammering out my column.

That June summer evening, Jamey, Maria, and I cozied up around the patio table in the backyard. A sweet breeze blew from the East, balmy and warm. Paper towels, brawny enough to stand up to thick pizza sauce flapped in the wind beneath the weight of plastic forks and knives. One paper towel launched air born; Willow attacked. The quilted pillows etched in the paper towels smudged with pizza sauce were no match for a puppy. Willow had a ball shredding the paper towel from one end of the backyard to the next. His bark cracked with each effort like a teenage boy whose voice is beginning to change. Maria lit citronella candles to ward off mosquitoes. One bloodsucker buzzed near my ear. I lit another candle, burned the tip of my finger with the lighter and then freshened our plastic tumblers with more crème soda. I squashed the buzzing varmint to smithereens.

A single slice of pizza flopped onto my forearm; I licked the sauce from my wrist. Jamey beat Maria to the punch when he tossed me the paper towels and said to me, "Here, Grampa, catch!"

"Thank you," I said then tossed the roll back to him. "Tear me off one or two, will ya?" I purposefully waited until Jamey had a mouth full of pizza crust before I asked him, "So, Tiger, what do you want for your birthday?"

He swung his feet beneath the chair, anxiously rocked his buns back and forth and chewed his pizza with the speed of a chipmunk. Swallowing, he blurted out, "I want Play Station 2 and the *Harry Potter and the Chamber of Secrets* video game."

"That's a tall order."

"Johnny got it already. It's way cool, Grampa."

"Play Station 2, huh?"

"It's awesome."

"If you say so," I agreed. Begging for pepperoni, Willow sat at attention between my feet. Each time Maria turned her head I sneaked him a piece. "Jamey, Gramma Peg told me you want to go visit," I told him.

"Yeah."

"She's coming over Sunday to pick you up for a couple of days. You want to take Willow with you?"

"Grampa Rob said no. When he's big and potty trained then Grampa says it's okay."

"That sounds reasonable enough. Your Gramma and Grampa and I talked to the judge today. You wanna know what she said?"

"Okay," he answered as he stuffed a second slice of pizza into his mouth, dragging cheese across his chin.

"The judge decided that you and me are gonna be buds for the rest of our lives. You're gonna live with me."

Jamey jumped into my lap and marked my shirt sleeves with pizza sauce handprints. "Excellent!" he confirmed with excitement and conviction as only a six-year-old can. He pushed his nose against mine and smudged the lenses of my glasses. Our shared commitment to one another remained true until my dying day.

I strained to see him through my foggy lenses and asked him, "Know what else the judge did today?"

"I don't know."

"She read your letter, the one you wrote to Dr. Aldrich, out loud to all of us."

He sat straight up on my lap and asked me, "Did she like it?"

"Let me put it this way," I said to him, "one day, I am convinced that you are gonna set the world on fire. I think you're gonna be a writer, like your old Grampa."

"I already know that. It's here . . . herd . . ."

"Hereditary," Maria jumped in.

"That's it, hereditary," he agreed.

"Mr. Jack, tell Jamey about Saturday," Maria encouraged me.

"Oh, yeah. Jamey, an old friend of mine is coming over to have dinner with us."

"Okay," he said and grabbed another slice of pizza.

"Guess who's coming?" I asked.

"Maria told me already," he informed me.

I slid my specs to the tip of my nose and stared over the wire rims at Maria. She pretended to be innocent, tilted her head back and gazed at the evening sky.

"She's the lady in the big white car," Jamey said.

"She flew all the way from New York just to see you. She's your Gramma, Gramma Margo."

"Nah, uh, I only have one Gramma, Gramma Peg."

I had hoped that Maria would have stepped in to help me explain this one. She lit another citronella candle and eased back into her patio chair and then instinctively began swatting at the hovering insects.

"Is she your wife?" Jamey asked.

"No . . ."

"Then she's not my Gramma."

"Jamey, a long time ago, back in the olden days, Margo and I had a baby together, your mom. We were very young like your mom was. Margo wanted to move to New York."

"You got a divorce," he said, his reasoning keen and astute for only six.

"I suppose you could say that. I stayed in Los Angeles with your mom when she was just a baby."

"How come she never came for Christmases?"

"I'm not really sure, but I'll bet if you ask her she'll tell you why."

I copped out to my own grandson. Normally, I could explain anything to him and he'd buy it; but this time he was on his own. Margo was about to meet her match.

"One favor from you, little man," I said. "Before Saturday, I want you to pick up your room and hide your sneakers from Willow."

Jamey rolled his eyes, blew a sigh of "I have to do everything, Grampa" when the phone rang. "I'll get it," Jamey said and rolled his eyes one last time, a jab meant only for me and then darted into the kitchen. "It's for you, Grampa," he shouted through the kitchen window, "It's Uncle William."

"Bring the phone out here," I said. Jamey leaped out of the back porch and made a perfect landing on the edge of the lawn without dropping the phone.

"Thank you, Jamey." I wiped a glob of pizza sauce from the phone's receiver. "William, I thought maybe you lost my phone number. I've been waiting for you to call."

"Congratulations! Justice has prevailed again. What are you guys doing to celebrate?"

"Pizza and crème soda," I moaned, then burped, "excuse me," I apologized.

"Sounds like Jamey planned dinner and sounds like you need a Pepcid AC."

"Carbonation . . . does it every time. Have you talked to Kevin?"

"Just got off the phone with him. Some courtroom drama Margo played out, huh?"

"I think drama is probably the right word. So what's this I hear about you and Kevin?"

"I guess Kevin spilled the beans. He's coming home." I scratched my beard and reached for my smokes. Five or ten seconds passed in silence and then William asked, "Jack, you there?"

"Oh, yeah, sorry. That's great." I choked back the jealousy that welled in my voice. "When does the happy reunion begin?"

"August, I'm flying out on the 8th. I'll be there a couple of weeks to help Kevin sell his condo and pack. We'll get together, you and me. There are some things I need to discuss with you."

"Like what?"

"It can wait until then. Don't fret about it, it's no big deal."

Rather than press the issue, I asked, "How's your mom?"

"She left yesterday to go back to LA. I love her, but she drives me crazy. When she comes to visit it's usually for months. This time she only stayed a couple of weeks, a first."

I reached for my cigarette; it stuck to the bottom of the ashtray; dripping candle wax had squelched the cherry. I fired up the nasty butt and blew a cloud of smoke over the phone.

"You're smoking again, aren't you, Jack?"

"Only when I'm upset."

"You've nothing to be upset about today, am I right?"

"William, you're always right."

"That's right. Okay, good-lookin'. I'm meeting some friends for dinner. I'll call you in a few days. Give Maria and Jamey a huge hug from me. Love ya."

"Love you too." I butted my cigarette out, citronella and menthol, not a pleasant smoke, so I lit another one.

Mulling over my conversation with William had interrupted my sleep most of the night. I'd doze off, wake up to go to the bathroom, toss and turn in the bed, doze off for thirty minutes and then back to the bathroom again. Too much crème soda.

*   *   *

Three days later, Johnny's mom dropped her son off at the house to play with Jamey. Sleep and I were not getting along very well. Saturday morning cartoons without ample sleep called for a double latte. "Jamey," I said, "instead of watching cartoons, why don't you show Johnny your birthday present."

"Oh, yeah, I almost forgot," he said.

Johnny ignored the Transformer battle blaring on the TV. "What did you get?" he asked Jamey.

"Play Station 2," his tone matter-of-fact.

"Excellent!" Johnny beamed.

They nearly knocked each other over in the hallway to be first to Jamey's bedroom. A herd of charging buffalo made less racket than these two animals. I punched the remote and terminated the Transformers. What a pushover I was. I wanted Jamey to have his birthday present before we went to Northern California with Maria and Henry.

The two high tech wizards tossed a coin to see who had first dibs on the only controller. "Johnny, heads or tails?" Jamey asked.

"Tails."

"Heads! You lose. I go first," Jamey triumphed. The battle between them began; Play Station 2 had initiated the challenge. They played for two hours, immersed in Pottermania until I interrupted them, "Sorry, guys, it's time to take Johnny home."

"Grampa . . . please, just ten more minutes, please, please. I'm kicking Johnny's butt!"

"You wish," Johnny exclaimed.

"Okay, guys. Ten minutes, then we wrap it up."

While I drove Johnny home that afternoon, Maria straightened Jamey's bed and played a video game. Jamey had picked up his room as well as a six-year-old can, the comforter, cock-eyed, the down pillow tossed at random. Later that evening, Maria boasted that she had helped Harry Potter destroy the snake. She also told me that Willow had fought his own battle in the back yard away from her evil eye. He had sneaked one of my sneakers from under my bed and chewed the shoestrings to shreds.

Evidently, Margo had arrived at the house before Jamey and I got back. We pulled into the driveway behind her convertible. Willow tore ass up the driveway to welcome us home; puppy naps are short and intermittent and easily distracted. The doggy door that I had installed in my office's sliding door was a brilliant idea, but brilliant only when I remembered to disengage the lock panel. Scaling the porch with Willow at his heels, Jamey jumped three steps at a time. He ruffled Willow's ears then turned his attention toward me. "Come on slow poke," he teased.

"Hold your britches, buster. Help me carry these groceries in," I said.

He leaped down the porch steps just as he had scaled them. I handed him the gallon of milk. I carried two grocery bags, one under each arm. Jamey flung the screen door open, wide and hard and leaped over the front door threshold and then into the living room. Before it slammed shut, I caught the door with my butt, one of the grocery bags slid down my side. "Jamey, here, take this bag before I drop it."

"May I help?" Margo asked.

"Margo, you're early," I said surprised to see her.

"And you're right on time. My how some things do change," she said with a playful dig. "Let me take that bag; Jamey's hands are full," she insisted.

Margo leaned her cane against the fireplace mantel. She moved one step forward and accidentally nudged the bottom of the cane with her shoe. The solid teak staff fell to the hearth. Its marble crown chipped one of the caramel veined fieldstone tiles. "Jack, I am so sorry. This cane is such a nuisance," she apologized.

Jamey scurried to rescue the cane and dropped the gallon of milk onto the floor. The plastic top popped off flooding the hardwood floor under a river of non-fat milk.

"Oops!" Jamey apologized. Willow lapped up the creeping milk.

I dropped the grocery bags onto the couch and shouted, "Willow, get out of there!" He ran to the kitchen and left a trail of white paw prints that faded with each step on Maria's polished hardwood floors. I snagged several beach towels from the hall linen closet to sop up the mess. Margo covered her mouth with her free hand to stop her laughter. Her other hand still clutched the photograph. Her laughter grew louder infecting Jamey. "I give up, you guys," I said, cracking up at the vaudeville circumstance. The three of us keeled over and cackled like a bunch of silly old hens.

Holding two espresso cups mounded with creamy foam, Maria stood at the doorway of the dining room. Interrupting, she said, "You could have invited me to the party." She stepped lightly across the floor to avoid the spill and offered the latte to Margo.

"Thank you, Maria. I hope there's enough milk for later," Margo said.

"Where's mine?" I complained.

"Here, Mr. Jack, take mine, I'll make another. By the way, when you're done cleaning up the mess be sure to wipe up the paw prints."

I snatched up the bags of groceries and tossed a dry towel to Jamey. "Bulls eye!" It landed on his head. "Okay, Tiger finish up here and don't forget the paw prints. Margo, follow me to the kitchen, it's safer in there."

After Jamey cleaned up Willow's milk tracks he sat down at the kitchen table across from Margo and stared at her without uttering a sound. Margo was not one to be beaten at any game so she stared back at him, also without uttering a sound. While they stared each other down, I fired up the barbeque for the tri-tip, a tender, succulent cut of beef that had been marinating in the refrigerator for thirty-six hours. Maria stirred the sauce simmering on the stove releasing the aromas of Garlic, Thyme and Oregano. My stomach growled interrupting the silence. "All these good smells make me hungry," I said as I sampled the sauce with my fingers.

Memories of Margo tumbled in my brain; words stuck in my throat. She sat only two feet from a hug that I fought to share with her. I had once loved this woman, embraced her, listened to her bullshit in college, and choked in our apartment from her chain smoking. She had been my best friend. My jumbled thoughts began to unscramble. "Margo, thanks for coming," I said.

"Thanks for inviting me."

Jamey scooted his chair away from the table and marched over to Margo. He grabbed the bull by the horns and introduced himself. "I'm Jamey. Grampa says you're my Gramma. How come you walk with a cane?"

"Jamey, mind your manners," I said.

"It's okay, Jack," Margo interrupted, the tone in her voice permissive. "Jamey, I walk with a cane because I had an operation on my hip."

"Do you have a scar?"

"A doozy."

Jamey opened his mouth wide and stretched the corners of his lips with his middle fingers and mumbled, "I had my tonsils out when I was five. See."

"Yep, they're gone, not a tonsil in your throat," she confirmed.

"Did your operation hurt?" he asked.

"Not until it was over."

"Me too. My throat hurt for a long time and then it went away. Can I see your cane?"

"Sure you can," she said then tilted the cane toward him.

Jamey balanced his palm on the crown of the cane, tilted it to the left and then to the right. He inhaled one long breath and then handed the cane back to Margo. "If you're my Gramma how come you never came to visit me before?" he asked.

"Sometimes, Jamey, people get wrapped up in their own lives," she explained.

"Wrapped up like a present?" he asked with curiosity.

"Yes, just like a present. I was trapped inside a box covered with pretty paper and couldn't see the good things waiting outside. From up in heaven your mom opened the box that I was trapped in . . . and you . . . you are my present." She tickled Jamey's ribs and tickled my soul. Maria sipped her coffee and smiled at me.

"You wanna see my birthday present? Grampa gave it to me."

"Lead the way."

"Easy, Jamey," I cautioned, "your Gramma can't run as fast as you can."

Jamey assisted Margo down the hallway and into his bedroom. He cradled her good elbow under both of his hands to steady her walk. Cub Scouts of America would have been proud. It cracked me up, this pint sized little boy caring for his invalid grandmother, a grandmother he had just met. Waiting near the hallway, I leaned against the door to eavesdrop on their exchange of wits and video prowess.

Jamey sat on the edge of his bed and switched on his 13" color TV. The set was an electronic dinosaur I had moved from Los Angeles to Laguna twelve years ago. It crowded the center of Jamey's desk; the connection of his birthday present to the outdated video screen permitted a cramped writing workspace for his homework, letters and doodling. Pre-remote control, the plastic channel selector had vanished twelve years ago somewhere along the 405 Freeway during the move to the beach house. Jamey stored a pair of pliers in his desk drawer for changing channels. Channel surfing in my house belonged to the head of household, Maria; she controlled the remote in the living room. But I had put my foot down, no cable allowed in the bedroom; channel three sufficed Jamey's video games.

Margo and Jamey wedged themselves hip to hip at the foot of the single bed. Poised with the game controls on his lap, Jamey demonstrated the intricacies involved in the wrist and thumb action for Margo. "Gramma, I only have one controller. I'll go first and show you how to do it."

I tiptoed down the hallway to peek in on them and heard Jamey break the ice with his Gramma.

"My mom was sick. She didn't have a operation. Were you sick too?" he asked.

"In a way, yes I was."

"Did your Grampa take care of you?"

"No, Jamey, my Grampa has been gone a long time."

"Where did he go?"

"When I was about your age, my Grampa was on a ship in the Atlantic Ocean. He was in the Navy. He got very sick. I never saw him again."

"Did he die and go to heaven?"

"Yes . . . ," she paused for just a moment then continued, "he did, Jamey."

"Your Grampa is in heaven with my mom and my dad and Willow."

"I thought Willow was here."

"Oh, he's my new Willow. He's a boy. The other Willow died in our backyard. She was a girl. Willow loved my Grampa. I hope my Grampa never goes away."

"I think your Grampa is gonna be around for a very long time, long enough to see you become a daddy someday."

"No way!"

"Way!" she bantered back.

The smell of smoking mesquite and grilled tri-tip drifted through the house. I slipped off my sneakers and then in my stocking feet silently left Gramma and her grandson to their techno meeting of the minds. I dropped my sneakers onto the office floor and slipped through the slider to flip dinner before it scorched.

*   *   *

A couple of hours later the four of us lazed around the kitchen table, overstuffed and refused Maria's temptation.

"There's cheesecake. Baked it fresh this morning," Maria tried to tempt us as she carried the decadent dessert to the table.

"Maria, you're a genius. And dinner . . ." Margo kissed her fingertips and extended the gesture to Maria then said to her, "but I couldn't swallow another bite."

"Mr. Jack? You never turn down dessert."

"I'm all full up, Maria."

Jamey wiped his fork with his napkin and settled back into his chair. "I'll have some, Maria."

Maria sliced two wedges of creamy white chocolate cheesecake cradled in Maria's special pecan crust. "I'll join you Jamey," she said.

"What I need is to move around a bit," Margo said as she stretched her leg and inhaled a long, deep breath. "Jack, let's go for a walk."

"What about your hip?" I asked.

"The stretch will do it well. Just to the end of the block and back."

"Okay with you, Jamey?" I asked, not wanting him to feel left out.

"Grampa, I'm eating cheesecake."

"I can see that." I brushed my chin with my finger hoping he'd get the clue. "Graham cracker crust is all over your chin, Mr. Neat Nick."

Jamey wiped the crumbs from his chin with his napkin, ignored me and savored each bite of Maria's best.

"Margo, you want me to grab you a sweater?" I asked.

"No, the air is delightful."

"Okay, hang on a minute. Jamey, make sure Willow goes outside to go potty. Your Gramma and I won't be long."

I stole a cardigan from the hall closet just in case.

Margo carefully placed one foot at a time as we descended the porch steps together. "You're so blessed, Jack," she said. "What a wonderful kid Jamey is."

"He's somethin' alright. He'll wear you out if you're not one step ahead of him. I don't remember it being so tiring when I was twenty-five. So, Margo, how long are you gonna be in town?"

"I fly back to New York tomorrow."

"Cancel your flight. Stay until Jamey's birthday, the fourteenth of July."

"I'd love to but . . ."

"No buts. Henry has invited us to spend the Fourth of July at his summer place up in the wine country. Come with us. Jamey would love it. I'd love it."

"So would I, but my hip; it's screaming for physical therapy. I have an appointment Monday. I'll be back in October. Jamey invited me; we're going to trick-or-treat together."

Margo rested at the corner. The discomfort in her hip began to slow her down. She furrowed her brow; she was hurting. The unforgiving lines of middle age creased the corners of her eyes, her only sign of fading youth. The smooth unwrinkled skin of her hands had resisted the cruelty of time. "Jack, tell me something," she said.

"Alright."

"Kevin's here. Where's William?"

"They split up last Christmas. William still lives in Maine. We talk on the phone every week."

"You're still in love with him, aren't you?"

"I never stopped loving him."

"Does he know that?"

"I'm sure he must."

"So what are you gonna do about it? You gonna spend the rest of your life alone?"

"I'm not alone. I have Jamey, good friends; it's a good life."

"Tell him, Jack. Get on the horn, no better yet, get on an airplane to Maine and tell William how you feel about him."

"It's too late. He and Kevin are getting back together. William is flying out in August to help Kevin get his affairs in order. Sell the condo, pack and leave."

"Take it from someone who's been there. Take the risk."

"I don't know, Margo. My fight has fizzled. My life is here."

The sidewalk began to incline. A single sprawling eucalyptus root, gnarled and thick from time had unearthed one cement slab of the sidewalk, an exhilarating jump for skateboarders but dangerous to a tenuous step. Margo caught her heel on the uneven sidewalk. She broke her fall with her cane.

"You alright?" I asked.

"Just a hitch in my get-along; I'll be fine." She clutched my arm. The sweet smell of lavender in her hair drew my head closer to her.

"Jack, help an old lady back to the house."

"Okay, Granny."

Arm in arm we moseyed down the block. "Margo, why now, after all these years, you and me, here?" I asked.

"I can't twitch my nose and change who you are. There was a time when I would have sold my soul for your love."

I must have had sucker written across my forehead. Margo was slick, slick as any three-piece suit lawyer with a Harvard degree, martini lunches and smoking cigars with the big boys. She had played with me like a hooked fish when she was on the witness stand and had reeled me in until this final testimony. I wasn't buyin' it; I knew better. Margo's soul was sacred to her and to her alone.

"You had my love once, Margo."

"I wanted more. When I walked out on you and Annie my soul stayed in LA locked inside a funky apartment. You and Jamey gave it back to me today. Jamey . . . he called me Gramma."

"You're right; he did."

Margo's performance at the house had conned Jamey and Maria. I pretended to buy into it, but only for Jamey's sake.

Chapter Sixteen

B y 6:00 a.m., July 2nd, Jamey and I had packed the Cruiser, crated
Willow in the back seat and were headed north climbing California's
Grapevine, the truckers' lifeline in and out of the LA basin. We followed
five car lengths behind Henry's car for four hundred miles along California's
Interstate 5. Maria drove; Henry navigated. I drove the Cruiser; Jamey
popped in five compact discs, three for him and two for me. Random play
helped me to tolerate Jamey's taste in music whenever Karen Carpenter
booted out the last track. Her voice soothed away my pained frown and
restored my temporary hearing loss from some new age rock 'n' roll,
electrified, if-you-were-under-twenty-you-might-recognize-the-band noise.
I continued, with limitations of course, to allow Jamey to make certain
choices. The CD player in the Cruiser, however, had my name engraved on
the select button.

Six-and-a half hours later and one-hundred-eighty miles south of
the Valley of the Moon, California's Central Valley baked under an
unforgiving July sun. The California Aqueduct, the farmers' lifeline for
growing almonds, cotton, lettuce, strawberries and cattle bordered
Interstate 5 like a serpent winding through the desert, an oasis providing
water for Southern California's thirsty swimming pools, golf courses
and dirty cars.

Speeding at seventy-five mph and gaining additional two car
lengths ahead of us, Henry's Mercedes hummed along. I kept checking in

my rear view mirror for California Highway Patrol cars. I called Maria's cell phone. The caller ID must have flashed my name across her mini screen because she answered, "Hello Mr. Jack."

"Maria, slow down you're gonna get us a ticket."

"I'm only doing seventy-five."

"The speed limit is sixty-five, so when the cops pull us over, you can do all of the explaining."

"You are such a worry wart." She slowed down to sixty-five and must have set the cruise control because from then on her speed remained constant.

Jamey changed the CD; I popped three aspirins. "Grampa, I have to go potty," he said.

"Me too. I'll bet Willow could use a patch of grass himself." I rang Maria's cell phone again.

Annoyed, she huffed oozing a sigh into the phone, "Mr. Jack, I am doing the speed limit."

"And a fine job of it at that. Pull off at the next rest stop; we have a boy and his puppy that need to do their business." I passed a green highway sign, 'next rest stop, 20 miles'.

Big rigs and semi's crowded the parking lot of the rest stop. I parked in front of a patch of brown, sparse grass designated for pets. Henry walked Willow. Maria made a beeline for the women's facility while Jamey raced to the men's room with me on his heels. We ran past a family who were enjoying a picnic under the shade of an aging oak tree. Jamey and I had enjoyed our own picnic earlier; in the car we had snacked on corn chips, Dr. Pepper and peanut butter sandwiches. It was a ten hour haul from Laguna Beach to Henry's place in Kenwood, so Maria had brown bagged our lunches for the trip. "No stopping," she said earlier that morning, "except for gas and potty breaks." My Maria, short and bossy.

Jamey put Willow back in his cage. We buckled up and followed Maria and Henry toward Lodi and Highway 12, the scenic route into paradise. The temperature continued to rise as we turned off Interstate 5 and traveled west into the Sonoma wine country. Jamey and I were city slickers. Even though we lived at the beach, tall glass office buildings leased to attorneys, dentists and mortgage brokers lined a twenty mile stretch of coastline from Dana Point Harbor to Corona del Mar. Throughout Orange County one township border blended into the next one, and most days a hazy gray from too many cars, diesel busses, charcoal barbeques and lawn mowers filled the sky. But according to a brochure

I read describing the Valley of the Moon, we had entered God's country, no skyscrapers and no concrete, just acres of wealth waiting to be bottled.

The outside temperature dropped two degrees and the smog-free sky was an endless expanse of opal blue. Highway 12, a two-lane, meandering country road took us through the landscape of rolling hills, either side dressed in a profusion of vineyards. The highway mimicked the gentle rolls and curves of the hillside as we drove through the wine country. I eased up on the gas; we slowed down from forty-five mph to twenty-five. "Jamey, put your Game Boy down. Look out the window; tell me what you see."

"A bunch of little green trees all lined up in a row and blue sky," he said, bored with the view.

"Close enough. Go back to your game."

Focused on the mini screen, Jamey asked, "Grampa, are we gonna be here for my birthday?"

"No, we're going home Monday. Your Grampa Rob and Gramma Peg want to take you to Universal Studios for your birthday."

"Are you gonna come too?" he asked.

"I think I'll wash and wax the Cruiser that day if that's okay with you."

"Okay, but don't forget my birthday cake, yellow with chocolate frosting."

"It's number one on my list. I'm gonna bake it myself."

"Uh oh. You better ask Maria to help you," he cautioned.

"Get outa' town," I said and then thumped his ear with playful intent. It was Jamey's chuckle, that little-boy-tickled-amused-with-him laugh that made everything all right for me no matter what.

Engaged in our culinary discussion I had lost sight of Maria. Beyond the next curve she had pulled off to the side of the road and parked her car where a row of grapevines ended. They gave way to an abundance of rose bushes that flourished under the July sun, painting the highway in crimson, pink and yellow. The Mercedes pulled back onto the road with Maria's hand waving from the window, signaling to me that she was okay.

Jamey remained focused on *Wizards and Dragons* or some such hand held video baby sitter. His idea of nature was virtual grass growing on a video screen. "Grampa, are we there yet?" he asked.

"I think we're getting closer," I said as we drove past a highway sign that read, 'Welcome to the Valley of the Moon.'

Kenwood, rural suburbia, retired and relaxed was located in the heart of Northern California's billion dollar wine industry. Turn of the century million dollar farm houses graced the foothills of this post card community. Eighteen miles of vineyards, wineries and trendy restaurants welcomed Highway 12, the only direct connection from Sonoma to Kenwood. Henry's summer get-away was one mile in from the main highway. An iron gate, twice my height, opened inward; on them the name of his estate was divided into large letters: TO ME. The late afternoon's sunlight filtered through the oak canopy that shaded the private driveway for a half-mile. Ahead of me, Maria's brake lights fluttered like a strobe under the dancing sunlight that filtered through the trees.

Maria slowed down to a crawl. I could see her lean over the steering wheel; her head and neck tilted back so that she could see the full scale of the turret that towered above the double, etched glass front doors of Henry's mansion. The winged doors of the Mercedes opened, but only Henry got out of the car. Chivalry was not dead; he walked to Maria's side of his coach and helped his princess step out. Maria had an astonished expression when she said, "Henry, I thought you told me it was a little summer house."

He rolled his shoulders and said, "So I exaggerated a smidgen."

"Your idea of smidgen is a smidgen different than my idea of smidgen, Mr. Parker."

"Well, Miss Ibleto, what d'ya think of my little summer house?"

"I think you tell tales that are taller than the rooftop," she said and raised her eyes toward the gabled peak that towered above the porch.

Jamey wasted no time escaping from the car to rescue Willow. He egged the puppy on and then chased him around the expansive, manicured front lawn. Henry warned Jamey, "Keep near the house, you guys. Critters live on the property."

"What are critters?" Jamey asked.

"Varmints."

"Grampa calls mosquitoes, varmints," Jamey said.

"These varmints are bigger than mosquitoes. There's skunk, voles." Henry pointed to the mountain rising from the backyard. "See up on those hills? Gaggles of wild turkey live up there. And if you're lucky, early in the morning, right over there under the dogwood trees you might see a mama doe and her baby fawn."

"Really?"

"You bet. Just as sure as lemons make lemonade. How 'bout it pardner, let's have some lemonade."

"Oh yeah, I'm thirsty."

"Maria, Jack? Some lemonade?"

Maria and I both nodded. I wiped the sweat from my forehead. Maria was trying to cool off by fluttering the opening of her blouse.

"Henry," Jamey asked, "do you think we'll see a vole?"

"There's a good chance. They're nocturnal, ya know."

"What's nocturnal?" he asked with blank curiosity.

"That means they only come out at night."

"I never saw one before. What does it look like?"

"A cross between a rat and a gerbil, tiny ears and no tail. Looks like Willow might be on the vole trail right now."

I snagged Willow's leash. His nose and curiosity were headed toward the vineyards. I tethered him to a rung on the porch railing and then leaned the heels of my hands on the banister and stared in awe of the view. Married to the land, meadows of wild mustard blazed into a floral bonfire of color. Hues of burnt orange and sunset yellow erupted between precise rows of seventy-five-year-old Zinfandel vines. The heat must have gotten to me. I watched Kevin and William stroll arm in arm beyond my reach, a mirage. A tap on my shoulder erased the hallucination. Tugging at my shirt tail, Henry asked, "Jack, you in there?"

"Yeah, it's this view, I drifted off somewhere."

"Have some lemonade. It'll cool you off, bring you back to reality."

He leaned against the railing next to me and rocked on the heels of his boots. I guzzled half the tumbler of iced refreshment. "Damn, brain freeze," I said.

"Don't ya hate it when that happens?" he asked.

I sucked in deep breaths of the warm air to melt the freeze from my eyes and brain.

Maria had cozied up to Henry's side. He pressed his forehead to hers while I guzzled the last half of my lemonade and buried my blush inside the tumbler.

Jamey dangled his feet swaying them leisurely on a ladder back rocker. He imitated a plantation owner sipping his cold drink with his pinky pointing north. "Grampa," he said, rocking, sipping and milking the role, "this is the life."

Henry and Maria chuckled. I just shook my head. "You're too much," I said. I ruffled his hair and bent down to kiss his tousled mop. "Whew! Somebody needs a bath. You smell like an old puppy dog."

"Na, uh!"

"Na, huh!"

Maria pushed up her sleeves. "Alright, you two."

"Jack, Maria and I are gonna go to the market. Cupboards are bare. Any requests for dinner?" he asked.

Jamey blurted out, "Macaroni and cheese and hot dogs."

"You heard the man," I said.

"And a salad, young man," Maria added.

"Can I bring you back anything? Pack o' smokes?" Henry asked.

"No thanks, I quit again two weeks ago. I'm giving my lungs a chance to heal before Thursday's race. Jesus, 7:30 in the morning they'll fire the gun. I'll sleep-walk through the course."

"Two days from now I guarantee you'll tear up the course. The quiet in this valley will rock you to sleep at night like a newborn baby," Henry assured me.

"I'm too old to remember what it's like to sleep like a newborn baby," I confessed.

"I forgot, you're closing in on retirement age. Pretty soon you can play golf everyday and wear polyester plaid pants."

"It'll never happen. The polyester pants . . . no way."

"I have a pair just in case you want to try them on," he kidded me.

"I'll pass."

Jamey and I walked the two lovebirds to the car. Stretching his leash to its limit, Willow barked for attention. I pointed my finger at him and commanded with a firm voice, "Willow! Go. Go lay down." He responded to my hand commands better than yelling. He finally sprawled out on the porch; his nose poked through the rungs of the railing and whined a poor-pitiful-me sob. I raised my free hand to my forehead to shade the blaring sun from burning my eyes. "Jamey, have you seen my sunglasses?"

"I saw 'em in the glove compartment," he said.

"Would you get 'em for me please?" I then turned to Henry and asked him, "By the way, when do we get to meet your daughter, Melissa?"

"At the Home Town Parade on the Fourth. She's tied up at the winery right now. I invited her to dinner tonight, but she can't get away. She sends her apologies and told me that she's looking forward to meeting you guys."

"I'm anxious to meet her too. Tommy sings her praises. She sounds like a wonderful gal."

"She is. She sponsors local communities to benefit needy kids. Every year she hosts a face painting booth on the Square. All the money is donated to send kids from less fortunate families to summer camps throughout Northern California."

"We'll add to the summer camp pot. You hear that Jamey? Maybe Melissa can paint you up to look like Spiderman."

"Yeah! Did you pack my Spiderman shirt?"

"We never leave home without it."

Henry smiled down at my boy. "Okay, Spiderman, macaroni and cheese, huh?" Henry asked again.

"Don't forget the hotdogs," Jamey reminded him.

"Sure thing, pardner." He turned to Maria and said, "I'll drive."

"No. I'll drive, you navigate," she said.

Ducking beneath the wing door, Henry glanced over his shoulder. "Women," he said to me and rolled his eyes.

"Come on Jamey, let's have some more lemonade," I said. He wrapped his arm around my hip as we took refuge from the heat inside the mansion.

*   *   *

For the next two days, Henry's hospitality made up for Jamey's gastronomical choices for dinner. Maybe it was the macaroni and cheese; maybe it was the hotdogs; or maybe it was the unsettling peace and quiet of the countryside. Either way, insomnia helped me roam around Henry's house for two nights. Willow followed me from room to room. To avoid waking the non-insomniacs who slept through the night, in my stocking feet, I quietly shuffled along the hardwood floors. The countryside also slept through the night; not a cricket, not the croak of a frog or the buzz of a mosquito could be heard; only the ticking of the grandfather clock in the entry broke the silence.

I was beat. Hours had passed while I tried to shut off the tug o'war in my brain, the possibility of Margo coming back into my life and William and Kevin getting back together, both a mistake. At two a.m., Thursday morning, I finally crashed in my bed. Before I dozed off I checked the e-mail on my cell phone. I had hoped for a message from William, but all that came up was an e-mail from Tim: "Jack, I went by the house today, nobody home. Congratulations on winning in court and Happy 53rd. Frank came home last night. Love, Tim."

My body sank into twilight; the cell phone lay silent on my chest. Hope replayed an old dream of mine: William lying next to me, the curve of his back molded against my hips while we slept together. I could feel the deep measured breaths of his sleep on my neck, the soft wind of a love I would, now, never have. The warmth of his feet warmed the chill of my heart's exposure. It felt so right, so safe, so calm. Dreams are born out of fantasy and desire, not reality. William's love belonged to Kevin; my love for William belonged to a dream. And then there was Margo. She made her grand entrance into my dream. I distrusted her motives. Shattering the images of my intimate night with William, Margo's advice echoed in my head. She strutted across the stage, gorgeous, fifty-three, what a bitch! "Tell him," she said, "tell William how you really feel about him."

"I will Margo, soon," I said aloud in the darkness of my room and imagined Margo sitting in the window seat, waiting.

Tiny taps at the bedroom door shifted my dream from twilight to daylight. Margo's image vanished and a balmy breeze blew past my bed as a trio of tone deaf voices sang happy birthday to me.

The strained a cappella woke me before the alarm clock went off which I had set for five a.m. Balancing a coconut angel food cake ablaze with one candle that illuminated the number 53, Jamey stood next to the bed. Their rendition of Happy Birthday came to a climax, "Happy Birthday, Dear Grampa," Henry emphasized 'Grampa', "Happy Birthday to you!"

"Make a wish, Grampa," Jamey said impatiently.

I made my wish and sent it to Maine. "Blow out the candle, Grampa," Henry said with a shit-eatin'-grin. The cake teetered in Jamey's boyish hands. Maria snatched the plate before it fell to the maple hardwood floor. I blew out the single candle with one breath. Jamey leaped onto my lap, chanting, "Paybacks, paybacks are worse than gets." He tackled me down on the bed, tickled my bare ribs and sang, "Happy Birthday, Grampa. You give up yet?"

"No way, Jose." My hands wrapped around his waist from finger to finger. I tickled the little shit until he screamed, "I give! I give!"

"What's that? I can't hear you," I continued relentlessly.

"I give. I give!"

"Alright, I'm gonna let go." I pushed him to the side and jumped off the bed to escape any retaliation from him. Obviously, I didn't move quickly enough because he jumped up on my back, wrapped his arms around my neck and blew noogies in my ear until I almost said, "I give." But instead, I grabbed his ankles that were locked like a pretzel around my hips and threatened to turn him upside down. He gave in. "Good morning, everyone," I said and hummed the happy birthday tune to myself.

"Jack, sorry to get you up so early," Henry apologized, "but the race starts at 7:30 and parking is a challenge during this event. Twelve thousand people attend this celebration, all of them packed into a small park at the Town Square. Up and at'em, breakfast is served."

I covered my bare chest with my robe, found one slipper near the bed, the other under the vanity in the bathroom, hidden there by Willow. The smell of country sausage sizzling on the stove filled the house with the comfort of family.

"A hearty breakfast will keep those legs runnin'," Henry said as he served me a hungry man portion.

Groggy from only three hours sleep, I implored Maria, "Make my latte a double, please."

Craving a cigarette, I asked Henry, "How come you never smoked?"

"They're nasty little things. Besides, they're fifty bucks a carton now. I could have brought you back a pack."

"Nah, I'm delirious. Caffeine will snap me right of this." I reached across the enormous pine table. "The *Chronicle*, may I?"

"Sure thing. I picked it up for you at the market last night. Pass the OJ will ya?"

"Grampa, can I have the funnies?" Jamey asked.

Eyeballing for the *Peanuts* cartoon strip, I thumbed through the newspaper, found the comic section and then handed it to Jamey. "Here ya go, Tiger." I slid the entertainment section loose for my own perusal, snapped the crease, crossed my legs and sipped my double shot of espresso.

Jamey folded the funnies onto his lap, snatched a crisp slice of bacon from the Lazy Susan, guzzled half his orange juice then asked Henry, "Do kids like me get to do the pillow fights?"

"Well, pardner, the rule is, you gotta be at least fourteen."

Fighting disappointment, Jamey scrunched his mouth. "But I'm gonna be seven. They can see how big I am," he argued as he stretched on his tiptoes.

"And bigger by the day," Maria said, "and seven years from now you'll probably become the next champion."

"Seven years? I'll be way old."

Under the table I nudged Jamey's leg with my toes. "In seven years, you'll be an old fart like me."

"Fine," he pouted and proceeded to read the funnies.

"Jack, it's almost 6:30. We need to hurry along. The race starts in an hour," Henry said.

"Okay, I'll scoot. By the way, Henry, twelve thousand people; that equates to twelve thousand cars. Where are we supposed to park?"

"The Whittaker's driveway; they're old friends of mine. Their place is an easy three-block stroll to Plaza Park, the starting point for the race. We better get a move on. You'll need to sign in, stretch, and do whatever you runners do before a race." He motioned for Maria with his finger. She rested her arms across his shoulders. "Jack," Henry said then reached for Maria's hand, "before we head out I have something I must ask you."

"You bet."

"Maria has been with you a lot of years, you two are practically married," Henry said.

Short and bossy stood tall behind Henry and squeezed his hand in hers. When she kissed him on his neck my heart filled with happiness for her, but sadness for me. "Practically . . . I don't know what I would have done without her."

"I'm asking your permission to marry Maria."

Even though I wasn't surprised, I rejoiced, "Wow! I'd better confer with the other boss." I nudged Jamey's leg from under the table, "Jamey, put the funnies down for a sec. What do you think? Should we let Maria marry Henry? It'll just be you and me roaming around in that big, big house all by ourselves," I said with a little dramatic license.

Jamey folded his paper neatly, set it on the table, then sipped his orange juice. Dragging out his response, he wiped his mouth with a napkin one corner at a time. He scooted his chair away from the table and approached Henry, his expression stern and serious.

Henry played into Jamey's prank, wide-eyed and nervous as if he were asking to take Jamey's daughter on a first date. "Well, pardner, what d'ya say? You gonna let me marry Maria?"

Jamey winked at me from the corner of his eye. Rubbing his chin, he contemplated, "I think it will be good. But Grampa will have to learn how to cook."

"Congratulations to both of you," I said and waited in line behind Jamey to hug the bride to be. "Okay, buster, my turn," I interrupted and bumped Jamey to the side. "Maria, you are the love of my life. I'm so happy for you. Have you guys set a date yet?"

They both spoke as one, "September 20th."

"I'll be darned, Maria's birthday. Some present, huh, Maria. Henry, before I bestow my blessings . . . two conditions."

"Name 'em."

"Get married in my back yard and supply the wine."

"That's it?"

"Unless you're gonna let Maria work for me part time, that's it buddy."

"Hire the band, Jack; we're puttin' on a weddin'!"

Time was getting away from us so I tossed my keys to Henry. "You drive. I'll grab my shoes."

By 6:45 we had parked in the Whittaker's driveway. The sun had already peaked above Mt. Hood, nature's fortress protecting the Valley of the Moon. I tossed my sweatshirt to Maria. She snatched the hood in midair and tied it around her waist. "Too warm to wear," she said.

Unlike Laguna Beach where the chilly morning air mandated a warm up before a run, the morning temperature in Kenwood was already a delightful seventy degrees. Nine hundred plus athletes and their families and friends had gathered in Plaza Park, a two-acre picnic oasis. The front-runners were easy to spot; zoned, toned, stretching hamstrings and practicing self-chiropractic to their necks. They lined up in front of the bank of porta-potties with their competition numbers safety-pinned to their tank tops. Jamey wriggled the potty dance while we waited in line. "Jamey, you come in with me. I don't want you out here by yourself," I said. We squeezed into the potty closet, took turns and then hustled to find Maria and Henry.

"Over here, guys," Henry called out. Near the starting line, they lounged on a park bench with the Whittakers. Jamey snuggled in between Maria and Henry. Singing above the noisy crowd, a local band played, "Hit the Road Jack." I felt honored. The runners began lining up. I had a few 10K's under my belt, one win, four third places in my age division which allowed me to start in the front of the line. The band quit playing and a microphone screeched before a welcoming voice came over the loudspeaker. "Good morning everyone and welcome to the 37th annual Kenwood Fire Department's Fourth of July Celebration, the Kenwood Foot Race and the World Championship Pillow Fights. Let's hear it for the 'Belmonts' and their rendition of "Hit the Road Jack." The crowd's shrill whistling, hooting and howling drowned out the announcer. He adjusted the volume on his microphone and hollered above the noise of the crowd, "We're ten minutes away from the starting gun. To be fair to the front runners all other runners please position yourselves further back in the crowd."

Jamey stood on top of the park bench and blurted out, "Grampa, kick their butts!" The runners howled with laughter and the announcer dropped his microphone as he searched the crowd for Jamey. Once he retrieved his mike he announced, "Someone is a big fan of his Grampa. Where are you, Grampa? Raise your hand."

I turned four shades of red and raised both my hands above my head. An anonymous voice from the crowd repeated Jamey's cheer. The announcer broke in, "Okay, Grampa, don't let your boy down. We have fifteen seconds. Everybody get set. When I fire the gun begin the race. Five, four, three, two, one!" The firing of his pistol evoked childhood memories of me shooting cap guns at a neighbor, an old curmudgeon who hadn't run a mile in his life.

Forty of us bolted from the starting line as one huge mass, but eventually merged into distinct groups of amateur athletes and weekend warriors. The younger athletes, the twenty-year-olds, left me in the dust while pacing five and six minute miles. For the first mile I paced a seven-minute mile behind two other runners. The first two and a half miles were uphill, a killer. One of the guys I was pacing gained a hundred-yard lead, the other, ten feet in front of me. He was a young stud, all of forty if he was a day. I was sweating; his stride, effortless. He was aware that I was pacing my race with his stride. Every twenty strides or so he'd look over his shoulder and grin. Unlike most of the runners, his legs were unshaven, hairy, lean and long. I focused on the loose fit of his shorts and paced my run to keep a short distance behind him, but he picked up his pace to a six-minute mile. "Mind out of the gutter, Turner," I said to myself and quickened my pace to keep up with him. The peak of the hill was another two hundred yards away. He looked over his shoulder one last time. Winded, I slowed my pace to a seven-minute mile. He was in his zone, passing three runners while the three-mile marker left me isolated between the front runners and the pack. After taking a mental cold shower I dismissed my lustful curiosity and concentrated on the race and the road.

Shedding Spanish moss peppered the country path. Rotting twigs that had fallen from the oaks crunched beneath my shoes as I pounded the pavement. I picked up my pace to a six and a half-minute mile and clocked myself against my watch and the mile markers. A three-percent downhill grade waited beyond the crest of the hill. The welcome descent lowered my heart rate; my breathing became less labored. I maintained that pace even at the risk of shin splints from the downhill. After all, my grandson instructed me to kick their butts.

My controlled breaths and the impact of my worn shoes on the road emphasized the restful solitude of the morning forest. A few blue jays rooted me on. A lone jackrabbit perked its ears in my direction and then sprinted across the road. Fifty yards ahead and a mile above Plaza Park volunteers cheered me on offering cups of cold water and encouragement. I guzzled three paper cups of water. Running and drinking is like rubbing your belly and the top of your head simultaneously; I spilled more water than I drank. I waved my hand above my head to say thanks and gained on two runners, old farts like myself. I passed them which assured me third place in my division. My heart rate increased, lactic acid burned in my calves and quads; I ignored the pain and slowed my pace. My right calf knotted stressing the Achilles tendon. I stopped dead center in the road, bent forward and raised my toes to relieve the cramping pain. My glasses slid to the end of my nose, sweat from my brow stung my eyes. The two old geezers caught up with me, stopped and then surrounded me. "Thanks for stopping," I said without looking up. Continuing to massage my leg, I asked, "Maybe you fellas could . . ."

Before I could look up, I felt a double-fisted blow pierce my shoulder blades. I tried to protect myself, but the blow had knocked the wind out of me. I skidded five feet along the coarse, rain eroded black top and then collapsed; the heels of my hands were poor substitutes for brakes. Torn skin came off my shins and knees and left flesh and blood on the road. Blood from my hands streaked my cheeks as I searched my face for my glasses. I turned my head to identify the aggressors. Without my specs all I saw were legs and well traveled running shoes. One of them rammed the side of my face into the pavement; my teeth tore the inside of my mouth. The other assailant bludgeoned my left side and kicked my ribs repeatedly. My left rib cage cracked, my chest collapsed to the pavement. Crouched in the fetal position I protected my head with my hands and fought to maintain consciousness. Blood dripped from my elbows and then onto the scabbed muddy earth. My eyes began to sting from the touch of my salty hands as I tried to wipe the blood from my battered face. Even though the assault had ceased, I anticipated another blow to my ribs so I remained crouched.

"That's enough," the man to my right said. "Let's get out of here before the runners catch up."

The other assailant had an English accent. He tucked his filthy shoes under my ear to lift my head. He bent forward and whispered in a cockney dialect, "Happy Birthday from Rob, faggot!"

I struggled to raise myself from the pavement to try to identify them. I managed to prop myself to my knees oblivious to the loose gravel embedded in the wounds. Their footsteps faded into the forest, their faces hidden from me. Their crime and message rang in my head, a threat and a name, nothing more. It would be Rob's word against mine. I cradled my ribs to support them and shouted, "Fucking bastards!" I blindly scanned the roadside for my glasses. I could make out only a blurred mass of bodies running my way. One runner stopped; the horror in her voice heightened my awareness of how badly I was hurt. She leaned forward but hesitated to touch me, "Are you okay?" she asked then looked at my battered face and exclaimed, "My God what happened to you?"

Four or five runners stopped, but the mass continued the race. A deep, baritone voice, much like William's, instructed one of the runners to head back to the watering station to call for emergency. His paternal manner and strength calmed my fear. He asked, "I don't know if we should move you before emergency gets here."

"Please, help me to stand. I think I have a broken rib on the left side, but my legs are okay."

"I don't know, you're pretty banged up," he said.

He supported my waist with one arm and lifted me from the ground. I rested my right arm around his shoulder. He assisted me to the side of the road and helped me sit down on a stump from a felled oak. The man, who gave up his race, whose name I would recall later, asked one of the runners to head back to the station for water. "Hang on," he said to me while waving his arms to flag down the emergency medical van cresting the peak of the hill.

"This probably sounds crazy to you," I said, dozing in and out and slurring my words. "Do you see my glasses near the road? I can't see jack shit without them."

Two Emergency Medical Technicians assisted me to the back of the van. One of them dressed my shins and knees to stop the bleeding. The other instructed, "We should take you to an emergency room. Memorial is the nearest hospital from here."

"Not necessary," I insisted. "If you just take me to my family; they're waiting in the park. I'll have them take me to emergency."

The gentleman who had forfeited his race to help me approached the back of the van. "You don't look half bad cleaned up," he said. The tone in his voice let me know that he was flirting with me.

I smiled and said, "I'd like to return the compliment, but you're pretty much a blur without my glasses."

He unfolded his hand. "These must belong to you."

"Thank you. You're a saint. AH! The frames are bent; at least the lenses aren't shattered."

"By the way, I'm Ethan," he said.

I started to raise my arm to shake his hand. "It's okay, man," he said, "don't make it hurt any worse than it already does."

"I'm Jack."

"You're the Grampa, the kick your butt Grampa."

"Yep, that's me, Grampa Jack."

"You're in good hands. I'm gonna finish the race. See ya at the bottom of the hill."

"Thanks, Ethan."

"Ciao!" I said and then remembered who he was. Kevin had introduced him to me when he waited our table at the restaurant that final day in court.

The crowd in the park cleared the road and all of them strained their necks to see if the injured might be a family member or a friend. Jamey, Ol' Eagle Eye, spotted me limping from the emergency van. He darted in and out of the maze of legs crowding the square and screamed, "Grampa!" On his heels, Henry and Maria headed toward me.

Maria reached out to hug me and to comfort herself. I flinched; her light squeeze to my ribs took my breath away. "Oh, Mr. Jack, I'm so sorry. How did this happen to you?"

"I tripped over my own feet. I fell." Maria's hazel eyes saw right through me. She knew that I had lied. "Henry," I said, "how 'bout a lift to the hospital?"

"Stay put. I'll bring the car around," he said and then ran as fast as his cowboy boots would allow.

I took a load off my feet and eased my shaky body onto a park bench. Jamey scooted his butt close to mine. "Grampa, are we comin' back for the pillow fights?"

"Next year, Tiger . . . next year."

Chapter Seventeen

L aguna's lazy August afternoons healed my wounds. I was glad to be home rocking on my front porch and melting into the solitude of my life. I lit a cigarette, sipped on raspberry iced tea and waited for Maria and Jamey to return from the market. Willow lazed alongside me, his head resting on his tender puppy paws, his eyes half-mast and his tongue licking in and out, a dog thing just before a nap.

A new Mercedes SLK with the top down pulled up curbside. Karen Carpenter's voice blared "Ticket to Ride" rockin' the block and waking me up. Unfazed by the intrusion, Willow slept. Margo had arrived two months ahead of schedule.

She remained in her car for a moment, tamed her wind blown hair with both hands and shook her head back, not a hair out of place. Maybe it was her cocky attitude; maybe it was her quirky charisma, but I still loved her in spite of all the negatives. She pushed the car door shut with her hips, polished the smudges from the door jam with a tissue, tipped her sunglasses and waved at me with a single forefinger. Even in capris, a sleeveless blouse and strapless sandals, Margo was a class act. She brushed a single strand of hair away from one corner of her mouth. She wasn't wearing any make-up; her tanned face looked more beautiful than I had remembered. A French manicure tipped her slender fingers, her feet were pedicured, her toenails unpainted. A gentle summer breeze carried the scent of her familiar perfume to the porch. She stopped at the foot of the steps and greeted me, "Hello, Jack."

"What are you doing here, Margo?"

"Happy to see you too," she said with a curt response.

Her sarcasm evoked a grin from the corner of my mouth. Choking back a good laugh, I said, "Oh, God, I am a real bastard, aren't I?"

"That's not the word I was thinking, but it'll do."

"Sorry, Margo." Favoring my left leg, I descended the steps and held my right arm snug to my ribs. I gave Margo a one-arm hug. "Come on in. How 'bout some iced tea?"

"Love some. Are you hurt?"

"A little bruise, nothing much."

She wrapped her arm around my waist and rested her head on my shoulder. "It's good to see you, Jack. Where is that boy of yours?"

"He and Maria are shopping for dinner. Watch your step," I warned. "Between Jamey and Willow, the living room looks like a toy store after a hurricane. So what brings you back to the West Coast so soon? I didn't expect you until Halloween."

"Personal business," she said casually.

I led Margo into the kitchen. She leaned against the counter while I took two glasses from the cupboard. I pressed one of them against the automatic ice dispenser of the refrigerator. Ice cubes overflowed the glass and slid across the floor. Willow batted the cubes with his paws through the living room, down the hallway and into Jamey's bedroom. The ace bandage supporting my ribcage loosened. I pulled off my tank top with my good arm and asked Margo, "Please help me secure this bandage."

Margo's jaw dropped open. She muffled a gasp with her hand and stared at the yellowing bruises beneath my arms. "Jesus, Jack, who beat the shit out of you?"

"No one. I fell."

"Liar," she accused, gently pressing the Velcro.

"Drop it Margo. It's not important." I slid my tank back over my head.

"What did you do, fall off a cliff?"

"No, I just fell."

"Suit yourself," she said with obvious disbelief. "Anyway, to answer your question, I'm moving back to California."

"Back to LA?"

"No. I bought a house in Monarch Bay."

"Why Monarch Bay?"

"Jack, the house is spectacular. It sets on the bluff, the views . . . the views are to die for . . . on a clear day, Catalina, the night light view down the coast . . ."

I stopped her cold. "You don't get it, do you, Margo?"

"Get what, Jack?" she asked, confused.

"Monarch Bay. That's where Annie lived . . . that's where she died."

Margo gripped my hand, her palm, moist and warm, her green eyes, a remembrance of Annie. "I had no idea, Jack," she said, her tone sincere and apologetic.

"Of course you didn't," I said, my tone equally apologetic. "Well, we can look on the bright side. Johnny lives there."

"Who's Johnny?"

"Jamey's best buddy. So when Jamey comes for a visit . . ." I felt a cold chill come over my neck, my cheeks flushed. "I need to sit down," I said.

Margo pulled one of the kitchen chairs out from under the table. "Jack, are you alright?"

"Yeah, this will pass; it's like having a hot flash." I pressed the cold, wet glass to my forehead and said, "Let's go outside on the porch."

"Leave it to you to have a hot flash," Margo chuckled. "I'll clear a path through the living room for you." She pushed a Transformer robot, a soccer ball, Willow's half-chewed tug rope, a pair of sneakers and a beach bag to the hearth. Willow snatched the tug rope and dashed between my legs. Margo held the screen door open; Willow beat us to the front porch. Margo dragged the matching wicker rocker next to mine, crossed her legs and stirred the ice cubes in her tea with one finger. Staring into her glass, she asked me, "How many were there, Jack?"

"How many what?"

"How many ganged up on you?"

"There were two men. I never saw their faces. It happened when we were in Sonoma. Henry had invited us to spend the Fourth of July weekend with him and Maria at his summer place near his winery. I competed in the Kenwood 10K Foot Race that morning. How these two men singled me out of nine hundred runners with a window of time when no one was around is beyond me."

"Did you file a police report?"

"Wouldn't have done any good. There were no witnesses."

"This makes no sense, Jack. In a public event, at random, two men seek you out to beat the shit out you? I don't buy it."

"I suspect who's behind the assault," I said then removed my glasses and massaged the tender bridge of my broken nose.

"Why haven't you said anything?" she asked with a motherly tone, the kind only a woman instinctively knows how to express.

"This is between you and me, Margo; even William doesn't know this. Maria didn't buy my falling down story either. One of the attackers gave me a message before he ran off. I can still smell his fowl breath when he said to me, 'Happy Birthday from Rob, faggot.'"

"Fitzpatrick? Are you sure?"

"I heard the message loud and clear. I couldn't see either of them, but I sure as shit heard them."

"You can't let Rob get away with this."

"Margo, I can't prove it."

"Horseshit! We'll hire a criminal lawyer; investigate the son-of-a-bitch!"

"I'm done, Margo, done fighting. He got his fuck-you-jab in. I have Jamey. Rob is the loser."

"I think you're mistaken. Peg is the loser. She needs to divorce his sorry ass."

"Peg will never divorce Rob. I don't know whether to admire her or pity her, but she loves him."

Margo sipped her tea and reached for my pack of smokes that were lying on the table. "Love is overrated," she confessed then lit her cigarette.

I too lit a cigarette and said, "I'll smoke to that."

Margo blew a gray cloud of smoke past her lips. "I hate these things," she complained but took another drag. "Jack, come to the new house with me."

"Not today. I'm not up to it."

She butted her cigarette out and said, "I insist." She then snatched my cigarette from my lips, tapped the full ashtray with her fingers and asked me, "Been chain smoking, have we?" We both extinguished our cigarettes in the ashtray heaped with ashes and stale butts. "Besides," she continued, "I've found something you need to see."

"You just don't give up, do you, Margo?"

"And I never will, Jack."

"Let me leave a note for Maria; I'll just be a minute."

I crunched my battered body into the cockpit of Margo's miniature hot rod which took some doing. My long legs stretched out with little room to spare; my healing ribs were unforgiving. Margo buckled me in; my bandages were a nuisance, stiff and restrictive. She flopped into the driver's seat, flipped her hair back, cocked her sunglasses onto her nose and quickly glanced at herself in the rearview mirror. Leave it to Margo to drive a six-speed manual transmission. Her hip replacement had been an obvious success.

"So, Mr. Turner, what do you think of my new ride?"

"Pretty sweet. Definitely reflects your style: compact, packs a punch, beautiful to look at, pricey."

"You know me better than I thought; I'll take all that as a compliment."

"And you should. So, you're moving back to the West Coast, huh? Is this a permanent move for you?"

"I'll probably stay here nine months out of the year. I've maintained my flat in the Big Apple. I love Autumn in New York."

"Autumn in Laguna isn't so bad."

"I know, but the fall color change in Central Park, the tease of the holidays inviting the brisk evening air, shopping along Fifth Avenue, store windows dressed in red, gold, silver and unrivaled fashion. But I'll return to California for Christmas. You'll have to pull the reigns in on me so I don't spoil Jamey."

"He's easy to spoil," I admitted.

Margo slammed on her brakes. I jolted forward; the seat belt locked pinning me to the seat. "Easy, Margo, my ribs."

"What an asshole. He cut me off before the stoplight. There's too much traffic on Pacific Coast Highway; spoils a good ride," she complained.

"It's still summer. It eases up come November," I assured her.

We crawled for two more blocks before Margo had to stop for a red light. The Little Shrimp was to the right of the intersection. A small choir of bare chested men crowded the bar's entrance. Half lit from an afternoon of sun and booze; they sang happy birthday, out of key, embarrassing a gay man whose face was beet red which I doubt was from sunburn. Coming up the street from the beach entrance, Frank walked hand in hand with Tim. And choking on a short leash, their pooch dragged them toward the singing party. Salty, moist sand coated their feet and flip-flops. Tim tapped his heels with a Frisbee to loosen the packed sand and then tethered his mutt to the side porch of the bar's entrance. The light turned green before Tim saw me, but Frank spotted me and waved as Margo sped away. From the side mirror of the car I watched them for about a block while the convertible breeze cooled my receding hairline. "Good for them," I whispered to myself.

"What? I can't hear you with the top down?" Margo said.

"It's nothing, just thinking out loud," I said, my eyes remained fixed on the mirror.

Three miles ahead Monarch Bay awaited us. Tuning out the car stereo and Margo's babble, I zoned out over the ocean. Memories of Annie teetered on the bluff of my sanity's threshold.

"Jack . . . Hello Jack . . . You in there?"

"Just enjoying the view and the ride," I said, my thoughts still wandering.

For the next three miles I stared out over the ocean, my mind's eye skimmed over the rolling surf. Reflections of the afternoon sun shimmered like an evening starlit sky. I lowered my sunglasses over my exposed forehead and rested them on the tip of my nose. I tilted my head back; the headrest cradled my neck. With my eyes closed I mapped the highway by rote; Monarch Bay was the next light.

"Here we are, Jack." Margo pulled up to the security gates and rolled down her window.

The security guard dropped his phone call and then bounded from his cubicle of authority toward Margo. "Ms. Evans, what a pleasure to see you twice in one day," he said beaming. Then he saw me and smiled courteously, "Mr. Turner, good to see you again, sir."

"You too, John," I said and attempted to shake his hand, but the pain in my ribs stopped my reach.

We drove past Mockingbird Circle, the street Annie had lived on street. As we turned the corner I told Margo, "I remember Jamey sprinting to that curb on a school morning last January. That was the last time I saw Annie alive." Margo gently put her hand on my leg. The tender squeeze of her fingers against the healing wounds of my knee made me recall the tenderness we had felt for each other so many years ago. I suddenly remembered W.H. Anden's beautiful line, "In the desert of the heart/let the healing fountain start".

"Jack, it's straight ahead." She pulled into the circular driveway to her house on Bluff Drive. She popped the clutch before coming to a stop and stalled the engine. "Oops," she said, "I haven't mastered the clutch thing yet."

"No, but you've sure mastered the art of real estate. Look at this place."

"Wait until you see the view," she said nervously. Her right hand trembled slightly as she struggled to remove the key from the ignition. It slipped from her hands and wedged itself between the seat and the console. "Damn! I didn't need that fingernail anyway," she said, digging for her keys. "Come on, I'll give you the tour."

"Margo, slow down, you're shakin' like a leaf."

"A little adrenaline rush. I am so anxious for you to see all this."

She left the car door open and ran up the front steps of her new house. It took me a while to release the unfamiliar seat belt. Once freed, I eased my sore body out of the car and made my way to the driver's side to close Margo's door. A letter from William had fallen onto the cobblestone driveway. I grabbed the opened letter before the wind blew it across the street. I waved the personalized stationery addressed to Margo above my head and asked her, "Margo, what's this?"

"I don't know. I can't see that far."

"It's a letter from William," I shouted. "Since when are you two pen pals?"

She either ignored me or didn't hear me. She opened the twelve-foot teak entry doors then raised her arms above her head and shouted, "It's mine, all mine and I have the pink slip!"

I tossed William's letter onto the front seat. "Title, it's called title, Margo," I hollered, correcting her.

"I know that. Pink slip was for your benefit. Hurry along Gramps, there's something here I need to show you."

"Watch who you're calling Gramps, Granny."

"I prefer Nanna."

"Nanna, Granny, Gramma, still means you're an old fart. Alright Nanna, I challenge you to a battle, one month from today."

"Name it, Gramps."

"A foot race on the beach. The winner eats crow and buys dinner, winner's choice of restaurant."

"Buy some new shoes because I'll whoop your ass."

"No shoes. Barefoot," I challenged her.

"Fair enough, but I pick the beach." She crossed her arms, tapped her foot on the top step and raised one eyebrow. "Need some assistance up the steps . . . Gramps."

"What a bitch," I said, bolting out a good laugh. "I made it to the top. I'm all yours, proceed with the tour."

The rubber soles of my sneakers screeched on the polished marble floor in the foyer. Margo's voice echoed off the walls of the empty house. "Watch your step going down into the great room," she warned.

At the top of the landing my knees locked, my shoes stuck to the floor. Standing before a wall of glass spanning the back of the house, William watched my reflection. His bushy black hair streaked with silver shone like marbled ebony in the sunlight. I turned to Margo. "What is this about?" I asked.

"Lock the door on your way out. I'll call you tonight."

"Margo . . ."

"Remember my advice? Tell him." She slid past the front doors. I listened to the hum of her car turn the corner and felt my heart racing in my chest. I hesitated at the top of the stairway and cleared my throat. "William, what are you doing here?"

"Enjoying the view. Margo has fabulous taste." Barefoot, William stepped to the center of the great room. He gripped the carpet with his toes, his sandals dangling from his hand. He smoothed his mustache, partially gray, matching his hair. "Heard about your tangle in the woods. Nasty fall, huh?"

"Who told you?"

"Maria."

"Snitch."

"Jack, Maria loves you. She knew that you wouldn't tell me."

"She's right. You have enough to deal with. Speaking of which, is Kevin packed?"

"Come down here so I can have a closer look at you," he said.

One step at a time I inched my way toward William. He waited for me at the foot of the steps. "Where can I hug you so it doesn't hurt?" he asked.

"The waist."

"Can you believe this view? Look beyond the bluff, out over the ocean. Tell me what you see, Jack," he said and then drew me close to his side.

"A buoy, two people paddling on a surfboard and two guys making out on the beach."

"Where, I didn't notice them," he said, stretching his neck to take a second look.

"Gotcha," I said. "What do you see, William?"

"Let me borrow your glasses." William slid my specs snug to the bridge of his nose and too close to his eyes. "Whew! These will make you seasick. Here we go; it's coming into focus now. I see a gangly, sort of good-looking newspaper reporter sitting Indian style on a grassy quad writing notes for a story while thinking rude thoughts about my knobby knees."

"Give me back my glasses. And you do have knobby knees; although, your taste in shorts has evolved, good choice," I said, tugging at his Polo walking shorts. "And what do you mean, sort of good-looking?"

He grinned and pressed his hands to his lips as if to pray. "This is really hard for me, Jack," he confided.

"What is?"

"Kevin. Kevin is not coming back to Maine with me."

"What did he do? Run off with another jock?"

"No. I did."

"Holy shit! I don't believe this. You and Kevin, it's always been the two of you."

"Not anymore. Kevin knows him. He told me, "I'm surprised you waited this long.""

Drunk from the punch of William's confession I wavered toward the window. I feared that his new beau would come jogging out of the kitchen and push me aside. I swallowed Margo's advice and drew from the past to be happy for William. I continued to stare out over the ocean and asked him, "What's he like?"

"Well, he's older than Joey."

"There is a God," I sighed with relief then pressed my palms together and lifted them toward the ceiling.

"You didn't like Joey, did you?"

"Let me put it this way . . . Billy?"

"I thought it was sweet."

"It was an age thing, wasn't it?" I teased.

"We're all entitled to one small life crisis," he said vindicating himself.

"Only one?"

"Maybe two," he admitted. "Jack, I want you to meet the new love of my life."

I rummaged through my pockets for my cell phone. "Yeah, that'll be great, maybe tomorrow," I bowed out. I tried to dial out on my phone. "Damn, the battery is low."

"An urgent call?" William asked.

"Just a cab."

"Jack, you just got here. I haven't seen you in months."

"Jamey and Maria will wonder if Margo kidnapped me. I better get home."

"Maria knows you're here with me," he said.

"Maria conveniently seems to know things before I do these days."

"I'd guess after twenty-five years, it's part of her job description."

"Hmm . . . I suppose so." I dialed 411 for directory assistance and connected. "Yes, Laguna Beach . . . the phone number for Yellow Cab . . . Thank you." William grabbed the phone from my hand and pressed the power button off.

"Cancel the cab. I'll give you a lift home."

"Good, then you can see Jamey. He's shot up three inches since the last time you saw him. But what about this guy you want me to meet. We can't just leave him here."

William acted as though he hadn't heard a word I said. "Jamey's probably up to my chin by now, huh? Before we leave, step out in the backyard with me, Jack. You won't believe this."

The automatic sweeper skimmed the surface of the pool while William dipped his foot into the cool water. Leaving his wet footprints on the flagstone walkway, William followed the edge of the lawn to the bluff. He stopped at its edge. A wrought iron fence with leaves reminiscent of a Tuscan wine vineyard bordered the backyard; beyond the fence was a fifty foot drop to a private beach. He gripped the ornamental leaves that topped the fence. I sneaked up behind him, laid my hand on his shoulder and asked him, "Where is it? Where is this unbelievable thing that you and Margo have conspired?"

"It's about this guy I met . . . His name is Jack. He knows this great kid who calls him Grampa."

"Grampa; nice name . . . I'm sure he's a great guy."

William reached for my hand and entwined his fingers with mine. I pressed our grip to my cheek, and then rested my chin on his graying, bushy mane. "William, how long can you stick around?"

"I bought a one way ticket."

Acknowledgments

My deepest gratitude to my editor, Jim Wade, who encouraged me to write critically and to push my ego aside during the process; to Gary Cockriell, Attorney At Law, for teaching me the lingo, the power and the protocol of the courtroom; to Fran George, Marriage Family Therapist, for her insightful wisdom, experience, dedication and love for children; to my friends and family who toiled through endless manuscript readings; and finally, a very special thanks to a wonderful boy named Max.